Praise for *Take Me Home*

'Full of romance, humour and a touch of mystery ... another engaging tale by the reliable Karly Lane.' —*Canberra Weekly Magazine*

'Karly Lane is back with another beautiful, cosy story that will sweep you away on a journey.' —Noveltea Corner

'Such a fun read ... Karly has smashed the contemporary fiction genre with *Take Me Home*.' —Beauty and Lace

'*Take Me Home* is a delight to read. I loved the change of scenery while still enjoying Karly Lane's wonderful, familiar storytelling.' —Book'd Out

Praise for *Something Like This*

'Another unmissable rural romance story of pain, loss, suffering and the power of love ... Karly Lane is firmly on my must-read list.' —Beauty and Lace

'A great book from an author I love ... Karly Lane never fails me.' —Noveltea Corner

'There is more to this narrative than rural romance; this is a multi-faceted exploration of loss, grief, families, second chances and courage ... I loved this!' —Reading, Writing and Riesling

'An engaging story, set at a gentle pace, told with genuine warmth for her characters and setting, *Something Like This* is a lovely and eminently satisfying read.' —Book'd Out

'Engaging, genuine, with a storyline we can all relate to ... Karly Lane has the wonderful ability to bring the many facets of everyday existence to life. Another fantastic story.' —Blue Wolf Reviews

Praise for *Fool Me Once*

'I adore Karly Lane's books—they always signal a wonderful time curled up on the couch with a cup of tea . . . Lane writes compelling characters and relationship realities, and I'm all here for it.' —Noveltea Corner

'With its appealing characters, easy pace and happy ending, I found *Fool Me Once* to be another engaging and satisfying rural romance novel.' —Book'd Out

'*Fool Me Once* is a guaranteed perfect light read . . . Karly Lane has woven a delicious tale of lust, love, betrayal, consequences and chasing dreams, which as time passes often need to be reconsidered.' —Blue Wolf Reviews

'Karly Lane's affinity for the land shines through in her stories . . . *Fool Me Once* is a feel-good story not to be missed.' —The Burgeoning Bookshelf

Praise for *Return to Stringybark Creek*

'Captivating, entertaining and most enjoyable, this return visit with the Callahans encourages the understanding that sometimes there are, even from the darkest of times, huge positives to be discovered.' —Blue Wolf Reviews

'Lane has added additional depth to this story that highlights the plight of Australian farmers and farming communities who are under strain . . . I'm grateful for the calm and considered way Lane has approached the topic. The Callahans have become a favourite book family of mine . . . they define family and friendship and it's been a real pleasure to read their stories.' —Noveltea Corner

'Karly Lane creates likeable, warm characters as she twists and turns her story . . . an entertaining read with an intriguing love story set against the challenges of farming and its stresses.' —*The Weekly Times*

Once Burnt, Twice Shy

Karly Lane lives on the mid north coast of New South Wales. Proud mum to four children and wife of one very patient mechanic, she is lucky enough to spend her day doing the two things she loves most—being a mum and writing stories set in beautiful rural Australia.

ALSO BY KARLY LANE

North Star
Morgan's Law
Bridie's Choice
Poppy's Dilemma
Gemma's Bluff
Tallowood Bound
Second Chance Town
Third Time Lucky
If Wishes Were Horses
Six Ways to Sunday
Someone Like You
The Wrong Callahan
Mr Right Now
Return to Stringybark Creek
Fool Me Once
Something Like This
Take Me Home

KARLY LANE

Once Burnt, Twice Shy

ALLEN&UNWIN
SYDNEY•MELBOURNE•AUCKLAND•LONDON

This is a work of fiction. Names, characters, places and incidents are products of the author's imagination or are used fictitiously. Any resemblance to actual events, locales or persons, living or dead, is entirely coincidental.

First published in 2021

Copyright © Karly Lane 2021

All rights reserved. No part of this book may be reproduced or transmitted in any form or by any means, electronic or mechanical, including photocopying, recording or by any information storage and retrieval system, without prior permission in writing from the publisher. The Australian *Copyright Act 1968* (the Act) allows a maximum of one chapter or 10 per cent of this book, whichever is the greater, to be photocopied by any educational institution for its educational purposes provided that the educational institution (or body that administers it) has given a remuneration notice to the Copyright Agency (Australia) under the Act.

Allen & Unwin
83 Alexander Street
Crows Nest NSW 2065
Australia
Phone: (61 2) 8425 0100
Email: info@allenandunwin.com
Web: www.allenandunwin.com

 A catalogue record for this book is available from the National Library of Australia

ISBN 978 1 76087 850 4

Set in 10/12 pt Simoncini Garamond Std by Bookhouse, Sydney
Printed and bound in Australia by Griffin Press, part of Ovato

10 9 8 7 6 5 4 3 2 1

 The paper in this book is FSC® certified. FSC® promotes environmentally responsible, socially beneficial and economically viable management of the world's forests.

In memory of the many heroes who rose from the ashes of the fires that decimated much of Australia in the summer of 2019–2020

One

Samantha Murphy pushed the last bale of hay off the back of the ute. She wiped a hand across her sweaty forehead as she watched the cattle jostle for position around the fodder on the dry brown earth below.

She was hot and uncomfortable with her shirt sticking to her back; her clothes were filthy and she was pretty sure she had bits of hay in her ponytail, which had been neatly pulled back this morning but now resembled a rat's nest. If she had seen herself like this at any other time, she would have been horrified.

Two weeks ago, she'd left the Sunshine Coast in Queensland and returned to her parents' property in the farming belt of the Mid North Coast of New South Wales. Gone were the long lunches with friends, the salon treatments and the beachwear, replaced by jeans, boots and her dad's floppy old Akubra. She grinned a little at the thought of her fifteen-year-old self even contemplating wearing her father's hat; she would have burnt to a crisp before putting the sweat-stained relic on her head. Her forty-—*cough*—closer to fifty-year-old self, though, was far more terrified of sun damage and wrinkles than what she looked like or what she might catch from wearing it. The bright, fashionable beach fedora she'd left hanging on her hallway hat rack wouldn't have lasted a day here even if she had remembered to pack it. Not that this was a holiday.

She was supposed to be housesitting while her parents were away on a round-the-world trip they'd been planning for three long years. But considering their house included a couple of hundred acres of farmland and livestock, the job was a little more involved than watering house plants and feeding the odd cat.

Sam had expected it to be a bit of a culture shock, coming home and doing so much physical outdoor work after so many years away, but somehow it felt . . . familiar. It really shouldn't. She wasn't the farming type—hadn't been since she was old enough to leave school—and yet, so much of what she was doing made her feel as if she had been thrown back in time. It was second nature. Or maybe she'd become better at adapting.

She'd had a bit of experience with that over the past few years. Her divorce had been unexpected and painful, but it had given her a new path to follow. She'd finally found the courage to follow a long-held dream to open her own homewares shop. It had been the most exciting, scary and worthwhile decision she'd ever made. She'd never imagined she could turn her passion for home decorating into something she could make a decent living from—or that she would actually be good at it. She had loved sourcing the perfect pieces for her store, and she soon carved out a niche for herself that had taken her from a small, poky shop in a backstreet to a prominent shopfront in the high-end tourist neighbourhood among some of the biggest names in fashion and business.

Sam jumped down from the back of the ute, moving gingerly through the herd of her father's prized black Angus cattle. They chewed their feed noisily, making low mooing sounds as they jockeyed for prime position around the bales of hay she'd thrown out. She climbed into the driver's seat with a sense of satisfaction. She'd been thinking about the cold beer in her fridge since lunchtime and now, after finishing all but one of her chores, she would finally be able to sit and enjoy it. Her muscles ached, and she'd given up thinking it would get better after a few days. She was coming to the uncomfortable conclusion that the muscles she had as a woman in her late forties were not as adaptable as they'd been as a teenager—which was the last time she'd done this.

She stopped the ute in front of the gate and pulled on the handbrake. The downside to driving alone on a farm was the gates. As kids, the job had fallen to her and her brothers, Thomas and Alex, as the passengers for their dad. They'd grumbled about it back then, and it wasn't any more fun now. As she drove through and then closed the gate behind her, she took a moment to look across the paddocks and let out a small sigh. It was so dry.

As a rule, the coast was greener than inland Australia, but the drought that had continued its stranglehold for two years hadn't spared the coastal areas. Sam, like the rest of the country, had watched as feed dried up and dams evaporated, leaving livestock to fade away in paddocks and crops to die in the fields. The whole country was praying for rain and yet it hadn't come, and there was no sign that it would.

The Murphy property was a small family farm, but the effects of the dry were starting to show here too. Sam had noticed it the last time she'd been home for a visit—the usually lush green grass was faded and the trees looked wilted—but this time, it was blindingly obvious that things had got worse. What little was left of the grass was brown, the dams were almost dry, and her parents, like most of their neighbours, were almost totally dependent on handfeeding livestock.

Sam pushed away from the gate and climbed back into the ute. She drove along the dirt track through the paddock, worn by years of cattle and wheels, then followed the road as it wound its way across the lower flats and through a gully between two hills. This was the place that always brought back a sharp, happy memory: it was at this spot on the property that Honey, her very first pony, would always pick up speed as she caught the first sight of home on a ride. Sam would have to hold on tight and be ready as the little golden palomino lurched from a docile walk to a full gallop in the blink of an eye. As she drove out of the gully, Sam saw the house further up the hill, and she smiled. It wasn't grand, just a three-bedroom fibro and brick farmhouse with a verandah, but it was home. No matter how many years passed, this little house would always hold the memories of her childhood and family within its walls. Now that she was a grown woman with children of her own, she could appreciate just how special her childhood had been here. As a teenager, she'd taken this place for granted, been impatient to leave—she wanted excitement and adventure—but as an adult, she enjoyed the simple beauty in a slower pace.

Sam hung her dad's hat on the peg inside the back door and kicked off her boots. It was strange coming into the kitchen and finding it so quiet. Usually her mother was in here cooking or on the phone to someone about one committee or another. Now, it was silent except for the echoing tick of the wall clock and the soft hum of the fridge.

Washing her hands and taking out the beer, Sam went outside and sank into one of the rustic old cane chairs that had been part of the verandah furniture for as long as Sam could remember. They were deep with the perfect armrest height and had recently undergone a facelift with a new coat of white paint and some brightly coloured pink, green and blue striped fabric on the padding. She released a long sigh as she put her feet up on the chair across from her and leaned back.

If her father were here right now, he would tease her. She'd barely done half of what he did every day around the place and she was exhausted. Well, she'd never claimed to be a farmer. Up until a month ago, she'd been a boutique-homeware store owner—a far cry from pushing bales of hay off the back of a dilapidated old ute.

There had been a few significant changes in Sam's life lately. The business. The marriage. And here she was, a recently divorced mother of two almost-grown children. She frowned at the thought. She had a twenty-one-year-old daughter, for goodness sake—how was that even possible? It didn't feel like so long ago that Mackenzie had sat here unwrapping Christmas presents when she was three and Brooklyn was just a baby. Now, Brook was nineteen and both girls had moved out of home and were living their own lives. There was no denying it: Sam felt old.

As she stared out into the distance, the sound of the dogs barking was suddenly followed by a commotion of loud screeching.

Bloody guinea fowl.

Her mother's latest pride and joy. And Sam had forgotten to lock the stupid things away. She jumped to her feet, hopping around as she struggled to pull her boots back on. The guinea fowl had become something of a hobby for her mother in recent years, and Sam was still trying to figure out what her mum found so endearing about them. To Sam, they seemed to be the love child of a drunken night between a turkey and a vulture. They were the ugliest and least intelligent creatures she had ever come across. Chooks, she loved—they laid eggs, they clucked about in a soothing, calm manner and they were quite therapeutic to sit and watch from the verandah throughout the day. Guinea fowl, on the other hand, were like a swarm of mindless imbeciles who would launch into a panic at the slightest movement and run frantically in a crisis, seemingly forgetting they could actually fly.

Her mother's argument for their usefulness around the place had been that they were great at eating pests, including ticks, and helped keep snakes away. Her father had to be getting soft in his old age, because she hadn't heard him question how effective the fowl were in either department since their arrival, and keeping the working dogs away from them was a round-the-clock security issue. Sam had lost track of how many replacement fowl her mother had bought due to dog misadventure.

'Tess! Max!' she yelled, calling the dogs out of the chook pen where they were running about excitedly, chasing their feathered foes. Sam could see why the dogs enjoyed a good chase—guinea fowl were so loud and mindless, they were practically begging to be pursued, though with a kelpie and a blue heeler the end result was never a good outcome for the guinea fowl.

Reluctantly, the two dogs moved away from their game and Sam herded them out the gate with a stern reprimand and a curse as she realised she now had to track down the birds that were scattered around the huge chook yard; if she didn't tuck them safely back into their coop they would likely be taken by a fox. No mean feat when the twelve little creatures were hiding in a variety of places up in trees and behind low bushes.

'Bad dogs,' she growled at the two animals sitting hopefully on the other side of the gate, waiting for an opportunity to come back in and play.

With a resigned sigh she headed for the feed shed to find some food to lure the birds back into their coop. She was tempted to just leave them out, but then she thought of how disappointed her mother would be when she returned home to find her little flock gone.

'Here guinea, guinea, guinea,' Sam called, walking around tossing out grain. She put a small trail of the feed at the doorstep of the coop, feeling like Wile E. Coyote for her efforts.

All she needed now was a wooden signpost with an arrow and 'This Way' written on it.

After twenty or so minutes, the fowl began to call out and emerge from all parts of the yard and trees, regrouping and slowly making their way back to their nightly abode. At least they were good at remembering a routine, Sam grudgingly admitted. Usually they would put themselves to bed and all she was supposed to do was shut the door for them each afternoon and open it again in the morning. Unless, of course, a pair of dogs decided to come along and mess up the routine.

Patiently—far more patiently than she thought she was capable of—Sam waited and watched as the guinea fowl pecked and scratched at the feed trail and eventually moved inside the coop. 'Two, four, five, seven, nine, ten, eleven,' she counted out loud and frowned . . . there were supposed to be twelve. She did a quick recount and still came up with eleven. Where was number twelve?

She scoured the area, praying the dogs hadn't got hold of one of them before she'd intervened, but found no pile of feathers or evidence of a body. *At least it's not dead*, she thought, before looking up into the big gum tree in the centre of the yard.

'Bugger,' she muttered.

Two

Jack Cameron gave the two dogs a quick pat before opening the gate and walking up the concrete path. His hands felt sweaty and he had a weird feeling in his stomach—kind of like the day after chilli night at the pub, only not quite so bad.

He took a deep breath before lifting his hand to knock on the screen door, but there was no answer.

The sound of someone yelling drew his attention and he followed the noise around to the back yard.

'I swear to Christ, Dave, if you don't get down from that bloody tree, I'm going to kill you myself.'

Jack gave a small, surprised chuckle at the unexpected sight of a woman standing below a gum tree, holding up a mobile phone that was emitting loud, high-pitched honking noises.

'Ah . . . Sam?'

He watched as she turned and gave a small yelp, dropping the phone, before quickly bending to pick it up and turn off whatever she had playing, cursing softly as she fumbled with the device.

'G'day Sam.'

'Hello, Jack. How are you?' she asked, clearly trying to hide her surprise and sound as though him finding her standing under a tree hurling abuse at someone named Dave was completely normal.

'Yeah, good. I, ah, heard you were back home.'

'Yep. Just keeping an eye on things while Mum and Dad are away.'

'And how's that going?' he asked, raising an eyebrow.

'Just fine,' she said briskly.

'Who's Dave?' he asked after a brief silence.

Sam pointed at the tree branches and Jack looked up, taking a minute to locate the spotted, grey-feathered bird perched on a limb above them. 'Your mother's guinea fowl is named Dave?'

'No, I just think he looks like a Dave.'

'I see,' Jack said, not really seeing at all. 'So, what are you doing, exactly?'

'I'm using guinea-fowl mating calls to lure him down,' she said in a tone that added silently but quite clearly, *dumb arse*.

'Oh. Fair enough. Is it working?'

'Not exactly. But maybe I'm using a male mating call and not a female one . . . it's hard to tell which is which.'

'That might be the problem.' Jack nodded, wondering if she was actually serious.

'Here,' she said, walking across to him. 'Can you throw this?' She handed him a stick, then looked at him expectantly.

The few times Jack had briefly seen Sam over the years, she had always looked as though she'd stepped from the pages of a glossy magazine—nothing like the Sam he used to know. Today, to his surprise, she looked more like the old Sam he remembered, with dusty jeans and her hair falling from a ponytail in wisps around her face. 'Throw it?' he replied. 'Where?'

'Up there. At Dave. I tried, but I can't throw it high enough.'

'You want me to throw a stick at the bird?'

'Well, yeah. If he won't fly down on his own, then we'll have to make him.'

'Why don't you just leave him up there and wait till he comes down on his own?'

Her words came out in a rush. 'Because I've spent over an hour out here trying to coax the little jerk down and I don't fancy having to tell my mother when she calls that Dave's dead because I forgot to shut the gate and the dogs got in the pen and terrorised the guinea fowl and now she's only got eleven.'

'Fair enough,' Jack said, suddenly sorry he'd asked. Taking a wide backswing, he let the stick go, hearing the crack as it connected with the branch the bird had been perched on before it bounced and knocked the fowl to the ground.

'What are you doing?' Sam yelped as Dave stood up and took off running low to the ground, head extended—straight into the fence.

'You wanted it down.'

'I didn't mean to *knock* it down. I meant to scare it.'

'Well, I didn't think I'd actually hit it,' Jack said, scratching his head. 'How dumb are these birds not to fly out of the way?'

'They're *really* dumb,' Sam replied as they stood side by side and watched the animal repeatedly run at the fence and bounce back like a pinball when he couldn't get through it.

'Help me round him up, will you?' she asked eventually with a sigh, and together they walked towards Dave, steadily moving step by step until the bird was in front of the coop where it belonged. 'And it *still* can't find the doorway,' she said.

Jack gave a slow shake of his head as they stood back watching. Inside the coop, the other birds were calling out, and Dave, hearing them, and only having to step through the wide open door in front of him, continued to run back and forth in front of the coop, searching for a way in.

'I swear to God,' Sam said in disbelief, 'every time I think they can't get any dumber . . . they do.'

They stood there for another five minutes, until eventually Dave fell through the doorway by accident and suddenly realised he was back with his mates.

Jack gave a small, amused grunt as Sam shut the door and let out a soft curse.

'I don't know about you,' she said, 'but I need a drink after that.'

'Lead the way,' he said, grinning. This had not been how he'd imagined it would go, seeing Sam for the first time in too many years to count.

'Take a seat,' she said, nodding towards the verandah while she left him to bring out two beers.

'Thanks,' he said, reaching out to take the offered can, noticing the water beads that ran down its sides.

'So, what brings you out here?' she asked as she took a sip from her can.

'I told Henry I'd look in on things while he was gone.'

'I see he had complete faith in his daughter's abilities, then,' Sam said wryly.

Jack rubbed the back of his head. 'He does. It's not that, I just told him I'd be around in case—'

'It's okay, Jack, I was just pulling your chain.' Sam grinned, and for a moment his heart flip-flopped in his chest. He'd almost forgotten the power one of her smiles used to have on him—still had on him, apparently. It was like being back in high school again, only this time he couldn't blame rampant teenage hormones on his reaction.

'But guinea fowl don't count,' Sam went on. 'Those things are just ridiculous.'

Jack quickly cleared his throat, forcing himself to shake off the past. 'I'm with you on that. Beats me why anyone would want to have them.'

'Maybe my mother's having a late midlife crisis or something.'

Jack smiled. 'So, how *are* the jetsetters?'

Sam waved a hand. 'They're doing great. Got over their jetlag and onto the tour. They're in Ireland at the moment, I think.'

'That's good. I didn't think they'd even go. The last few months things have been pretty tough with the drought, and your dad was talking about postponing the trip.'

'I think Mum would have killed him if he'd tried,' Sam said simply.

'Yeah, they've been planning it for a while.'

'They sure have. In all honesty, though, I wasn't sure Dad would really leave either.'

'What'd they have to do to get you to come down and babysit the place?' Jack asked, sipping his beer and enjoying the cold crispness of the bitter taste.

'I offered.' She shrugged. 'Actually, I was planning on coming down for a while anyway. I sold my business, and Brook moved out of home a few months ago to start uni. She's living with Mackenzie, and my place was getting a bit too quiet. So I figured I may as well be here doing something useful.'

Jack knew she'd sold her business and that her girls had moved in together—Margaret kept him up to date with all her daughter's major milestones. He wasn't sure if Sam knew how much her parents talked about her to him—or if she'd even care. Once, she might have; when she'd decided that a life with him was too horrible to even contemplate and left town. He was pretty sure she'd put a gag order on her parents back then. They'd made it clear, each time he'd come over and asked for her address or a phone number to call her, that she wasn't coming back and he needed to move on. So, eventually he had, and life had gone on. As the years had passed, they'd both started families, and their childhood romance had faded into a memory, and now her parents occasionally talked about her to tease him.

'You still remember how to do it all?' he asked Sam now.

'Don't worry, Dad made me do everything under his supervision before he was convinced I could handle it. It was a jillaroo crash course,' she said with a laugh, and the gentle tinkle of the sound once more sparked long-forgotten memories.

When he was younger, whenever he went to the swimming hole where they'd spent their summers as kids, if he closed his eyes and listened really hard, he'd swear he could hear that laugh floating on the breeze. He'd never admitted that out loud to anyone—they would think he was losing his mind—and it had been years since he'd thought about it . . . until now.

'Oh yeah? So, you'll be right to do pretty much everything, then?' He grinned.

Sam wrinkled her nose in a way he remembered her doing as a kid. 'If the cattle need anything more than feeding and watering, I'm just going to hire someone to come and do it.'

'I guess that's where I come in.'

'Dad had your number written down and underlined multiple times, *In case of an emergency, call Jack*,' she said, barely hiding her eye roll.

'I'm here if you need me,' he said. 'Just give me a shout.'

Jack watched as she drank her beer and found himself wondering how she could look almost the same now as when they were kids. Her hair was different. It used to be lighter, not blonde but a shade of golden wheat, and longer. He remembered her running along the beach, her hair flowing out behind her, tanned skin and blue eyes shining. She'd been eighteen then. Now, her hair was darker, a warm brown with expensive-looking highlights. He knew from his ex-wife that these were done in a hairdresser's salon and that they weren't cheap. Cilia may have liked to spend money, but he was willing to bet even her hairdresser's bill would probably have been a bargain compared to Sam's. The Sunshine Coast was a whole other level of high maintenance, which is why he found it strange that she'd decided to come back here and feed cattle for her old man.

'So, how have you been?' Sam asked, settling back in her chair and snapping him out of his thoughts. 'I don't think we've ever really sat down and talked, in . . . well, I don't know how long. When would I have last seen you?' she asked, tilting her head slightly.

'I dunno. Maybe your mum's sixtieth?'

Sam frowned a little. 'That was years ago.'

'It's been a while.'

Even then they hadn't actually talked. They'd stood in a circle of old friends and exchanged hellos. They'd both been married then, and he hadn't been any more impressed with her husband than he'd been the first few times he'd met the bloke.

'A lot's happened since then,' she said, as if reading his thoughts. She glanced up at him. 'Mum and Chelsea have kept me up to date with the local news. I was sorry to hear about you and Cilia.'

He wasn't surprised to hear she'd been kept abreast of all the gossip—this was Burrumba, after all, and Chelsea Graham was Sam's best friend. 'Yeah. Well, shit happens, I guess,' he said, shrugging.

But when it happened he hadn't been able to shrug it off. It had side-swiped him completely. He hadn't seen it coming. The fact that Cilia had managed to move on and find a new bloke so soon hadn't lessened the sting.

'How are the kids?' Sam asked.

'Good.' He nodded, sitting back further in his chair. 'They've settled in pretty well down there. Seem to like it.'

'How old are they?'

'Tasmin's twelve and Bianca's fifteen,' he said and felt a wave of emotion wash over him. He missed his girls. Cilia had moved back to her family in Newcastle, taking his daughters away from the only home they'd ever known. It was only four hours away, but it felt as far as the other side of the world. The house had never felt so empty.

'Do you get to see much of them?'

'They come home most school holidays, though Bianca had too much of a social life last time, so it was only Tasmin.'

'They go through that stage,' Sam said with a small grimace of sympathy.

'Luckily I can still blackmail Tasmin by holding her horse hostage,' Jack said with a grunt. His youngest was a country kid through and through. She loved horses and swimming in the creek and was still happy to hug her dad in public. His older daughter, though, had suddenly grown up. She had a part-time job, and visiting her old man didn't seem like much of a priority anymore.

'I'm pretty sure Dad does the same thing with me.'

'I can't believe old Matey is still kicking. He has to be almost thirty?' Jack remembered when she'd got him. That was the night they'd slept together. Sadly, that's all they'd done—sleep and watch over a pregnant mare in a freezing-cold stable—but he hadn't cared. He'd got to spend the entire night with her as they'd watched Matey come into the world. Had it really been that long ago?

'Almost,' she agreed with a smile. 'I can't imagine this place without him.'

'He's a tough old bugger, I'll give him that much.'

'Remember the night he was born?' she asked quietly.

He gave a small start. It was like she was reading his mind. 'Sure do,' he said, holding her gaze. They'd been seventeen years old and he'd been head over heels in love. The mare had a difficult, drawn-out delivery and had required around-the-clock supervision before finally giving birth to a long-legged buckskin foal. They'd sat together, side by side, watching mother nature do her thing. Even though Jack had gone on to witness more births than he could remember over the years, that one had been special. They'd also been caught making out by Sam's father, who'd told Jack not to come back for a few weeks, but it had been worth it. 'Your dad reminds me now and again that my time is coming, now that my girls are both teenagers,' Jack groaned. 'I think he's looking forward to me suffering a bit.'

Sam gave a low snigger. 'I hope for your sake they don't take after you, then.'

'I don't know what you're implying,' he said with a haughty air.

'Uh-huh,' she said, nodding sarcastically. 'You were an angel.'

'I'm pretty sure I was until I was corrupted by you.'

'Right,' she drawled, but her smile lingered and for a moment, as they looked at each other, he felt an old stirring inside.

'Sometimes I wish I could just go back to that time,' she said, tipping her head up and closing her eyes. 'We couldn't wait to grow up and do whatever we wanted . . . remember?'

He gave an easy smile as he watched her.

'Well, just look at us now,' she said, throwing her hands in the air and shaking her head.

'Aw, come on, Sam, you haven't had such a bad run.'

'No,' she said with a sigh. 'But life was so much simpler back then. I don't really like this adult gig anymore. Making big decisions; kids growing up; worrying about everything.'

'Yeah, the kids-growing-up thing takes a bit of getting used to,' he agreed. 'But I'm pretty sure you've still got a few good years left in you.'

She gave him a reluctant smile before finishing her drink. 'I guess so. I don't know, Jack, for some reason coming back this time seems to be dragging up all the old ghosts.'

'Maybe it's life trying to tell you to slow down a bit. Sometimes you need a bit of peace and quiet to hear the things you haven't been able to hear before.'

She grinned. 'Look at you sounding all grown up and wise.'

'I was always wise—you were just too blinded by my rugged good looks and charm to notice before.'

Sam rolled her eyes at him but kept on grinning, and Jack leaned back in his chair and smiled, that weird feeling in his stomach flaring once again.

Three

Sam looked at the man across the table from her. There wasn't much of the boy she'd once known in his adult features. He'd grown up. And yet his eyes remained the same; those denim-blue eyes. She'd seen them lighten as he laughed, and darken when he was focused on something. His hair was a little longer than the last time she'd seen him—swept back from his forehead. It was still as dark as coffee, but she noticed a few lighter greys showing on the sides and in his scruffy-looking beard. He looked different . . . older, yes, but there was a hardness about him too, something standoffish that would discourage people from getting too close.

Inwardly, she rolled her eyes. How could she possibly know that? Once, maybe, she could have read him like a book, but that was years ago. She didn't know what kind of man Jack had turned into. He was a stranger to her now.

They'd bumped into each other now and again over the years, but not as often as she might have expected considering he was her parents' neighbour. Then again, whenever she'd come home with Andrew and the girls they'd only stayed a few days; there was never enough time to catch up with old friends.

Andrew hadn't really enjoyed the farm, preferring to spend any time off he had with his boats and jet skis on the canals behind their lavish Mooloolaba home. His property-investment business had been a lucrative but time-consuming enterprise, and the lifestyle that went along with it—socialising and networking—was not something Sam particularly enjoyed.

It had always been a bone of contention between them, but Sam had devoted herself to their children, and eventually she and Andrew had come to lead separate lives. It shouldn't have come as a surprise to discover Andrew had had numerous affairs over the years, but it did. At least he'd tried to keep them quiet, until he met the one woman who refused to play by his rules and made herself, and their relationship, known publicly, and Sam could no longer ignore what a hollow shell her marriage had become. It had hurt at the time, but looking back, she wasn't sure where the pain stemmed from: heartbreak, or the fact that Andrew had continued to pretend their marriage had been important. She'd been so stupid; oblivious to the fact he had happily discarded their marriage whenever it suited him while she had continued to be the loyal wife holding down the fort at home. But beneath the hurt, there was also a touch of relief. She could finally acknowledge that she'd fallen out of love with the man she'd married. She wasn't sure when it had happened, just that it had.

'How are you handling the quiet?' Jack asked her. 'Be a bit different from where you come from?'

'I don't miss the noise,' Sam said adamantly. 'I've been catching up with Chelsea, which has been nice. It's strange not having Mum and Dad here, though.'

'I know the feeling.' He nodded. 'When Cilia and the girls left, the old place felt like a damn mausoleum. It takes some time to get used to.'

'That's kind of what made my mind up about coming down here. A house just isn't the same when the kids go.'

'So, you're an empty nester,' he said, eyeing her from across the table.

'I guess I am.'

'That doesn't seem right. You're too young to have kids leaving home.'

'It sneaks up faster than you'd think.'

Sam had left home at eighteen, moving up to Queensland to live with an older cousin before deciding to head further north with a group of friends to find work in a resort. At twenty-one, she'd been living her dream, spending a few wild years partying a bit too hard—a side-effect of bartending on too many of the Whitsunday Islands—until at twenty-four she'd met Andrew, who, just like in some romantic chick flick, had swept her off her feet.

He'd been part of a high-flying, hard-partying crowd, and even after a whirlwind romance, quickly followed by an elopement, their life had continued to be one long, never-ending party. Until Sam discovered she was pregnant.

She hadn't planned it, but Andrew had been older and they'd been in love back then. Her parents hadn't been sure about it all at first, but their headstrong daughter had found a self-made man with a job and money to provide for a family, so there was little to substantiate their concern. Except now, looking back, Sam knew that their parental instincts had detected something untrustworthy about Andrew that she hadn't. Or maybe they'd just been concerned about how fast she'd fallen for someone they didn't know. She suspected they'd always thought she would marry a local. It was a lot less risky when everyone knew your family and where you came from.

That was part of the reason she'd been determined to leave Burrumba as soon as she could. The constant judgement of a small town had always driven her crazy.

'Especially considering you were the one who apparently didn't want to be married off and be barefoot and pregnant.'

Jack's words snapped her back to the present and she glanced across at him, but he didn't meet her surprised gaze. 'Not at eighteen,' she said pointedly. She knew exactly what his words, and his tone, meant. She'd broken his heart when she'd left town after high school. 'I got all the rebellion out of my system and it turned out I was ready for it a few years later,' she added quietly.

'Well, that's something, I guess.'

'It was a long time ago, Jack.'

'Yep. Water under the bridge,' he agreed, draining the last of his drink and putting the can on the table. 'Thanks for the beer. I better get going.'

His abrupt mood change left her slightly off balance. One minute they'd been reminiscing about old times and the next, he was slamming the door shut on their past and making it clear he couldn't wait to get away. She rose from her chair, following him with a frown, and almost ran into his back when he stopped suddenly and turned around.

'Let me know if you need a hand with anything,' he said, looking down at her.

His face had lost the laidback, friendly expression he'd had earlier, but his nearness sparked a sudden flare of something that made her feel slightly giddy and tingly, before she remembered he'd just acted like a bit of a jerk. She took a quick step away. 'Thanks. But I'm sure I'll be fine.'

He opened his mouth as if he wanted to add something, then changed his mind and closed it, turning away.

Sam stood at the back door as the sound of his car faded, before returning to the verandah to collect their empty cans, pondering the strange rollercoaster of emotions Jack's unexpected visit had created. 'Welcome home, Sam,' she murmured under her breath as she headed inside to find something for dinner.

Jack swore as he slammed his door shut and turned the key in the ignition. What the hell was wrong with him? Everything had been going fine until he opened his big mouth about the past. He hadn't expected it to still hurt so much. He hadn't even meant to bring it up. One minute they were talking about their respective kids and the next, he suddenly remembered with disconcerting clarity the night she'd run away, right after they'd been talking about *their* future together and the possibility of *them* having kids.

One day she was here and they were together—Sam and Jack; Jack and Sam—and the next, he got a Dear John in the form of a postcard from Queensland. She hadn't even said goodbye.

'It was almost thirty years ago, for Christ's sake,' he muttered. It shouldn't even be something he remembered and yet, he did. She'd broken his damn heart.

Back then, there had only ever been two things in his life he'd known for sure: the first was that he was going to be a farmer, and the second was that he was going to be Samantha Murphy's husband. He'd had a simple outlook on life even as a teenager, and nothing had changed in him as a man. He was still happy with a simple life. He just hadn't counted on it not being enough for Sam.

And now, she was back.

He'd never imagined what it would be like if Sam were ever to return to Burrumba. It seemed an impossible thought. She had the perfect life—everything she'd ever wanted, it seemed. Maybe it had crossed his mind briefly the day Henry mentioned in passing that Sam was getting a divorce, that maybe . . . just maybe, she might bundle the kids into the car and move back home with her parents. But then, he knew she had a business and a life, and any minute hope that may have briefly flared, withered and died.

But now, here she was—back in town only a handful of days and already she'd managed to reawaken old memories and stir up emotions he'd thought he'd forgotten. He would have laughed if it wasn't so bloody depressing. That old adage of 'Be careful what you wish for' had never been truer than it was right now.

Four

Sam woke to the sound of a loud engine near her ear, only to open her eyes and discover it was Mr Buttons. It was slightly unnerving to realise that the slow, sleepy-eyed feline had been watching her while she slept. Mr Buttons was renowned for his dislike of men, which made Sam think the whole nine-lives thing wasn't a myth after all. Her father had tried many times to remove the cat . . . unsuccessfully. To this day, Mr Buttons still hissed at him whenever he walked past—and had done so ever since her mother had found him as a stray kitten beside the road seven years ago.

Around women, though, it was a different story. He curled up on Sam's lap at night as she watched TV and occasionally slept on the end of her bed. Sam loved being back in her old room. It had had a makeover since her teen years—gone were the twin single beds in matching pastel pink bedcovers, replaced with a queen bed; and the lace curtains had been updated to a set of vertical blinds—but it was still her room. Her mother hadn't changed the colour of the walls; they were still unashamedly pink. Her dad had painted her room for her tenth birthday, and she loved it as much today as she had back then.

Sam got up and headed to the kitchen, dodging the now meowing cat as it threaded its way between her steps down the hall. She was not naturally a morning person, but she tended to wake up early when she was here. There were certain things she enjoyed about mornings: the sunrise, the quiet of a house before the morning rush . . . but what she enjoyed most was caffeine. 'Okay, okay, I'll feed you. Just wait,' she said, her attempt to reach the fridge for his tin of food hampered by Mr Buttons under her feet. With relative calm soon restored when the cat was fed, she switched on the kettle and set about making coffee. Later, as she sat with her mug on the verandah, she listened to the sound of chirping birds and clucking chooks mixed with the noisy racket of the guinea fowl in the chook pen.

Bloody guinea fowl.

It was only just after eight o'clock but the temperature was already rising. For the past few days it had been well into the high thirties—summer weather in the first week of October.

The noisy hum of insects made the day feel even hotter as she looked across the lacklustre paddocks and landscape. Surely it had to rain soon.

Sam's thoughts were interrupted by her phone buzzing on the table next to her, and she smiled as her daughter's face filled the screen.

'Morning,' Sam said as the video call connected.

'Morning, Mum,' Mackenzie said, before the phone moved and a second face appeared.

'Morning, Mum,' said Brook, waving.

'Hey, you two,' Sam replied, her heart swelling with love as a wave of homesickness washed over her. She'd been a little concerned when they'd raised the idea of sharing an apartment together when Brook was accepted into her university course. When they were younger they'd fought like cat and dog at any given opportunity, but so far things seemed to be working out, and Sam was quietly impressed.

'So, how's the farm manager gig going?' Mackenzie asked.

'Just fine. I don't know why anyone was ever worried I couldn't do this. I *did* grow up here you know,' Sam added with a haughty tone while trying to keep a straight face.

'But that was a *long* time ago,' Brook said with a cheeky grin.

'Don't listen to her, Mum. *I* have always had complete faith in you,' Mackenzie cut in.

'Well, thank you. I'm so glad someone believes in me,' Sam said sarcastically.

'You know I'm only joking, right?' Brook said, her smile dropping. 'Are you okay though, Mum?'

'Of course I am. I'm loving being back down here.' And she was. Each time she'd brought the girls to visit over the years, she found herself wondering what it would be like to move back, but by the time they returned to the coast she would be swept back into hectic school schedules and social activities, and all thoughts of home would be pushed aside.

However, in the lead-up to Brook moving out with Mackenzie, Sam had been feeling more and more unsettled, and coming back to the farm had shown her how much she'd missed her home town. She assumed that her divorce had been the catalyst behind her unrest, but losing a close friend to a melanoma around the same time had also made her realise how precious life was, and she found herself growing annoyed by the sun-worshipping, body image–focused environment she lived in. Her husband leaving her for a twenty-something with perfect eyebrows and boobs that hadn't yet started to sag *could* also have been the underlying reason, but whatever it was, she was tired of the Sunshine Coast lifestyle. Even the business she'd started almost five years ago had stopped bringing her joy.

Creating a homewares business had been something she'd scarcely dared to dream about. She loved decorating, but she hadn't realised she had a knack for it until she started receiving compliments from so many of Andrew's clients when they came to the house. In the early days, prior to having Mackenzie, Sam was easily bored. She found that changing the rooms around and finding the perfect knickknacks and finishing touches gave her something to do. She loved hunting around for the perfect chair, the right lamp or the best coloured placemats to set off a new table setting. They were small touches sometimes, but they made all the difference. Once the girls had grown older and didn't need her so much, she began to play with the idea of starting her own business. At first Andrew had been against it—there were risks in investing money in a new business, and what did she really know about running a business anyway? His words had hurt a little, but she had to admit he had a point. All she knew how to do was be a mum. She'd been venting over the phone one night to Chelsea, who had abruptly put things into perspective.

'Of course you know how to run a business,' Chelsea had snapped. 'You've been a treasurer on the school's P&C committee, haven't you?'

'Yes, but that's hardly—'

'Who buys the groceries and pays the bills? Who hired the gardeners and landscapers to create that amazing tropical garden you designed?'

'I did, but that's nothing to do with running a business,' Sam had protested once she managed to get a word in.

'Rubbish. Running a business uses the same skills you've been using to run a household. You know how to deal with people—you've been entertaining your husband's hoity-toity clients for years,' Chelsea added in her no-nonsense Chelsea way that had made Sam smile on the other end of the phone. 'If this is something you want to do—you should go for it.'

Chelsea's words gave Sam renewed confidence, and she'd sat down to plan and research, and within months she presented her husband with a business proposal. Looking back, she suspected Andrew had probably been giving it some thought of his own and decided that the more distracted Sam was, the less likely she would be to interfere in his private life.

Little did she know then that her business would become the foundation of her new life. Through the breakdown of her marriage, the business was there. Through her daughters' horrid, trying teenage years, the business welcomed her every morning with open arms. When Mackenzie left home, the business kept Sam focused on something other than thinking about her eldest baby moving out. The shop saved her sanity, it gave her purpose, and it was something that was truly her own in a marriage that had been heavily geared towards her husband and his success.

Which was why her decision to sell had surprised everyone, including herself.

As her shop had grown, so had her workload and she'd needed to employ more people, but in doing so she found that she was spending less time doing the fun things she wanted to do, and more time sorting out staffing issues and paperwork. The joy the business had once brought her when it was small and manageable had changed as it had grown, and she no longer felt the same thrill and excitement when she walked into her gleaming showroom.

After another long day spent behind a computer dealing with accountants, Sam had gone home to a lonely dinner for one in an empty house. That's when it hit her—she was alone. Suddenly everything felt wrong. A bottle of wine probably hadn't helped, but for the first time in years, even her little shop couldn't make her feel better. She just felt . . . redundant.

Sam had put the business on the market the next day, just to see if there would be any interest. It had sold within a fortnight, putting an end to any lingering indecision.

'You just haven't seemed yourself lately,' Brook continued.

'I think I needed to get away for a bit,' Sam said. And she had. For so long she'd been the strong one. It came with the job of Mum, but it hadn't always been easy. Navigating the way through the divorce for herself and the girls had left her exhausted, both mentally and emotionally.

'But isn't it kind of boring being there all by yourself? I mean, what do you *do*? There's not really anything there . . . you can't even go shopping.'

Sam bit back a chuckle. Her daughters' upbringing had been so different from her own, yet they were exactly like her in many ways. When she was a kid she couldn't wait to leave Burrumba and go where all the action was. Now, though, she craved . . . quiet. She hadn't missed shopping or going out for lunch or seeing a show. 'I'm catching up with old friends and reading. I'm really happy being back here, and I spend a lot of time with Matey,' she told them.

'Oh, Matey,' Mackenzie sighed. 'I *do* miss him.'

Sam smiled. At least one of her daughters shared her love of horses—to a degree. Every trip home, it would be Mackenzie who spent her time with Sam's old gelding. Sam had often regretted not being more vocal about buying somewhere they could have horses, but Andrew already had boats before they were married and wanted a house on the canal to moor them. It just never seemed practical to sell up and move. Still, having had the past few weeks to dote on her old friend, Sam realised how much time she'd wasted not following her own passions.

'Mum!' Brook's voice cut into her musings.

'Sorry? What?'

'I said, we have to go, we're going to the beach.'

'Oh. Okay. That sounds like fun. Be careful, and put on sunscreen,' she added.

'We're, like, adults now, Mum, you don't have to remind us to do that anymore,' Brook said, rolling her eyes.

'So you've packed the sunscreen, then?' Sam asked, raising an eyebrow.

'We were just about to,' Mackenzie said with a sheepish grin at her mother.

'Uh-huh, sure you were. See, you do still need your mum for some things.'

'We'll *always* need our mum,' Brook said solemnly, and for a moment Sam felt a sting in her eyes as she looked at the two beautiful faces of her children, now almost all grown up.

'I love you. Take care of each other.'

'We will. Love you, Mum,' they chorused, before the screen went blank and only the sound of birds surrounded her once more.

She didn't mind being alone. Silence didn't bother her—in fact, she often craved it—but it was the *constant* silence she'd noticed the most once both her girls had left home. Through the day when they were at school or out on weekends, the quiet of the house always followed the bedlam of the morning rush—music playing in bedrooms, muted phone conversations with friends at night, or a TV show being played too loud and Sam having to yell for it to be turned down. That's what she missed the most: the prelude to silence. Once she was on her own, there was nothing to break up the quiet.

On the farm, it was the same, only it wasn't. Here, it was never truly silent. The hum of insects that grew louder as the day got warmer was sometimes so noisy that she had to close a window. The cattle would call out now and again in the distance, and the chooks in the yard were constantly cackling or screeching in protest over a nest hog who was taking too long to lay an egg. And the guinea fowl . . . the bloody, noisy guinea fowl—they never shut up. This wasn't the sterile, noise-reduction-window kind of silence that blocked out the rest of the world in her own house. She liked this kind of quiet.

Sam lugged a heavy bucket of feed from the shed, cursing softly as she splashed some on her jeans. She'd forgotten just how messy animals and farm life could be and soon realised with a sinking heart that her expensive, designer-brand jeans would now be declassified into *work* jeans, with some designer patchwork stains.

She walked across to a gate that led to a big shady paddock and called out to Matey. There was no movement, and it took another three calls before his white head popped up over the hill and the old horse made his way closer to her. With a mixture of love and sadness, Sam watched his slow, steady gait, his head bobbing in time with each step. He was looking old. In horse years, he was ancient. Even in people years, he was an old horse. But he was hers and she loved him.

'Hey, old man,' she crooned when he reached her. She leaned over the fence to feed him the bananas she'd bought especially for him, letting them get brown and squishy just the way he liked them. 'I don't like it when you take so long to come up. I was worried about you,' she said, rubbing his head. One day, she knew, he wouldn't come up at all. Each day she hoped it wouldn't be while she was in charge. She wasn't sure she could cope with that alone.

She buried her face against his white neck and breathed in his musky horse scent. There was nothing like horse aromatherapy. If she knew how, she would bottle the scent; just one bottle could fix everything from depression to stress and anything in between.

She put the bucket down at his feet and leaned against the rails to watch him devour his feed. The loud washing-machine-like sound he made brought a fond smile to her face. It was funny how something as simple as keeping a horse company while he ate could make her feel so contented.

There was a breeze picking up today, but not a cool, refreshing one. The wind was warm as it moved through the trees and across the dry countryside, sapping what little moisture was left out of everything it touched. It was barely nine-thirty and already the sun held a significant sting. It was going to be another long, hot day.

Five

Sam drove slowly along the washed-out dirt driveway, doing her best to avoid the worst of the potholes. In the distance, a row of fat, healthy cows were plodding from the dairy back into the paddock after the morning milk.

Her childhood best friend, Chelsea Mitchell, had married Troy Graham, a boy they'd both gone through school with, and for the past twenty-odd years she had worked alongside him and his parents, running the family's dairy farm. It was a true love story. Before Chelsea had married Troy, she moved away from Burrumba to become a teacher and went on to travel after she'd graduated, before returning home to her high-school sweetheart. Troy had been happy to work his farm and wait for her. The arrangement had worked well for them—unlike for Sam and Jack. She thought briefly of Jack's reaction to the memory of their break-up—it had been over almost the exact same thing. The key difference was that Sam hadn't wanted Jack to wait for her—she knew she wasn't coming back. Not then.

Over the years Sam and Chelsea had remained close, but they hadn't really been able to do more than catch up over a quick coffee during Sam's visits home . . . until now. Sam was loving her new freedom to drop by Chelsea's place whenever she felt like it. They had fallen back into their old friendship, as if it hadn't been years between visits, and it made Sam realise just how much she cherished having a friend who'd known her so well growing up. It was different from the friendships she had as an adult. Grown-up friends had in-jokes and could exchange looks when certain people began to rabbit on in long committee meetings, but they didn't have the old stories—the important ones that became memories.

Sam parked the car and greeted the dogs that bounced around her legs: an enormously fat Labrador named Molly, and a small, wiry-haired mix of terrier and God-only-knew-how-many-other-breeds called George. It always amused her how farmers tended to have two completely separate types of dogs—the house animals and the working ones. The Grahams were no different; their five kelpies, lean and athletic, were almost a different species from these two. If Sam had to come back as anything in her next life, she hoped it would be as the house dog of a farmer.

'Hey, you,' Chelsea called, coming out the back door with a smile.

'I was in town and thought I'd just keep driving out here for a visit.'

'I was thinking about calling you later,' Chelsea said as she embraced Sam. 'So that was good timing. Come inside, I'll put the kettle on.'

Sam loved her friend's house—the moment she stepped inside, it ceased being a house and instantly became a home. It was like walking into a hug. Photos of family decorated the walls, and kids' artwork adorned the fridge. Sam smiled every time she saw it. She missed those years, when her girls had proudly brought their paintings home from school. It had been a long time since her fridge had displayed anything other than bills and the occasional postcard. Chelsea's five children were spread out in ages, the eldest seventeen, a son, followed by a fifteen-year-old girl, twin boys who were almost eleven and a young daughter who had just turned seven.

'How're things going over your way?'

'Yeah, fine. I haven't managed to kill or lose any of Dad's livestock, so everything's okay for now.'

'What about your mum's guinea fowl?' Chelsea asked, lifting an eyebrow.

'Yep. All still alive,' Sam said.

'Damn, I see the assassins have failed yet again,' Chelsea said.

Sam watched as Chelsea pottered about the kitchen. 'They don't even *need* an assassin—they're a big enough threat to themselves as it is.'

'Seen anyone interesting lately?' Chelsea asked.

Sam narrowed her eyes at her friend as she took a seat at the kitchen bench. 'And by interesting, I assume you mean ... Jack?' Chelsea's attempt at wide-eyed innocence didn't fool Sam for a second. 'How could you possibly have heard about that?'

Chelsea didn't even bother hiding her grin as she crossed to the fridge to take out the milk. 'It's Burrumba.'

Sam kept her narrowed eyes on her friend. She'd only seen him yesterday afternoon. Even the notorious gossip mill around town wasn't *that* fast.

'Troy saw Jack this morning in town and he mentioned it,' Chelsea said with a laugh.

This shouldn't have surprised her—Jack and Troy had known each other all their lives—but it did.

'So? How did *that* go?' Chelsea prompted.

'Oh, Troy didn't say?' Sam asked with only a touch of sarcasm.

'Nope. Jack only said he'd stopped by your parents' place yesterday and saw you. You know men—they never bother to dig for any important info. So? What happened?'

'Nothing happened,' Sam said dismissively.

Chelsea rolled her eyes. 'Come on, Sam. You've gotta give me something. My life revolves around washing, cooking and milking bloody cows. I need something juicy to get me through.'

'Well, sorry to disappoint,' Sam muttered, then gave a small sigh. 'It was a bit weird. He's changed a lot since last time I saw him.'

'How so?'

'I don't know, maybe I wasn't really paying much attention last time, but he looks . . . harder . . . colder than I remember.'

'He didn't take Cilia leaving very well. We hardly saw him; he kept to himself for a long time.'

'That's understandable.' Sam nodded. She knew exactly how it felt being left behind, only she'd had the advantage of having her children around her to stop her sinking into depression. She'd had to get up in the morning and put on a bright smile for their sake. But she remembered avoiding social occasions as much as possible. She'd felt humiliated and hurt. Her husband's betrayal had been splashed across the newspapers' social pages, and though Jack's break-up wouldn't have made it into the local rag, around here it didn't need to—everyone knew everything that went on and it would have been just as mortifying.

'What did you two talk about?'

Sam gave her friend a frustrated glance. She knew there was no way Chelsea was going to give up on this. 'We talked about the kids mainly.' Except for the bit at the end, she added silently. Even now it surprised her that there'd still been something raw about their break-up. She didn't like that she'd hurt him then, or that it brought back painful memories for them both now.

'Right . . .' Chelsea said as she picked up the two coffee mugs. 'Bring those, will you?' she added, nodding towards the plate she'd just filled with cake and slices. They moved outside to the undercover patio beside the pool. Towels and swimmers hung over the fence drying in the morning sun, the smell of chlorine and sunscreen lingering in the air around them. It brought back memories of summertime fun and made Sam smile.

The sound of cattle in the distance and the shrill cicada song in the bush behind the yard filled the silence as the women settled themselves into chairs at the outdoor table.

'Are you missing the glitz and glamour of home yet?' Chelsea asked as they sipped their coffee.

'Not really,' Sam said, tilting her head slightly as she considered the question. 'I miss the girls, of course, but I don't really miss anything from up there.'

'Except your inbuilt coffee machine,' Chelsea said with an almost wistful look. On the one occasion Sam had managed to get Chelsea to visit her, her friend hadn't been able to get over the fact that Sam's kitchen had a coffee machine built into it. It still made Sam laugh when she remembered the look on Chelsea's face.

'I don't know how you could bear to leave that house behind. I mean, you practically lived in a damn resort. If I were you, I'd never have set foot outside my house.'

Chelsea was right; Sam's house had been beautiful. Andrew had made sure it had state-of-the-art everything, and with Sam's design flair it had looked like something out of a *Home Beautiful* magazine, but it had never felt like Chelsea's place, or even Sam's parents' home . . . it had lacked a soul. Because they used the house for entertaining and hosting Andrew's business parties, it was always more of an extension of the business . . . they didn't display family photos, and every piece of furniture or artwork had been selected to fit perfectly with the rest of the decor. It was a showpiece, not a home. Sam had sometimes thought her girls had missed out on having that. It wasn't as though they'd suffered—growing up in a luxurious home was hardly any kind of hardship—it was just different from her own childhood.

She'd been happy to move out after the divorce—the house itself meant nothing to her, other than the memories of the girls growing up there and the first few happy years of her marriage. She'd bought a smaller place nearby, where she could finally add the touches that she'd always wanted. The walls were full of framed photos of the girls and her family. Christmas photos taken with Santa over the years now adorned the walls and hallway tables, and furniture was chosen for comfort rather than photogenic appeal.

'Actually, I've been thinking for a while now that maybe I need a change of scenery.'

'You want to move?'

'I'm only thinking about it,' Sam said quickly. Saying it out loud suddenly made it feel a little too real. 'Since the girls left and I sold the business I've been feeling a bit lost. I just don't feel like I fit in up there anymore.'

'So, you'd move down to the Gold Coast, to be with the girls?'

'No, not there. I've been thinking about how I always wished I'd got the girls into horses when they were growing up—like we used to be. I really regret they didn't have that experience. Being back on Mum and Dad's place makes me feel as though maybe I've put off what I really wanted to do for too long. I'm thinking about buying a farm of my own.'

She saw Chelsea's eyebrow rise in response, and she instantly felt stupid for bringing it up.

'Not a working farm or anything . . . just a few acres for some horses . . . It's probably a stupid idea. It was just a thought,' she said, her voice trailing off.

'No,' Chelsea said firmly, leaning forward in her chair. 'It's not stupid at all. It just took me by surprise. I always thought you loved living up there.'

Sam shrugged. 'I've been living there for half of my life. It was exciting in the beginning and I did like it, but I don't know, I just realised I've been caught up in this world where everything has to be perfect all the time. Maybe it had to do with Andrew leaving the way he did. Maybe I felt like I was being traded in for a newer model or something, I don't know.' She waved her hand dismissively. 'I just want to be me, and I don't think I've been me in a very long time.'

'I always saw you,' Chelsea said quietly. 'The real Sam was buried under a lot of other stuff, but she was always in there. I think you know what's right for you. Follow your heart.'

Sam groaned, closing her eyes briefly. 'But I'm not sure I can just abandon the kids.'

'It's not like you're dropping them off at a church in a cardboard box,' Chelsea scoffed. 'They've left home. They're adults.'

'They're twenty-one and nineteen . . . they're *not* adults,' Sam insisted.

'What were you doing when you were nineteen?' Chelsea asked.

'It was different back then.' For a moment they shared an amused look before laughing.

'I think you need to give your kids a bit more credit. Either that, or they'll learn to grow up once you're not there to do everything for them.'

Sam pulled a doubtful face. 'They're only two hours away at the moment. If I move back here it's a five-hour drive.'

'Which is doable. It's not the end of the earth. They'll be fine. Besides, they have each other and their father's up there. It's not like they're on their own.'

She had a point. Only, for Sam, logic didn't really come into it. She was their mum and she had always been the one who fixed things.

'I can't wait for the day it's just Troy and me here,' Chelsea went on. 'No fighting, no mess, no extra washing . . .'

Sam gave a small grunt. 'You can't even imagine life without your horde around.'

'Okay, maybe not, but sometimes I do fantasise about lying back on my lounge with my feet up, and not having to make dinner or oversee bath time or referee a fight or make sure everyone's done their homework.'

Sam had no idea how she did it. Life was hectic, but Sam had seen first-hand how efficiently Chelsea ran her household, despite the chaos and noise. Maybe she had the occasional thought about all the peace and quiet she'd have once the house was kid-free, but Sam knew that the reality was nothing like Chelsea imagined. She still had a few years before she experienced the first of her children leaving home—her eldest, James, seemed destined to work alongside his parents on the property after he finished school, so they'd have a full house for quite a while yet.

'Any plans to see Jack again?' Chelsea asked before feigning innocence at Sam's loaded glance.

'No,' she replied firmly.

'You don't need some time to think it over first?' Chelsea hitched an eyebrow at Sam's quick response.

'We knew each other as kids. Now he's . . . well, not a kid. He's practically a stranger.'

'Nope. He's certainly not a kid anymore,' Chelsea agreed. 'But neither are you. Who knows? Maybe you can pick up where you left off?'

Sam gave a small snort.

'I'm serious,' Chelsea said. 'What's stopping you? He's single. You're single.'

'I'm so not even interested.'

'You so are,' Chelsea returned. 'Don't give me that innocent look. Jack Cameron is one hunk of a man and you two used to be crazy about each other.'

'*Used* to be,' Sam countered. 'Like, a hundred years ago in a different life.'

'That kind of thing doesn't happen very often. And I'm willing to bet it doesn't ever really go away either.'

'I think you've been reading too many romance books, Chels,' Sam said, shaking her head. Even in high school, Chelsea had been addicted to romance. She had devoured the Sweet Dreams and Sweet Valley High series and even now there was always a book lying around the house, its cover showing a bare-chested hero and a woman wearing an off-the-shoulder gown with quite a bit of leg exposed.

'Or maybe I just want the people I care about to be happy.' Chelsea shrugged, spooning a bite of cake into her mouth.

'I don't need to start messing my life up with a relationship.'

'Not all relationships are messy.'

'I'm finally in a place where I don't have to explain myself to anyone else. My kids are self-sufficient—mostly,' Sam added, taking a moment to savour the delicious carrot cake from her plate, 'and I have my independence.'

'Which is all well and good, but you can still have your independence and a man who makes you happy.'

'Not in my experience,' Sam quipped. Which wasn't exactly true. She'd been happy enough in the beginning with Andrew. She couldn't pinpoint the exact moment things began to change, but she suspected it happened gradually, as the girls began to take up more of her attention and she had less energy to spend going out with Andrew and doing couple things the way they had in the beginning. 'I'm glad you and Troy are happy, but I don't necessarily think being in a relationship is an idicator of being happy or not. That's up to me.'

'And are you?' Chelsea probed. 'Happy? Really?'

Sam considered her friend's question. 'I am. I went through a rough patch after Andrew left, and it took a while for me to find my feet as a single mum, but it opened up a whole new life for me. I threw myself into the shop and discovered I really loved owning my own business. And I miss the girls now, but I know I'll be okay without them.'

'Then I guess you've answered your own question about whether or not you could move back here and leave them.' Chelsea said with a shrug.

Sam gave her a small smile as she realised Chelsea was right. Maybe her crazy idea wasn't as crazy as she'd thought.

Six

Burrumba was the central town in a valley on the banks of a wide river, inland from the coast. The many arms of smaller creeks that branched off it included farming areas, places too small to be towns but which made up the general population of their region.

The radio newsreader launched into the top news stories of the hour, and Sam listened with half an ear. Mostly they covered the Sydney and national news but they also touched on the efforts of volunteers who were delivering donated hay out west, and she felt a glimmer of hope for humanity. For so long, each night the news bulletins had been filled with images of desperate farmers trying their best to feed starving stock as the drought continued to drain the country's spirit day after day. Now, the radio announcer mentioned the fire that was burning high up in the national park; it had started with a lightning strike a few weeks earlier, and firefighters couldn't bring it to an end. Her previous moment of optimism quickly sank. She'd been hearing warnings for the past few months about the dangerous fire season being predicted, and this seemed to verify it. It wasn't even summer and already fires were starting. When would this bloody drought end? How much more could farmers take?

The main street hadn't changed much; mostly it was just the shops that were different. Some had always been here but had moved premises, while others hadn't survived, and there were some new ones since she'd last been home.

The selection of cafes, hairdressers and beauticians indicated that locals loved coffee and liked to look good. They had the necessities: a chemist, a baker, a butcher, a supermarket and a bank and a few takeaway places; and even a few alternative health practices, which Sam thought was very progressive for the small town she'd grown up in. Clearly Burrumba had also been doing some growing and moving with the times.

Then, of course, there was the other side of business: mechanics and feed stores. These were the rural-focused industries the town needed to keep its farming population running. It may have been a small town, bordered by farmland and now bypassed by the main highway, but it had what it needed to keep the region working.

Sam pulled into the supermarket carpark and climbed out, the heat biting her shoulders. As she walked in through the sliding glass doors, cold air instantly cooled her hot skin.

The shop had changed considerably from when she'd been here as a kid. Nowadays, after an extensive facelift, it looked like a modern supermarket, not the crowded sardine can she'd grown up with. As she pulled out a trolley, she was so distracted by the fancy new layout that she didn't notice the woman who reached over to select some mangoes beside her, until she heard her name.

'I thought it was you,' the woman said with a smug smile. 'I heard you were back in town.'

It took a few moments but Sam eventually recognised her. Jennifer Howard. Sam's smile wavered slightly. 'Yep, it's me.'

'I bet you're finding it all a bit boring down here,' Jennifer said in a tone that immediately grated on Sam's nerves. Then again, Jennifer had always been one of those people who could be annoying for no particular reason other than that she was simply annoying.

'Not at all. I've always loved coming home.' Sam's face was beginning to hurt from the forced smile she was trying to hold in place.

'I'm sure it's not as exciting as the Sunshine Coast,' Jennifer persisted.

'Excitement is overrated,' Sam said, making to move away.

'So, what have you been up to?' Jennifer doggedly continued, blocking Sam's trolley with her own as she waited expectantly.

Sam studied the other woman briefly. They'd been classmates for a large portion of their school lives but they'd never really run in the same social circles. Jennifer had always been one of those kids who enjoyed getting into everyone's business—moving from group to group to get the goss and spread rumours. Apparently, she hadn't changed much.

'The usual—kids, work, you know . . . life.'

'Oh, I know,' Jennifer said, waving a hand and rolling her eyes dramatically. 'I'm so busy myself. I'm president of the P&C, and vice president of our local CWA branch. I'm on the town's advisory committee and the hospital auxiliary. Then there's the children's sports, although thank heavens that's almost at an end now that my older ones can drive.'

'You certainly sound like you have your hands full,' Sam said, trying for an interested smile and attempting to move her trolley, without success.

'Oh, I thrive on stress, you know? Some people just cope with a hectic lifestyle. That's me,' Jennifer said with a sugary smile.

Good on you, Jenn, you over-achiever, you. 'Well, I better keep moving.'

'Oh, and I was so sorry to hear about your divorce . . . that must have been hard.'

Sam couldn't help but bristle. 'Well, you know—'

'I'm not sure how I'd cope if my husband left me for a *much younger* woman,' Jennifer cut in swiftly. 'I'm sure that had to hurt. A lot. But I bet you had the last laugh with your divorce settlement. He was quite well off, from what I've heard,' she said with a conspiratorial wink.

Fuck you, Jenn.

'We must catch up some more. Maybe over a coffee one day while you're back?' she prompted as Sam was busy silently counting, rather violently, to ten.

'Sure. That would be fun.' *About as much fun as a dentist visit.*

'What day would be good for you?'

'Ah, I'm not too sure what I've got on, I'll have to check the calendar when I get home.' *Christ, this woman's pushy.*

'I don't leave the house without my daily planner,' Jennifer said, holding up a bulging diary from her handbag.

'I might have to get myself one of those,' Sam said, with forced politeness, pulling her trolley backwards. 'It was nice to see you, Jenn.' That lie almost made her choke. She manoeuvred around the other woman's trolley, clipping the edge with a small crash, ignoring the slight gasp Jennifer gave in her wake, and kept going.

She was still fuming as she threw an assortment of junk food into her trolley two aisles down. As she dropped a carton of milk into her trolley, a man dressed in work pants and a business shirt with the store logo printed on it smiled at her, delaying her progress yet again. This time, though, when she recognised his face, she smiled a genuine smile.

'Peter. Hi.' She almost didn't recognise her old school friend. It still threw her when she met people she'd gone to school with as grown adults, when she still remembered most of them as gangly teenagers.

'Hey, Sam. Good to see you. I figured you'd be in here sooner or later.'

'We've all got to eat,' she agreed. And this was the only grocery store her family had ever shopped at.

'How are your parents?'

'They're fine. Having a great trip. I'm not sure they even miss us.'

'Knowing your old man, I'm willing to bet he's making daily calls to check on the cattle.' Peter grinned.

'Actually, I think Mum's confiscated the phone.'

'You doing okay out there?'

'Yep, got everything under control. This farm-manager thing is pretty cruisy,' she joked. *If you ignore the guinea fowl incident.* 'So, you're store manager now?'

'Yep. About time, huh?' Peter had been working there since they were at school. Sam remembered waving to him as he collected trolleys in the carpark after school, like it was last week.

'I'd say that's the least you deserve after all those years of loyalty. You still enjoy it?'

'Yeah. I do. I know it may not seem like the kind of job most people would want to do long term, but I have the bushfire brigade as well, and between both of those, I'm busier than a blue-arsed blowfly.'

Sam grinned at his analogy before hearing someone call his name over the loudspeaker.

'See what I mean?' he said, rolling his eyes. 'Good to see you, Sam. Catch you later.'

Sam watched him stride down the aisle and disappear out the back of the store. Thank goodness for all the Peters in the world. And the Jacks. They were the kind of people who worked hard and gave up their time for the community without all the fanfare and carry-on of the Jennifers.

Sam hurried to get the rest of her shopping done before she bumped into anyone else from her past. She'd had quite a morning so far.

Depositing the last of the groceries into her boot, Sam hesitated before getting back into the car. It had been ages since she'd stopped to take a look around town. She locked the car and walked back down the main street. She loved that the town was undergoing a makeover. Slowly, the beautiful verandah awnings that had been torn down decades ago were being re-established. In an effort to reinvent the town and attract tourists, the council had secured a number of beautification grants, and the main street was gradually returning to its former glory.

She took her time browsing through the shops, discovering a gorgeous little shop that specialised in potted plants and gifts. She briefly wondered if there might be room for a new homewares shop in town too, but then she dismissed the idea. It was still too soon after selling; she wasn't ready to reinvest the time and effort it took to build a new business from scratch. And yet, there was something appealing about the idea of going back to something boutique-y. She wouldn't make the mistake of going bigger again. If she were ever to start a new business, she would keep it small and exclusive.

She wandered down to the riverbank where she'd spent countless afternoons after school eating hot chips at the picnic tables and feeding seagulls. This area had also undergone a transformation, and it was nice to see travellers and locals enjoying the space. Her gaze fell on a large tree nearby and she found herself thinking of Jack. That had been their spot. A flutter ran through her as she remembered the heady, all-consuming power of teenage love. She could picture them sitting under that tree, Jack's arms wrapped around her as they talked about their dreams and their future. A sad sigh escaped Sam's lips at the memory. *She'd* talked about her dreams. Jack had just listened. Even back then he hadn't been much of a talker.

With a quick glance at her watch she turned away from the last wisps of memory that lingered around the old tree, and headed back the way she'd come. She'd wasted enough time wallowing about in the past for one day. She had cows to feed before getting ready to head over to her brother's place for dinner. The past was the past; she had to live in the present.

Seven

'How's the farm, sis? Still standing?' Thomas asked as he poured her a glass of wine.

'Of course it is,' Sam said haughtily. 'Hence Mum and Dad trusted *me* to be farm manager while they were gone.' It had been a long-standing joke in the family that the favourite child would inherit their parents' farm one day, and the siblings took endless pleasure in claiming the right whenever the opportunity presented itself.

'Whatever,' her older brother dismissed loftily, handing her the glass and then passing another to his wife, Joanne, before picking up his own. Thomas looked like an exact replica of their father when he was younger and grew more like him every time Sam saw him. These days along with his work on his own property he was the local State Emergency Services unit commander, and today he had arrived home in his work truck.

'Been busy with the fires?' Sam asked.

'Yeah. Doing lots of prep and lending a hand with a few evacuations,' he said, taking a hefty sip of wine.

'Evacuations?' Sam frowned.

'Yeah. It's getting a bit hairy up there for a few of the more remote properties. Had to assist an older couple to get out the other day as a precaution. This bloody fire doesn't want to quit.'

'He's hardly been home the last few days,' Joanne put in.

'Got another meeting to go to tonight.'

'Which is why we're eating at this ridiculously early hour,' Joanne said, levelling a look at her husband—but it was softened by a smile.

Joanne was the epitome of a modern farmer's wife. While she worked alongside her husband when he needed her, she was also an English teacher at the local high school. Sam admired her sister-in-law, who had somehow managed to juggle a career, raising her family and working on the farm, all the while making it seem easy. Sam sighed with a small twinge of regret. Long marriages ran in her family—her parents were into their sixth decade, and Jo and Thomas were at twenty-seven years. When Sam had got married, she'd thought that one day she too would celebrate her fiftieth anniversary, but life didn't always run according to plan. Still, she was proud of her brother for being such a steady and dependable husband and a wonderful role model for his kids.

Lucy, Alison and Mitchell were older than Sam's girls, at twenty-six, twenty-four and twenty-three. Her brother and sister-in-law had been the family pioneers in everything: from the first married to supplying the first grandchildren to her parents, and on through all the other firsts such as kids getting their licences and leaving school and even becoming the first grandparents, with Lucy now married with two babies. Sam pushed that particular thought from her mind. She was *definitely* not ready to become a grandmother.

'How are the girls?' Joanne asked Sam while they waited for dinner to cook. Sam's mouth watered as the tempting scent of roast lamb wafted through the room.

'They're doing great. They haven't killed each other yet, which is a bonus,' Sam said.

'How's Brooky enjoying uni life?' Jo asked as she took down three plates.

'She's loving it,' Sam said, sipping her wine. 'I guess having Kenzie there helps.'

'Our kids refused to go to the same university,' Jo said, shaking her head.

'Yeah, nothing like spreading themselves around the damn country. Cost us a bloody fortune to visit them all from Queensland down to Victoria and up to Canberra,' Thomas muttered, although he couldn't hide the quiet pride in his voice when he talked about his kids.

As well as his looks, Thomas had a lot of their dad's personality in him. Farming ran in their genes and he'd gone out and bought his own property just after he and Jo had got married. He was a hard-working, gruff man—again, much like Henry Murphy—but unlike his father, none of his children seemed to be particularly interested in farming, which Sam found a little sad. They'd spoken about it once, and Thomas had been a lot more accepting of it than she'd thought he'd be. 'You can't choose your kids' paths, Sam,' he'd said with a shrug. 'Maybe one day down the track one of them might want to come back, but if they don't, then it's not the end of the world. I'll be a farmer till I can't farm anymore and they'll do whatever it is that makes them happy, too.'

Her brother's farm was a lot bigger than their parents' property. Thomas and Jo ran cattle as well as growing macadamia trees. The delicious nuts were worth a fortune and had become a huge success, and in the last few years they'd expanded, buying two other properties in Glenview, a half-hour drive south of Burrumba.

'How's everything going with the expansion?' Sam asked.

'Business is booming,' Thomas said. 'Best thing we ever did.'

'Despite the sleepless nights we had wondering whether we should do it or not,' Jo added with a touch of sarcasm. 'He always forgets the bad bits.'

'I think it's great that Alex and Marcie could move up to Glenview and manage the processing and packing sheds for you.' Their younger brother, Alex, and his wife had been looking for a new direction once Alex left his job in the Defence Force. The solution seemed to benefit everyone.

'They've been able to take a lot off our plate, and Alex has been amazing—designing new machinery and fixing anything that goes wrong,' Jo said. 'We're really happy with how it's all worked out.'

'So, no issues with anything over at Mum and Dad's?' Thomas asked, a little more seriously this time.

'Nope. Everything's fine. I promise if anything goes wrong, I'll call you. Dad asked everyone he knows to drop by to check up on me, so I should be fine,' Sam grumbled.

'Who's checking up on you?' Thomas asked.

'You. Jack. Alex,' she listed off pointedly.

'Jack dropped by, did he?' Thomas asked and Sam's eyes narrowed at the slight smirk on his face.

'Briefly.'

'Uh-huh. And how did that go?'

'It went fine. Why shouldn't it? He's Dad's neighbour.'

'He is.' Thomas nodded, but his grin remained.

'Would you knock it off? There's nothing happening between Jack and me.'

'I never said there was. You sound a little defensive there, though.'

'Leave her alone, Tom,' Jo cut in with a weary shake of her head. 'Ignore him, Sam. You know what a tease he is.'

Yes, she knew. She'd grown up with two annoying brothers who'd loved to rile her up endlessly for entertainment and still did. Usually she tried not to rise to the bait, but Jack was a bit of a sore spot.

'I'm just saying, you could do a lot worse than a bloke like Jack Cameron.'

'If I was *looking* for a bloke at all,' Sam emphasised.

'My advice?' Jo weighed in. 'Enjoy being single.'

'Oh, that's nice, that is,' Thomas said, getting up to pour everyone another drink.

'I envy you,' Jo said, sighing longingly. 'Not having to share a bathroom with a messy male. Cooking whatever you want without some fussy bugger complaining all the time. Having a bed to yourself and no one hogging the blanket.'

'Well, when you put it that way,' Thomas said thoughtfully, 'it does kind of make me wish I was single again.'

Sam grinned as she saw her brother dodge a plastic pear from the fruit bowl centrepiece his wife threw at him.

'Jerk,' Jo said, but laughed despite herself.

'Speaking of jerks,' Thomas said, turning his attention back to Sam. 'How's old Andy? You had any more trouble?'

Sam gave a reluctant twist of her lips at his use of her ex-husband's pet hate—the shortening of his name to Andy. 'Everything is much more civilised nowadays.'

'That must be a relief,' Jo said. The divorce had not been pleasant—not that divorces typically ever were, but Sam suspected that things would have been a lot more amicable if Andrew's girlfriend hadn't been behind the scenes pushing him to make life difficult.

'It's a lot less stressful now the girls are older and I no longer really have to communicate with him.'

The meal was served, so conversation moved on to other topics and Sam again realised how much she'd missed her family. If she moved down this way she would be able to do this more often: a tick on the pro side of her mental checklist of buying her own place. Maybe it wasn't such a crazy idea. She found herself thinking about it on the drive home and long into the night.

'Hello, darling,' her mother greeted her brightly on the phone early the next morning.

'Mum! Hi.' Sam blinked away the last remnants of sleep as she struggled to sit up in bed.

'Sorry, I know it's a bit early over there.'

'A bit early? Why aren't you up already?' her father's voice boomed over the phone.

'I'm not a real farmer—I'm a fill-in farmer,' she reminded him pointedly.

'We just wanted to call before we got on the train. It might be a few days before we get to phone again. We keep messing up the time zones. How is everything?'

'Good. Everything is fine.' Sam filled them in on her visit with Thomas and Joanne. She didn't mention the fires up in the mountains. They weren't a real cause for alarm down this far, and she didn't want to worry her parents needlessly.

As they prepared to say their goodbyes, Henry threw in, 'Remember, if you have any problems—you call Jack. He knows the cattle.'

Sam rolled her eyes heavenward and shook her head. 'Dad, stop worrying about your bloody cattle. I promise if I see anything out of the ordinary, I'll let Jack know and get him to come over to check them out.'

'Righto, then.'

'I love you,' Sam said, before the line went silent. She could imagine the scolding her mother would be giving her dad right this very minute. They were supposed to be enjoying a break away from the farm, but her dad in true farmer spirit wouldn't be able to stop thinking about his livestock no matter which wonder of the world he was standing in front of. She put her phone back on the bedside table and snuggled under her blankets, hoping to catch a few more moments of sleep before the sun came up.

Sam frowned as she stared out the kitchen window. The smoke was heavier this morning. The fire up in the national park was all anyone could talk about in town and the local Rural Fire Service was doing their best to get it under control.

She opened the old timber gate and walked into the yard to feed the chooks and collect the eggs. 'Here chook, chook,' she called, but she needn't have bothered; the girls had spotted her the moment she'd opened the gate and were running towards her from all directions. Sam threw a handful of laying pellets in a wide arc and the birds quickly halted, hungrily pecking at the ground. She tipped the rest of the pellets into the feed dish and went into the coop to gather the eggs from the nests.

Until a few weeks ago, she hadn't been inside this chook pen in years. It was her mother's domain. Sam smiled when she thought about how her girls had loved helping her mother feed the chooks when they were little. It had been a novelty for them, whereas Sam had always considered it a chore she'd had to do as a kid. But now, having taken over for her mum, it was a task she was finding strangely satisfying. The routine of feeding and watering the chooks then collecting the eggs felt rewarding. She fed the chooks and they fed her—with eggs. Unlike those other annoying things, she thought, searching for the herd of chattering noise-makers and finding them at the far end of the yard.

Bloody guinea fowl.

Sam looked up from watering her mother's agapanthus plants when the dogs started to bark. The postman slowed and slid some mail into her parents' large letterbox at the top of the driveway. 'Max! Tess! Come on,' she called, deciding she could do with a walk. 'You two are getting fat and lazy,' she teased, scuffing both dogs affectionately before sending them off ahead of her.

As she closed the letterbox, the sound of an approaching car made her glance up, and she raised an eyebrow in surprise as a white ute came to a stop beside her.

Jack sat in the driver's seat, an elbow resting on the open window as he nodded a greeting.

'You've been out with the fires today?' Sam asked as she noticed the smudges of black on his cheekbones and across his forehead. He was wearing an orange RFS shirt with the local brigade sewn on one side and his name on the other. A heavy orange jacket and a white helmet took up the passenger seat beside him.

'I've been out since last night.'

No wonder he looked exhausted. 'Have you got it under control yet?'

'Nope. We've got no hope of putting it out.'

'Well, that doesn't sound good. What's going to happen?'

She saw him shrug and for a moment she was distracted, following the movement of his wide shoulder. 'It'll burn until it rains. That'll be the only way we'll be able to get on top of it.'

'It's that big?'

'Yep. Most of that country's inaccessible. It's almost impossible to get in there and fight it.'

Sam sent a worried glance towards the mountain across from them. Saddleback Ridge looked exactly like a saddle on the back of a horse and was a dominating landmark in their area. There was no sign of fire, just smoke—lots and lots of smoke. She knew the national park covered an enormous swathe of land—she'd spent her childhood up there riding horses and four-wheel driving—and that despite the smoke, the fire was still a long way from them, and yet, as she looked up at that mountain now, she felt a prickle of fear.

'It'll be okay,' Jack said gently, as though reading her thoughts. 'It'd have to jump the ridge to get here, and so far the wind's blowing it the other way.'

She summoned a weak smile, though his confident tone made her feel a bit better.

'I hope you're heading home to get some sleep,' she said, studying him a little closer. His red-rimmed eyes were heavy with fatigue.

'Yeah, for a couple of hours after I feed the cattle and sort a few other jobs out. Then I'm back out there again later.'

It seemed crazy. These men and women who made up their local brigade were all volunteers and had jobs and businesses of their own on top of protecting the community against fires. Her father had been a member of this brigade most of his life too, and she remembered the bad summers when they'd barely seen him for days on end when he'd been out fighting fires—coming home to grab a few hours' rest then heading back out before any of the kids had woken up. Later, as her brothers got older, they too joined up and her mother then had three men to worry about each time they went out. She also remembered that her dad, unlike Jack, had a couple of sons and a wife and daughter at home to do the everyday farm work. Animals still needed feeding and watering even if their owner was dead on his feet.

'I'll come over and give you a hand,' she said, already pushing away from the side of the vehicle.

'You don't have to do that, Sam. I'll be fine,' he protested, his eyes narrowing slightly—she wasn't quite sure if it was with confusion or annoyance.

Well, too bad. It was all right for him to volunteer his time and energy to the community—surely she could do the same in return for him.

'I'll get the car and be over there in a few minutes.'

Clearly, he figured it wasn't worth the effort to argue—proof he really must be exhausted—and she didn't wait around to give him the opportunity, jogging back to the house to change into work boots and grab her keys.

It had been a long time since she'd been to the Cameron place. Despite them being neighbours, she'd never ventured over there on her visits home. Her mum and dad had been good friends with Jack's parents, and Sam felt a moment of sadness wash over her now as she thought of Julie and Bill Cameron.

Jack's father had passed away almost twenty years ago, she realised with a start once she worked out the dates. She remembered her parents taking it very hard. His mother had moved down to Victoria with Jack's older sister a few years after that, leaving Jack and Cilia to manage the property. Now it was Jack running it all on his own.

Sam looked at the house and noticed that the once well-tended garden—Jack's mother's pride and joy—had been taken out, leaving only a few shrubs and small trees growing inside the house yard. A wave of memories flooded through her at the sight of the leafy hydrangea bush. She'd once told Jack how the purple-blue flowers always reminded her of her nan and made her happy, and from that moment on, whenever they were in bloom she would find a hydrangea from Jack, left beside her bag or dropped on her desk at school.

The house hadn't changed a lot from the outside; it was just as she remembered it from her childhood. It was a bit strange being there, like she'd somehow stepped back in time.

She climbed out of her car and walked across to where Jack was now loading bales of hay into the back of his ute. She immediately started to help, but it was slow going. Over the past few weeks Sam had used muscles she hadn't engaged in a very long time and her arms had been almost constantly protesting. Loading up her dad's ute with hay bales each day to feed his cattle took a considerably longer time than it was supposed to, but now as she worked she felt grateful that she didn't have to load anywhere near as many bales as Jack did.

'How on earth do you manage to do this every day at your dad's?' Jack asked after watching her struggle with another bale.

'I manage,' she said defensively. 'It may not be fast, or pretty, but I get it done.'

His tired chuckle dulled the beginnings of indignation she felt growing in response.

'I'll throw this lot out once it's loaded, and you go in and get some sleep,' she said. 'Leave me a list of what else you want done and I'll do it when I get back.'

'Nah, I'll be okay.'

'Jack Cameron. March your arse inside that house right now,' she said, straightening to stand in front of him with a stern glare. 'I wasn't suggesting. I was telling you that's how it's going to be.'

He shot her a doubtful look and then once again decided it wasn't worth risking an argument because he reluctantly nodded and finished throwing on the last few bales before stepping back. 'Righto. That'll do 'em,' he said.

'Okay. Off you go,' she told him, making a shooing gesture as she went to move around him towards the driver's seat.

When he didn't budge, she stopped and looked up at him pointedly, only to find him watching her with an expression she couldn't quite fathom. For a few moments neither of them spoke, and Sam felt her heart rate start to do an uncertain little flutter.

Eight

Jack was beyond exhausted. This had been his third day straight of working eighteen-plus hours. The lightning strike that had started the fire up in the national park had been burning steadily for a few weeks, but it had only become a significant concern over the past few days as temperatures had started rising into the forties. Now, it had grown in size and ferocity, and nothing was going to stop it. All they could hope to do was contain it; divert it from burning towards the town and outlying properties. It was a full-time job, and the limited volunteers they had were already working long hours, juggling work commitments and fire shifts as best they could, but it was becoming obvious they weren't going to be able to hold it off much longer. Resources were already stretched in the area due to a number of other fires burning across the state, and until they got some reinforcements, there seemed no end in sight to the long hours.

He'd been driving past the Murphy place, thinking about Sam, when all of a sudden there she'd been. For a split second he wasn't sure if she was real or not. It was as though he'd conjured her up. He'd been battling to find the strength to finish the work he knew was waiting at home for him before he'd spotted her, and then almost like magic he'd had a second wind and the weight on his shoulders had all but vanished.

He hadn't realised just how badly he'd wanted to see her again after his last visit. He'd fought the urge to drop by and check on her—it had been a constant gnaw inside him, and if it wasn't for the uncontrolled bushfire that was keeping him occupied he probably would have been hanging around the Murphy place like a love-sick bloody kid.

It had been an automatic reaction to turn down her offer of help earlier. It went against every fibre of his being to allow someone else to step in and do his work for him. He'd spent so long handling everything, it felt a little strange to even consider the idea. And yet, here she was. He had to admit he hadn't put up much of a struggle and he felt a bit bad about that. The urge to spend more time alone with her outweighed his pride on that account. Just knowing she was right here beside him made him feel . . .

He pulled the brakes on. He had no idea where that thought was headed, but it couldn't have been anywhere good. He needed to keep his head straight where Sam Murphy was concerned. She was out of his league and would be out of his reach again once she returned to her swanky house on the waterfront. She might be finding it fun to relive her youth on her parents' farm for a few weeks, but that was it. Soon she would miss her real life and head back to all the beautiful people with their suntans and beach bodies on the Sunshine Coast and everything here would be forgotten again.

He had no right to feel disappointed by it. Sam hadn't come back here for him. She didn't owe him anything. And yet, it still hurt. Ever since he'd heard about her divorce from her arsehole of a husband, he'd been fighting the hope that maybe, just maybe, some day she might come back.

He blamed having too much time on his own for this stupid idea. He was turning into a crabby old man. His daughters were constantly telling him he needed to go out more before he became a hermit, but that was easier said than done—he worked long hours and there wasn't much point going out around here when everyone he knew, knew everything about him.

Every now and then he visited an old friend in Glenview with whom he had a mutually beneficial arrangement. She had her own life as an artist, her own set of friends and no interest whatsoever in committing to another relationship after being divorced three times.

Jack respected that. He didn't want to do the marriage thing again either. Cilia leaving him, for another man at that, had shaken his confidence more than he liked to admit. He knew he shouldered part of the blame in the breakdown of their marriage—he'd been working long hours and hadn't shared the responsibility and stress of managing the farm with her as much as he probably should have. She'd always said she didn't feel like an equal partner. In fact, the day she left, she told him she had felt more like his housekeeper and nanny than his wife, and that had struck home, hard.

He regretted that he hadn't realised how hard things had been on Cilia until it was too late. Maybe part of him hadn't wanted to realise. He'd always refused to look deep down inside himself and acknowledge the reasons he hadn't paid more attention to his marriage. He suspected she'd always known he hadn't been in love with her.

When they'd first started going out he'd been upfront and told her he wasn't interested in settling down. But only a few months later, Cilia had fallen pregnant with Bianca and he'd done what he needed to do. He'd tried to love her, and over the years they'd settled into family life, and he discovered that he loved being a dad.

His girls were his greatest achievements in life. And maybe he could have accepted that what he had with Cilia was enough—if he'd never been in love before. He knew logically that teenage love was just an illusion made up of overactive hormones and the innocence of youth, and yet, whatever he and Cilia had shared had never come close to making him feel the way he had with Sam. But he'd pushed past all that and had been content to live with what he had. He loved being part of a family and having kids, and so when it was gone, life suddenly lost all its sparkle.

Until now. The thought slipped through unexpectedly. Christ, he was tired. He had to be if he wasn't even up to arguing with his own wayward mind.

And now here Sam was, helping him finish his work so he could get some sleep. Dragging hay bales almost as big as herself around and getting more in the way than actually helping, but the fact she'd cared enough to try made his throat close up tight with emotion.

As he looked down at her, standing there holding her ground, he wasn't sure if he felt like laughing or crying. God, he hoped he didn't cry. Wouldn't that be just great. Then another emotion forced its way forward. He wasn't sure what it was. Lust? Desire? Gratitude? Maybe it was all three. Whatever it was, it compelled him to move closer and he watched as her eyes widened and her lips parted slightly before he no longer saw anything, only felt the touch of her soft mouth and lost himself in a kiss so deep and familiar that he found himself falling through time.

Sam's breath caught in her throat as sensation overwhelmed her. His kiss, tentative at first, had sent a tingle of electricity through her, which only increased in voltage as it deepened, until she found she could barely form a coherent thought. There were so many things rushing through her head. This was Jack . . . her Jack, only it wasn't. This was a grown-up Jack. It was a man she was kissing, not an eighteen-year-old man–boy. This was also a man with a beard. That thought, strangely enough, managed to rise to the foreground. She'd never kissed a man with a beard before. She found the experience fascinating. The contrast between the initial prickly and slightly scratchy sensation was quickly surpassed by the warmth of his lips as the kiss deepened.

His hands settled lightly on her hips, then moved to her lower back as he pulled her tightly against him. Jack broke their kiss, and Sam briefly opened her mouth to protest, but instead she let out a gasp as he dropped his mouth to the side of her neck. The combination of his beard, the fullness far softer than that around his mouth, tickled the sensitive skin of her neck, sending goosebumps along her arms and a shot of instant desire to her core, as he nuzzled and kissed his way back to her lips.

This was definitely not how she remembered it as a teenager.

Eventually, Sam eased back slightly, her breathing unsteady and her newly awakened desire protesting loudly. She was feeling out of control and reckless. One of them needed to rein things in before she ended up inside . . . on his bed . . . naked.

Stop it. What was wrong with her? Her libido was asking the same question as it pouted.

'I should get this feed out for you before it gets dark,' she managed, unable to look at him but finding the little tuft of dark hair below the undone top button of his shirt slightly mesmerising. 'And you should get to bed,' she said, making the mistake of lifting her gaze to find his dark eyes, even more of a distraction. 'To get some sleep,' she added weakly.

She swallowed hard and took a deep breath at the slow grin he gave her. He was heading back to fight fires later that night; the last thing he needed was to be side-tracked by . . . this.

'So, go,' she said, stepping away from him and finding a firmer tone.

'Okay. Fine,' he said with a reluctant sigh. 'But I'm not sure how much sleep I'll be able to get,' he added with a lift of his eyebrow.

'I'm sure you'll cope.' She hurried to climb into the ute and turned the key, hoping to put an end to further discussion. Things had just spiralled out of control and she had no idea what to do next. It was too much to think about. Jack leaned down until he was level with her, one arm resting along the open window, as he gave her directions to the cattle. Sam forced herself to listen, despite being completely frazzled by everything that had just happened.

'Okay. I'll be fine. Go get some sleep.'

'Thanks, Sam,' he said, not moving from the window. When she looked up at him, she felt her rattled nerves ease from the earnest look he was giving her. 'For the help.'

She smiled and managed a nod, not trusting her voice. She knew he was probably too proud to ask for help, just like most farmers around here, which is why she'd left him little option to protest in the first place. But it was endearing that a man like Jack, so proud and strong, could still be touched by something as simple as someone offering to take care of his animals for an afternoon. She put the ute into gear, and he stepped away as she drove off. A brief glance in the rear-view mirror showed that he was still standing there watching her as she headed for the gate, but she focused on the task at hand, ignoring the fluttery feelings that refused to settle inside her.

By the time she'd pushed off the last bale, Sam was breathing hard. Jack had a lot more cattle than her parents and it took considerably longer to distribute the amount of feed they'd loaded. She got back to the shed just before dark and parked the vehicle. She did a quick inspection of the dogs, who had been fed and tied up, and headed back to her car to go home.

Inside, on the front seat, was a flower. Sam smiled as she picked it up. It was a blue hydrangea from the old bush that grew by the back gate in Jack's mother's garden. Sam couldn't believe he'd remembered after all this time. She put her car into gear and headed home with a head full of memories and possibilities.

Jack woke up and stared at the dark ceiling for a few minutes. He hadn't thought he'd be able to sleep after leaving Sam to feed his cattle for him—he'd hated walking away, but at the same time he couldn't recall ever feeling as dead on his feet as he had been yesterday.

It had been a particularly brutal day for the volunteers, trudging through the bush and dragging hoses for almost twelve hours, and they'd had a few close calls—too close for comfort. This fire had him worried. It had a lot of people worried. It had been too dry for too long and the temperatures were too high for this time of year, which was making it difficult for the volunteers to catch a break. It didn't help that the bush had become overgrown. His dad and many of the other old-timers around the place had been saying for years that there was going to be a problem once the national parks locked up the forests and stopped the grazing that local cattlemen had been providing, as well as regular control burns to keep the undergrowth down. Jack feared their predictions might just be coming true. The bushland surrounding their valley was a tinderbox waiting for the right conditions to ignite it, and it seemed that this might be the year it happened.

Jack's mind went back to Sam, and he felt some of his tension dissolve. *That kiss.* He gave a small grunt as a tingle shot through his body at the memory. *What? Are you fourteen or something?* He hadn't meant to kiss her, it just kind of happened. All of a sudden there wasn't any here and now, they were just Jack and Sam—the way they'd been way back when. Only, it was even better than he remembered. As tired as he'd felt, that kiss had managed to stir more than a few emotions in both of them, judging by her glazed eyes and heavy breathing. If she hadn't stopped it . . . well, he was fairly sure he knew where he'd wanted it to end. In his bed. Seeing her again had made him realise there were still some lingering feelings there, but he hadn't been prepared for the force of attraction he'd felt once she was in his arms. It had kicked him with all the grace of a rampaging bull.

He'd reluctantly left her, convinced he would lie down and not be able to switch off his mind. But clearly he had. It was the last thing he remembered before waking up after a solid ten hours' sleep.

As he sat up, the smell of old smoke and soot filled his nostrils, reminding him that he hadn't bothered to have a shower before he'd fallen on top of his bed. He headed for the shower with a clean set of clothes, and when he was dressed he felt almost human again.

He'd be heading out this morning to relieve the other poor bastards who would be equally as tired as he'd been, and the whole thing would start again. He hoped he was wrong about where this fire was headed. He glanced up at the clear sky above him as he walked out to his ute. The early morning light hadn't quite touched the sky yet but already he could tell it was going to be another hot one, with no rain in sight.

Sam hid a smile as she listened to the banter between the two old men standing at the counter in the feed store. It was the same every time she came in here. The feed store, like most places around town, was where locals stopped to chat to friends and neighbours. She'd been caught many a time waiting in the car while her father would 'just pop in' for something but end up talking for an hour with someone he'd been meaning to catch up with. The earthy smells of feed and fertiliser and the slight chill of the cold cement floor threw her back to another time.

She'd woken hot and flustered from a dream this morning—the kind of dream she hadn't had in a long time. Even after a shower and coffee, she was still feeling out of sorts. It was that damn kiss stirring up old memories. And there was no denying that it had been a good kiss, too. Sam closed her eyes and could instantly feel the warmth of being held tightly against Jack's chest, his hands on her hips, his lips against her skin . . .

'G'day, Sam.'

Sam's eyes flew open to find Jack walking into the store, coming to a stop beside her.

'Hey,' she said, trying for a cheery, carefree greeting but fearing it sounded a bit too bright. 'Fancy seeing you here.'

Jack gave her a strange look. 'Probably the most likely place you'd ever find me around town.'

She winced slightly and struggled to shake off this stupid mood she'd found herself in.

'About yesterday,' he started and Sam quickly glanced around to make sure no one was close enough to hear them.

'Look, Jack. It's fine. It just happened. You were tired. I was tired. We've got all this history hanging around us, it was probably bound to happen at some point.' She heard herself babbling but was helpless to stop.

'I . . . ah . . . was going to thank you again for throwing out the feed for me.'

'Oh.' *Well, this is embarrassing.*

'But since you brought it up,' he said, sounding amused by her discomfort, 'I'm not going to apologise for kissing you.'

Once more Sam's head snapped around in alarm, hoping to God no one had heard him.

'Would you keep your voice down,' she all but hissed.

He laughed, and Sam stared at him blankly.

'I'm sorry if I'm concerned *the whole town* thinks we're sleeping together,' she said sarcastically.

'I'm pretty sure *the whole town* has better things to worry about than whether two grown adults are sleeping together,' he pointed out.

'Oh, and I'm the one who's been away from town too long? I think you've forgotten how Burrumba works.'

His face sobered at that. 'I kind of thought you liked it,' he said.

Under his watchful gaze, Sam felt herself fidget slightly. 'I did,' she eventually blurted. 'I was just offering you a dignified way out . . . if you thought it was a mistake.'

'It wasn't a mistake.'

Sam swallowed hard as she held his gaze.

'Can I help you?' a man's voice called, breaking the spell Sam had found herself wrapped in. She turned away and formed what she hoped was a completely normal smile that hid the fact she and Jack had just shared a moment that she couldn't quite explain.

'I need some laying pellets and dog food,' she managed to say, surprised she sounded relatively unshaken by the experience.

When she finished paying at the counter and walked past Jack on her way out, he smiled and nodded. 'See you around, Sam.'

To anyone watching, it would have seemed like a neighbourly farewell, but Sam knew better. There was nothing neighbourly about whatever had decided to flare back into life between them again. Nothing neighbourly at all.

Nine

Sam was awake early again, after another restless night. She tackled all her morning chores and then headed over to make a start on the work at Jack's property. She'd thought a lot about their last encounter . . . and the kiss. She had no idea where any of it was going, but the fact remained that Jack needed a hand while he was busy with the fire, and she wasn't about to let a little awkwardness get in the way of helping where she could.

She knocked on the screen door and let herself in. After placing the shepherd's pie she'd made into the fridge and leaving a note on the bench, she stood back and looked around.

It felt a bit stalker-ish going inside Jack's house uninvited, but Sam figured it was for a good cause. Like everything else about the place, some of it was the same and yet much of it was different. From where she stood in the kitchen, it seemed that Jack's parents' furniture was all gone, but what was left didn't look as though Cilia had chosen it either. Just the basics, and not much of it matched. No buffets or hall tables, no wall cabinets or display photographs—none of the little touches that made a house a home.

It smelled the same, though. She wasn't sure what it was—a mix of furniture polish and something else she couldn't name that was unique to this place. Maybe scents got trapped in the walls, because she couldn't see Jack as the type who would use furniture polish to clean the way his mother always had. Sam glanced down the long hallway and bit her lip as she considered taking a peek at the rest of the place. Her gaze fell on the door at the end and with a brief, guilty glance over her shoulder, she tiptoed her way towards it. Sam put her ear to the door and listened, but only the tick of the large grandfather clock in the living room sounded. She eased the door open. This had originally been Jack's parents' bedroom, and though she had briefly seen it as she'd walked to the bathroom on occasion as a kid, she'd never been inside.

There was no elegant cream embroidered bedspread on the large queen-sized bed as there had been in the past, just a jumble of sheets and a navy doona crumpled on top. 'Your mother would have a fit if she saw your bed left unmade like this, Jack Cameron,' Sam murmured as she let her gaze wander around the rest of the room. A roughly folded pile of laundry sat on the top of a long set of drawers, and the bedside table held a collection of loose coins and a few farming magazines scattered amid framed photographs of his daughters.

Sam took a step closer and picked up the first frame, noting the cheeky grins on both girls—they could only have come from their father's genes. Sam smiled at the two sets of chubby arms circling their father's neck as Jack held them. She loved that Jack looked so animated and happy—his hair had been shorter and a little darker back then. She picked up the second photo, taken fairly recently: Tasmin had her father's blue eyes and smile, every inch a Cameron, whereas Bianca looked more like her mother, with brown eyes and lighter hair. She seemed more serious. Reserved.

Sam carefully put the photo back and walked past the unmade bed to the door, easing it shut and resisting the urge to wipe her fingerprints from the knob when a sudden, loud boom sounded behind her, making her jump. She let out a startled curse, before realising it was the grandfather clock banging out the hour. Who the hell put up with that every hour on the damn hour? Having just lost a few years from her life, she hurried down the hallway, feeling suitably reprimanded for her intrusion into Jack's privacy, and let herself back out, heading for the shed.

It took a lot longer to load the hay this time and she had to make two trips because she couldn't lift the bales high enough to add a third layer on top—the way Jack had the day before—without the fear of them all toppling over. It was after one when she finally finished, exhausted and filthy. After a quick inspection of the water troughs, she headed back home.

Jack shrugged out of his jacket and hung it over the railing of the verandah to air out overnight and kicked off his heavy boots at the back door. His plan was to change out of his smoky, sweat-drenched clothes, feed the cattle and then come back and grab some more sleep, but he made the mistake of sitting down at the kitchen bench and suddenly he couldn't get back up. He was so bloody tired. He closed his eyes and pinched the bridge of his nose, rubbing his sore eyes before he sighed and opened them, noticing the piece of paper on the bench that hadn't been there when he left early that morning.

He picked it up and immediately brightened.

Cattle are fed and water checked. Dinner's in the fridge. Heat in the oven at 180 degrees for thirty minutes. Sam.

For a minute, Jack just stared at the note. She'd made him dinner. She'd fed his bloody cattle, again, and made him dinner. He felt a strange sensation in his chest, a warmth he hadn't felt in a very long time. The last remaining lump of resistance inside him began to melt. It'd been a long time since someone had done anything so simple as making sure he had a meal waiting for him after a long day.

The FaceTime ring tone sounded and Jack pulled his phone from his pocket.

'Hey kiddo,' he said, once his screen opened up and the face of his eldest daughter appeared.

'Hi, Dad. Wow . . . you look terrible,' Bianca said.

'Gee, thanks. Don't hold back or anything,' he replied.

'When did you last have a haircut? And I know you're kind of proud of your beard and all, Dad, but you really need to get that thing under control.'

'Jesus, kid. Brutal much?' He should have been used to his eldest daughter's blunt manner—she took after her mother that way—but it still managed to catch him off guard sometimes.

'It's not brutal, it's the truth. You need to start taking care of yourself or you'll end up being a lonely, grumpy old man.'

'I've been a bit busy lately, you know, fighting fires and running a property. I haven't exactly had time to book a haircut.' The sarcasm seemed to go completely over his daughter's head.

'Here's Tas. I'll be right back,' Bianca said, standing up to let her younger sister sit at the computer.

'Hi, Daddy,' Tasmin chimed in.

'Hey, sweetheart,' he said, then frowned. 'Hey. Hold up,' he called, halting Bianca's retreat. 'What are you wearing?'

She looked down at her short skirt and the cropped T-shirt that barely covered her chest with a confused look. 'What's wrong with what I'm wearing?'

'The fact you're hardly *wearing* anything,' he pointed out, his frown deepening.

'It's not that bad . . . the skirt almost reaches my knees.'

'It doesn't reach anywhere near far enough for my liking. Has your mother seen what you're wearing?'

'Mum bought it for me.'

'You better not be going out anywhere in that get-up,' he snapped.

Bianca rolled her eyes, and his jaw immediately clenched in irritation. 'You're so old-fashioned,' she told him with a disdainful air that irritated him even more as she escaped while the going was good.

Jack gave an inward sigh. He *felt* old with two teenage daughters. Maybe he was out of touch with teenage fashion and what passed as decent nowadays—he barely watched TV, and Burrumba wasn't exactly the fashion capital of the modern world, and yet he was sure he hadn't noticed many girls walking around town in what his daughter was currently wearing. He listened to Tasmin update him on the latest crisis within her social network and whatever injustices had happened at school that week, which changed from teacher to teacher depending on which subject she disliked the most at that point in time, before Bianca came back in to tell him they were about to have dinner.

'Love you Daddy,' Tasmin said, blowing him a kiss then disappearing from the screen before he had a chance to reply.

'Love you Dad,' Bianca said. 'Don't forget that haircut,' she added.

'Love you,' he said.

Running a hand through his shaggy hair, he went into the bathroom and grimaced as he took a long, hard look at his reflection in the mirror. Maybe it *was* time he started taking a bit of interest in the rest of the world again. He rubbed a hand over his chin and frowned. He *did* like his beard . . . but it was becoming a pain in the arse to fit his firies' mask over . . . and that was the *only* reason he was considering getting rid of it. A man had to have some kind of illusion that he had control over his life, after all.

He took the hair clippers out from under the bathroom vanity and eyed his reflection somewhat critically once more, before selecting a blade and releasing a half-hearted sigh.

Sam followed the same routine the next day, but as she walked into the shed she discovered the ute had already been loaded with hay. *When had he had time to do this?* she wondered, but she was secretly glad she wouldn't have to tackle that part on her own again.

Inside the car, on the seat, was another flower and a folded note. She opened it and found herself smiling as she read it.

> *I figured you'd be back today, since I told you I'd be fine. So, just in case, I've already loaded the ute. I owe you big time, Sam.*
> *Jack.*
> *P.S. Where'd you learn to cook like that! Dinner was great, thanks.*

She gave a small twist of her lips. He didn't owe her anything. She was helping because she wanted to. He wouldn't expect anything from the local farmers he was saving from the threat of fire, so he shouldn't think that she would expect anything either. He was a proud person, like most people she knew around here, her father included, and it was hard for them to ask for help, so this was a major step.

When she put a lasagne in his fridge, she saw the dish she'd delivered the shepherd's pie in, empty, washed and sitting dry on the sink. It felt good to be useful; she hadn't had anyone to take care of for the past few months. Not that Jack needed taking care of, but still . . . being a nurturer wasn't something she seemed to be able to simply turn off like a tap.

She finished early and took advantage of it by heading straight home to the shower to wash off the accrued sweat and dirt. Sam turned her face up to the lukewarm spray and closed her eyes as she felt some of the weariness of the day wash away. Her muscles were aching less now than they had over the first few weeks and she was feeling better than she had in ages. Her little farm break might have been just what the doctor ordered—more exercise and less stress. As she was towel-drying her hair, she paused. *Was that a knock?* She waited a few more moments, then swore as it sounded again. Someone was at the door . . . and she was stark naked and dripping wet. *Damn it.* Wrapping the towel around herself, she hurried down the hallway and stuck her head around the corner of the kitchen, biting back a groan. But as she spotted Jack standing at the door, she gaped.

'Oh. Hi. Sorry, I didn't hear you, I was in the shower,' she stammered. She was standing there in a towel with her hair dripping, but she barely noticed that—instead she couldn't help but stare at Jack. He'd shaved off his beard, leaving only a slight stubble that made him look . . . *like hot afternoon sex.* She quickly shut down that train of thought and switched to his hair, which he'd shaved close to his head. Gone was the shaggy, unkempt look, replaced by short, darker hair that her hand itched to reach out and touch.

'Come in and make yourself at home. I'll just—' She stopped, swallowing nervously at the glint of interest she caught in his eye as he stared at her. 'There's a beer in the fridge. I'll be right back.' She didn't stick around for an answer, just forced herself to walk rather than run back down the hallway to her room.

'You're an adult. Act like it!' she scolded herself under her breath as she frantically searched for something to wear. She'd been planning to pull on a pair of trackies and an old worn T-shirt, but Jack turning up changed that plan. She needed to do a load of washing; all her jeans were filthy, which only left a sundress she hadn't yet worn while she'd been here. She quickly pulled it on over her head and tried to do something with her hair.

When she came out, dressed and feeling back in control once more, she found Jack sitting out on the verandah drinking a cold beer.

'Sorry about that.'

'No worries,' he said, passing her a beer.

'You've had a haircut,' she said, taking a sip of her drink.

'Yeah.' He rubbed a hand across his head a little self-consciously and dropped his gaze. 'The girls were threatening to boycott video calls if I didn't get cleaned up. Apparently the hobo look isn't in at the moment.'

'You look different . . . without the beard.'

'Yeah, I'm still getting used to it. I had to let it grow back a bit; I looked like a sixteen-year-old with a clean-shaven face.' She followed his hand as he moved it from his head to his chin as he spoke. She remembered his face at sixteen, but there wasn't a whole lot of that boy left on the face across from her now. Without the beard, his jawline was more prominent and the dark stubble that remained highlighted the sharp edges, giving him a somewhat dangerous-looking appeal.

She blinked quickly when he looked up at her, halting her thoughts. 'I wanted to come over and thank you,' he said quietly. 'For all your help this week . . . and the food.' He grinned. 'I can't remember the last time I had dinner waiting for me when I got home.'

'It's nothing, I just figured with all the extra hours you've been doing with the fires, cooking dinner would probably be the last thing on your mind.'

'It's not nothing. Thank you,' he said, holding her gaze.

'You're welcome.' Sam took another hasty sip of her beer to cover the sudden attack of nerves his words had created. She was a grown woman. She should *not* be this flustered. It was just Jack, someone she'd known her whole life. Only, it wasn't. This was *hot* Jack, *dangerous* Jack. Older Jack. Trouble!

'So, how's the firefighting going?' *That's good, get things back in friendly neighbour territory.*

He shrugged a shoulder briefly. 'Still burning. At the moment it's creeping, but I'm more concerned about the forecasted weather over the next few days. No one knows what it'll do when that hits.'

Sam must have been looking as concerned as she felt, because Jack leaned forward and took her hand in his. 'It'll be okay. We'll get on top of it eventually.'

She looked down at the hand that sat on top of her own. Its warmth shot heat up her arm and into her chest, and her heart thudded against her ribcage. Slowly she lifted her gaze and met Jack's steady, watchful eyes. The air around them suddenly felt heavy—like the feeling just moments before a summer thunderstorm broke.

Without conscious thought, she moved forward and closed her eyes as Jack leaned in. The touch of his lips sparked a low, instant simmer of awareness. She found herself being tugged forward until she was seated across Jack's lap, his wide chest pressed snugly against hers as she wrapped her arms around his neck.

Ten

Jack Cameron was a sensible man. He could be patient and methodical—in farming, these were necessary attributes. He wasn't easily surprised, but right now he was struggling to comprehend the fact that he had Samantha Murphy in his arms, and they were making out like a pair of teenagers. What was most alarming was the need that had sprung up inside him. He wanted to do everything, touch everywhere, and do it all right now.

For the love of Christ, man, get a hold of yourself. Calm the hell down!

With the mental slap to the back of his head finally knocking some sense into him, he slowed down his kisses, savouring instead of devouring, and found that the raging fire soon settled into a steady burn.

Sam wasn't the same person she'd been at eighteen—neither of them were—and yet she felt familiar. The curves were in all the same places, but fuller, matured, not the lithe teenage body but something sexier, able to distract him with every movement. He'd found himself unable to drag his eyes away as she'd pulled and dragged the hay bales a few days earlier, admiring the way her jeans clung to her shapely backside and thighs. The gentle swell of her breasts under her T-shirt had him swallowing over a dry throat more than once, and he had to force himself to stop watching her like some desperate perv.

A moan escaped from her throat, and the sound was like a current of electricity shooting straight to his groin. She still had the power to drive him crazy without even trying. He felt her hands at the front of his shirt, impatiently trying to unfasten buttons, and he released one arm from where he held her to help. Within moments they'd managed to undo enough buttons for him to yank it over his head and detangle himself from the sleeves. The touch of her hands against his chest brought a grunt of encouragement from his lips as she leaned back in to kiss him once more.

The chair beneath him creaked under the strain of movement, and Jack hesitated, holding his breath as Sam lifted her head to smile.

'I think we should move this inside before we end up stuck in a chair frame,' she said.

'Good idea. I don't really want to try to explain that to the ambo guys.'

His body screamed its displeasure at the abrupt stop as he stood up, but she took his hand and he followed her silently through the house to her bedroom. He found himself amused that even now, after all these years, the scared sixteen-year-old inside him was jumpy at the thought of being caught in her bedroom by her father.

He was relieved to see that the room no longer had posters of eighties rock bands Blu-Tacked to the walls and that the single bed had been replaced by a queen. While the tasteful, neutral decor was far removed from the sticker-covered headboard and student desk of Sam's teen years, he found it amusing that the pink walls remained. He remembered how much she'd loved that paint.

He stood quietly before her, their hands loosely linked as he waited to see where they would go from here. He was sure she'd been as eager as him outside, but the last thing he wanted to do was move too fast and scare her off. Suddenly this had become very important and he didn't want to stuff it up.

His hands dropped from hers as she lightly moved them away, and he held his breath, too scared to breathe, as he watched them move to the zip at the back of her dress. She slowly pulled down the zip and then lifted the dress up over her head. His gaze traced the bare skin the movement had revealed. She reached behind her and the white lace bra she'd been wearing lowered and dropped to the floor, unnoticed as he again swallowed hard at the sight before him. She was beautiful. So beautiful that he found himself scared to touch her in case she vanished.

Soundlessly she stepped forward, closing the gap between them, and he felt the press of her soft skin against his chest. He lowered his head to catch her lips once more, and then nothing else mattered as the spark once again took hold and threw them back in time.

It was like the past twenty-nine years hadn't happened. Their bodies remembered each other like it was only yesterday.

Sam wasn't sure where she ended and Jack began. His broad shoulders and wide chest seemed to dwarf her now, different from the narrow youthful body he'd had as a teenager. His hands moved slowly up her waist and across her back, pressing her closer to him, and she felt a tingle of electricity spread through every inch of her at his touch.

When he released her lips to move to her neck, Sam found herself breathing heavily as a tidal wave of sensation washed over her. It had been so long since she'd felt like this . . . too long. She couldn't even remember the last time she and Andrew had really made love. The rush of emotions and excitement they'd had at the beginning of their relationship had been missing for a long time before their marriage had ended. The roughness of Jack's stubble across the delicate skin on her neck sent a quiver through her that she was unable to hide, and she felt Jack tighten his hold on her.

The sensations running rampant were all-consuming, and her normal self-control evaporated. Need and desire and something foreign and reckless filled her and suddenly she wasn't content with kisses anymore. She needed more and she needed it now.

Pulling back, she didn't allow Jack time to register his surprise at the abrupt movement. Instead, she tugged at his arm and pulled him down onto the bed behind them. The time for playful exploration was over. Her hands went to the button at the top of his jeans and she heard his harsh, swift inhale of breath at the touch of her cool fingers against his heated skin. Together they removed their remaining clothing and she gave a small gasp as he lowered himself back down against her, the pleasure intensifying at the touch of his hard body against the softness of her own.

His hands cupped her face gently and she stared into his gaze, watching those familiar blue eyes darken with desire. There was no need for words—everything they wanted to say was being felt inside them. Slowly they began to move, finding a long-forgotten rhythm, like a song they hadn't heard for years but suddenly knew all the words to without trying. It was part of them, and they were part of each other.

Sam rested her head against Jack's shoulder as her heart rate settled back into its normal beat. She was struggling to remember when sex had ever felt like that. There must have been times in the past when she'd experienced the same kind of pleasure, but she couldn't recall ever feeling this stunned by it before.

The silence that had fallen between them was stretching out, and Sam knew she couldn't avoid looking at Jack forever. What was she so nervous about? This was Jack. Although the saner part of her was trying to be logical, there were, in fact, quite a lot of reasons why she should be nervous. What if he hadn't liked it? What if this was pity sex, for old time's sake? She bit her bottom lip as she contemplated the best way to get this over with. *Just do it.* She took a breath in readiness to lift her head and meet his gaze, but before she could move she heard the thump of something landing on the bed, followed almost instantly by a high-pitched, shrill scream and Jack's loud yell as Sam was propelled off the bed, landing with an undignified plop on the floor.

She was too shocked to register what was going on until she saw Jack throw one of her mother's decorative cushions after the fleeing, scrambling form of Mr Buttons as he streaked from the room in an outraged fit of feline displeasure.

Jack stood beside the bed, tall, naked and breathing a little unsteadily. 'I hate that bloody cat,' he said, glaring in the direction it had run.

Sam bit down on her lip at the look of indignation on his face and dropped her eyes, finding a row of bright-red scratch marks oozing blood across his chest, before remembering she was sitting in a crumpled naked heap on the floor at the bottom of the bed. She quickly grabbed her short silk dressing gown from where it lay on the chair beside her.

When she got to her feet, Jack crossed to her side. 'Are you okay? Sorry, I didn't mean to knock you off the bed.'

'It broke the awkward tension,' she offered with a small smile. Nothing said graceful and seductive like being thrown from a bed like a rag doll. 'I'll get something to clean those scratches.'

'Nah, it's okay. They don't even hurt.'

'Okay, tough guy, but I'm still cleaning them. The last thing I need is to be responsible for you getting gangrene from an infection.'

'I'd forgotten how dramatic you could be.' He grinned as she walked past him.

'Why does that cat hate you so much, anyway?' she called behind her as she stepped into the bathroom next door. 'What did you do to him?'

'I didn't do anything to him. He just senses how much I hate cats.'

'I don't know why you would. They kill mice and rats. We've always had cats in the shed and around the house. You always had them at your place when your parents owned it.'

'And I hated them then too.'

'Maybe there's something buried deep down inside that you need to work on,' she said, coming back into the room with antiseptic and noticing he'd pulled on his jeans while she'd been gone.

He gave an unimpressed grunt before taking a seat on the edge of the bed. Sam carefully cleaned the scratches, which thankfully weren't deep, and put the antiseptic on, automatically blowing on the wound as she'd always done when the girls had been little.

She stopped and glanced up, seeing an amused expression on Jack's face. 'Sorry,' she said, clearing her throat. 'Old habit.'

'I wasn't complaining,' he said with a grin.

'It stops it stinging.'

'It does. It made it feel all better.'

'Mock all you want. Next time I'll leave it to get infected.'

He caught her hand as she put down the cream. 'Thank you,' he said and held her doubtful gaze. It may have started out as a bit of teasing, but it soon changed to something else entirely as his hand moved to the back of her thigh and he gently moved her closer, until she was standing between his legs.

Her heart rate picked up pace again as he moved his hand under the hem of the gown, lightly stroking the skin beneath it. She gave an involuntary shiver and closed her eyes, letting her head tip back as she surrendered to the onslaught of sensations Jack was creating within her. She couldn't imagine allowing another man to get this close to her in such a short space of time—but this wasn't just any man. This was Jack, and without even knowing she'd lost it, she'd found the piece of her that had been missing for far too many years.

Eleven

His chest was still stinging, but he would poke an eye out before he admitted that out loud to Sam. He'd been floating on a high, holding Sam and trying to form some kind of coherent sentence to express how amazing he was feeling when that shit of a cat had landed on his chest and scared the hell out of him.

He didn't even know where the little bastard had come from. He'd feared the moment may have been lost and everything would go to hell after that, but then Sam had insisted on tending to his wound, and one touch of her soft hands on his skin, close to a whole mess of sensitive nerve endings, and everything came bounding back to life in an instant.

He'd forgotten everything—the cat, the less than manly scramble from the bed—except that strange, magnetic pull that he'd felt around this woman for as long as he could remember. He couldn't keep his hands off her. All he wanted was to be near her, hold her and never leave this bloody bedroom ever again.

He thought that maybe the first time they'd been together had just been an unexpected surprise—that the electricity he'd felt and the power of his emotions had been wrapped up with their past somehow—but here they were, lying entwined on her bed, his heart thudding like a damn drum under her ear, and he felt just as floored by the experience as he had the first time.

A couple of weeks ago, before Sam came back into his life, there was no way he could have imagined feeling the way he was right now. It hadn't even crossed his mind that he could feel this kind of emotion again. He'd figured his life would just continue the way it had been indefinitely. And then Sam came home. Even so, after their first meeting he hadn't thought that there would ever be anything between them again. She'd brought back a few good memories and a whole bunch he'd like to forget, but he'd assumed she'd go her way and he would go his, and then she'd go home when her parents returned.

But then things changed. And now they'd changed again. He wished he was brave enough to ask her what she was thinking right now, but he wasn't sure he could handle the disappointment if it wasn't something he wanted to hear. Hell, he didn't even know what *he* was thinking, really. He only knew what he was feeling—happiness, fulfilment, peace. He was also smugly satisfied. Sam had never been able to hide her emotions; he knew she'd been just as caught up in it all as he had.

It took a moment for him to realise she'd fallen asleep. Her breathing had regulated a while ago and he'd been enjoying the simple pleasure of running his fingers gently across her back, but now he could hear her steady, soft breath. Part of him was relieved they could delay the after-sex talk. Unlike other occasions when he'd dreaded the post-coital pillow talk, this time it wasn't because he wanted to leave without having to discuss feelings or make awkward next-time plans. It was because he realised he had too much riding on the outcome of anything they talked about from here on in, and it terrified him.

Early the next morning, he woke up and lay still as he searched for what had woken him. Sam was tucked in beside him, one hand nestled under her chin, the other flat against his chest as she slept soundly. Instantly his body sprang into overdrive, sensing the unusual presence of a woman beside him in bed. *Down boy*, he cautioned. He was impressed that his body seemed to think he was still capable of a third time within a handful of hours, even if his head was rolling its eyes ruefully.

With a regretful sigh after checking his watch, he slowly eased himself out of the bed and went in search of his clothes. He was due back on the fire front. He knew it was going to be a long day, after a long and overly active night, but he didn't care. It had been worth it. After one last look at the woman snuggled in the bed, he turned and let himself out the back door.

When Sam came back in range of reception after feeding the cattle, her phone began to ping. Seeing the number of missed calls from Brook, Sam immediately went into panicked-mother mode. A million scenarios flashed through her head in the short time between seeing the name on her phone and the four or five rings before Brook answered.

'Mum! Where have you been?'

'Down the back, there's no reception. What's happened? Are you okay?'

'No. I'm not. I broke up with Guy,' her daughter said before bursting into tears.

Guy? Who the hell is Guy? Sam frantically searched her mind for the name.

'He dumped me in a text. Can you believe that?' Brook continued. '*A text.* Who even does that?'

Sam opened her mouth to console her, but Brook was apparently on a roll and continued to vent, her teary voice hardening into outrage.

'I wish you were here, Mum. I just want to come home for a hug and some chicken soup.'

'Oh Brooky, I'm sorry,' Sam said, suddenly feeling an overwhelming attack of guilt. 'But you couldn't really come home, you still have classes for the rest of the week, don't you?'

'Classes? Mum, how can I possibly concentrate on classes when I'm heartbroken?'

'How long have you been going out with Guy?' Sam asked hesitantly.

'In normal time, not long,' Brook said, 'but we connected. We had something special.'

Normal time? There are different measurements? 'Well, at least you have Kenzie there to keep you company,' Sam said gently.

'No, I don't. She just went off to work like nothing even happened.'

'So you didn't go in today?' Sam asked.

'Of course not, Mum. How could I? I knew you'd be like this. You and Kenzie are the same. Just because you two don't have any emotions, doesn't mean the rest of us have to put on a brave face and soldier on.'

Don't have any emotions? What the hell? 'Excuse me?'

'It's true, Mum. You and Kenzie, you're so alike. She wouldn't let anything get in the way of her stupid degree, and when you and Dad broke up, you didn't even cry. Well, I'm not like you two. I get emotional, all right?'

Sam was surprised into silence by her daughter's outburst. Is that how she'd seemed to her kids: like an unemotional robot? She'd shed plenty of tears over the end of her marriage, but she didn't do it in front of her children—they had their own grief to deal with and Sam didn't have the luxury of being a sad, miserable mother who felt like hiding away from the world in her bedroom until it all blew over. She still needed to get kids to school and buy food and do the after-school-activities drop-offs.

'I'm sorry you've broken up with your boyfriend, Brook, but you can't be angry at Kenzie for going to work. That's not fair.'

'Being dumped isn't exactly fair either, Mum,' Brook shot back with a sniff.

'No, it's not, but that's all just part of growing up. You're in university to get your degree. Boyfriends should come second to that. It's okay to take a day here and there when you need to, but I think if you take a long, hot bath, have something to eat and get an early night, you'll find by tomorrow that things will start to look a lot better.'

'Is a bit of sympathy too much to ask?'

'I gave you sympathy!' Sam said with an exasperated sigh.

'You gave me a lecture. All I wanted was my mum, and you're all the way down there.'

Kids always knew where to hit to score the most emotional damage when they were upset, and Brook was a pro. 'I think they call that bad timing,' Sam soothed. It had usually fallen on Sam to be the level-headed bad guy while Andrew got to do the spoiling. Brook and her father had always had a special bond—she could wrap him around her little finger, and did so whenever she needed to, even though Sam had hoped she'd grow out of it once she was out on her own in the real world. Clearly adult life was presenting somewhat of a culture shock still.

'I'm really sorry about your break-up, Brook. Truly. But he obviously wasn't worth it if he thought breaking up via a text was okay. You deserve someone who respects you a lot more than that. Going about your normal day will hit him harder than crying over him ever could. Hold your head up and go to your classes tomorrow—you're stronger than you give yourself credit for. Don't let some little limp-dicked shit make you feel like nothing. You deserve so much better than that.'

Silence greeted her statement.

'Did you really just call him a limp-dicked shit?' Brook said eventually.

'I'm sorry, but he must be, to break up with someone as amazing as you.'

'I can't believe you just said that,' Brook said, starting to laugh.

'If you tell anyone, I'll deny it.' Sam smiled, glad she'd managed to distract her daughter from the pity party she'd been throwing herself.

'I'm sorry, Mum, you're right,' Brook sighed. 'I *do* deserve better than that. I'm going to go get a makeover, then I'm going to go out tonight and post a heap of photos on Snapchat. He'll be sorry he dumped me.'

That wasn't exactly what she'd been saying. 'Ah, just don't go overboard . . . with the posting on Snapchat thing, okay?' Sam said nervously.

'Oh, Mum, please. I'm not in high school anymore.'

'No. You're not.' That's what Sam was worried about. High schoolers didn't go out to nightclubs and usually, at least, had to get past a parental inspection of what they were wearing when they left the house.

'Thanks, Mum, this is a fantastic idea. I gotta go and see if I can get into my beauty therapist. Bye, Mum. Love you.'

'Bye,' Sam said as the call disconnected abruptly and she was left looking at the phone with a concerned frown.

Twelve

Sam glanced up from the computer screen at the sound of an approaching car, and felt a smile tug at her lips. It felt like déjà vu. She was sixteen and Jack was driving down the driveway to see her. Only, she wasn't sixteen anymore, and there was no need to seek out privacy away from annoying brothers and watchful parents. She knew there had to be some bonuses to getting older.

'What are you doing over here at this time?' she asked, glancing at her watch. It was only just after lunchtime.

'I finished what I had to do early, and we're not on call today,' Jack said with a grin, leaning down to plant a kiss on her mouth, which left them both breathing slightly harder than they had been before.

'Go get changed,' he said. 'I want to take you somewhere.'

'Changed into what?'

'Swimmers.' His grin grew wider.

'Where are we going?'

'You'll see,' he said. 'I'll wait for you here, but if you're not out in five minutes, I won't be responsible for how long it takes us to leave this house after I come looking for you.'

'Five minutes to get changed.' She eyed him doubtfully. 'I don't even have make-up on. I'll need at least half an hour if we're supposed to be going out—'

'Four minutes,' he said, shaking his head without looking the least bit perturbed by her panic. 'And you won't need make-up where we're going.'

As they drove past Jack's place, Sam relaxed in her seat, a smile breaking out across her face when she realised where they were headed.

'Remember this place?' Jack asked as they climbed out of the car and surveyed the swimming hole, the water in the gravel-edged creek running clear over the white stones below. The Cameron place was further up creek than her parents' farm and still had water flowing. It was lower than Sam remembered it, though. Just like her parents' waterholes—everything was drying up.

'Vaguely,' she said, trying for an offhand shrug.

'Vaguely?' Jack growled, reaching for her. 'I think you might need a reminder to jog your memory, lady.'

This was the place they'd always escaped to for that much-yearned-for privacy away from prying eyes and protective parents. There had been more than one occasion when their interlude had been prematurely ended by the arrival of someone coming down to check on cattle or fences, but not today.

It was so hot, and a swim was one of the best suggestions Jack had ever made.

'Didn't you bring your swimmers?' he asked, watching her tiptoe into the water.

'These *are* my swimmers,' she said, looking down at the loose white shirt she wore over a bikini top and her denim shorts. 'Why?'

'Nothing. I just . . . nothing,' he said quickly.

Sam frowned a little. 'If you thought you were getting me up here for a perv, you've really missed out.'

'Can't blame a guy for trying.' He shrugged, and she shook her head at him as she walked deeper into the water.

Once she was brave enough to submerge her torso under the cold water, she felt her body relax and memories of long, hot summer days swimming in this exact spot came flooding back.

She let out a contented sigh when two arms wrapped around her, drawing her back against a solid chest. That sent even more memories flying through her mind, and she closed her eyes, listening to the shrill sound of cicadas echoing off the water from the dense tree line around them.

'You know what?' Jack's deep voice broke the peace and quiet surrounding them.

'What?' she asked lazily.

'You still look amazing,' he said, tightening his hold just a fraction and nuzzling the side of her neck. 'You're the same, but different. In a good way.'

His comment made her smile. There was no denying she was not the sixteen-year-old girl he remembered, but his words, so much like the man himself, were spoken with honest candour, and it gave her a thrill to know he still found her attractive.

'I haven't felt like myself in a long time. I guess I lost . . . something, after Andrew left.' She could feel Jack's displeasure at the mention of her ex-husband in the tightening of his forearms around her. 'It's my issue, not his. I began to feel as though I didn't fit in anywhere anymore. He left me for a twenty-something and, as clichéd as it sounds, I felt like a second-hand car being traded in for something newer.'

'He was an idiot,' Jack said in a low tone that vibrated through his chest into her back, and she smiled a little.

'It was a wake-up call.' She shrugged. 'I used to be caught up in the whole image thing. The Sunshine Coast and the Gold Coast seem to have this projection of perfection everywhere you go. Everything has to be waxed, and shaped, and hair and make-up has to be in place at all times. My wardrobe had to be full of name brands only, and everything always had to look perfect. There was an image to uphold.' She shook her head sadly. 'Then I lost a friend. She was in the prime of her life. She used to eat all the right things, work out constantly and then feel guilty if she missed a day at the gym, she stressed about the slightest wrinkle . . . then she died. And all I could think about was, how much time did she waste stressing about how she looked instead of just living? It really shocked me into taking a long, hard look at myself.' She traced a finger along his wrist and absently noted the scars and healing scratches. 'I don't feel as though I fit back in my old life anymore. I'm in my forties, and I don't want to be constantly comparing myself to twenty-year-olds. My kids are that age, for crying out loud,' she said, shaking her head. 'I don't want to end up one of those women who turn to plastic surgery just to fit into a society they *want* to belong to. I won't do that.'

'No. You don't need to do that,' he agreed.

She'd occasionally wondered, if she had gone down that road, would that have kept Andrew from wandering? She doubted it. After having their children, she knew that his interest had started to wane. He still wanted to party and entertain, and having a wife who was tired from running after two kids all day and didn't feel like dressing up and going out hadn't fitted his marriage expectations.

The cool water trickled around them as they floated, Jack's solid presence behind her holding her up. She let her legs straighten out before her and leaned her head back against his bare shoulder. She smiled at his farmer's tan: brown arms and face contrasting with his lighter chest, legs and feet due to wearing work shirts, jeans and boots outdoors every day.

'I'm really glad you thought to come here,' Sam said after a while, breaking the silence. 'You needed a break.'

'We all need a break,' he countered, and she knew he was thinking about the others still up there fighting. 'But this will probably be the last chance I get for a while.'

'Do you get scared?'

'Sometimes,' he said. 'Most of the time I don't—we've trained for pretty much every situation we're likely to get into, but occasionally things turn to shit and it gets a bit hairy. It's more the waiting that makes everyone jittery. My dad used to tell us it's an old bush legend, that fire's smart and knows when it's being watched by firefighters, so it waits for its chance to make a run. That's what this one's been like. For weeks it's been slowly burning away up in inaccessible country—keeping just out of our reach, like it's biding its time. That bit scares me.'

'Why?'

'Because I think it knows that we have the perfect conditions at the moment for it to unleash hell and it's toying with us.'

Thinking of fire in general had made Sam nervous enough—but thinking of it as an actual living thing terrified her. She couldn't stop the shiver that ran up her spine at the thought, and Jack's arms tightened around her.

'Don't listen to me—I'm overtired and talking shit,' he apologised. 'We're doing everything we can to keep on top of it. Don't worry, okay?'

She nodded and smiled, and after a few minutes the warmth of his body behind her soon erased her misgivings.

She could stay here like this all day, she thought, as the cicadas and insects serenaded them from the trees on the riverbank. As a kid, this is where she would spend pretty much her entire summer, every summer, with friends and family. She still preferred swimming in a creek to going to the beach, despite the fact it was a mere forty minutes away. The hard white rocks of the creek floor were as pretty as white sand, and the fresh water didn't sting her eyes like salt water did. Nope, deep down she was still a farm kid at heart.

After a few minutes she felt Jack's hands begin to move across her stomach and she smiled sleepily as he nuzzled her neck, until that flicker of desire lit up once more and she turned in his arms to kiss him.

She didn't see Jack again for two days after their all too brief, idyllic afternoon at the swimming hole. He was back to spending crazy hours in the bush trying to keep the unrelenting fire from encroaching on farms and homes. The news continued to report on the outbreaks of new fires in the area and a few that had started up in other parts of the state as well, as the dry, hot weather continued.

When Jack did come back for a day, he refused to sleep for too long, instead intent on ensuring both his property and her parents' farm were as prepared as possible and to attend a briefing at the local hall, where they were provided with contact numbers of various agencies who could assist with livestock management and evacuation sites.

'Can't we move the cattle somewhere? I heard the showground's taking in livestock,' Sam asked as they discussed the animals.

'They mean horses, cats, dogs, pet sheep and alpacas . . . that kind of thing. They don't have enough room to take in everyone's stock.'

'So, what do we do with them? We can't just leave them to fend for themselves.'

'Animals are a lot smarter when it comes to fire than you'd think,' he said and smiled at her doubtful look. 'There are safety measures we can take. Your dad's been through bushfire seasons before—he's prepared.'

'Well, he's not here. It's just me, and I have no idea what to do.'

'Henry, like most people around here, would use a safe paddock.'

'Which paddock is that?'

'One that's been eaten down and cleared so there's less to burn. We'll put the irrigation sprinkler in there with them and they'll be fine.'

'I'm worried about Matey,' Sam said, resting her arms along the top of the timber rail as she watched the old horse eat.

'Why, what's up?' Jack asked, eyeing him carefully.

'All this smoke, the fires . . . I get we can't move the cattle but I just don't think leaving Matey out there with them is a good idea. He's too old and slow. I think I'll find out about taking him in to the showground.'

'Probably not a bad idea. But maybe give it a day or two.'

They spent the rest of the morning setting up her father's so-called safe paddock and Sam tried her best to watch how to do everything should she ever need to implement their fire plan. Jack wasn't one to overreact, so the fact he was going to all this trouble made her nervous.

None of this had been in the back of her mind when she'd volunteered to come and farm-sit for her parents. The worst she'd thought she'd be dealing with was the bloody guinea fowl. Not a bushfire running through the place. Not having to evacuate livestock and animals on her own. They'd never had to evacuate animals before. Sam looked across at Jack, then let out a slow breath. She wasn't on her own. She had Jack, and plenty of other people she knew she could call on. Only, with everyone looking so worried—down-to-earth, sensible people who didn't scare easily—she didn't feel especially confident that she could handle something this enormous herself.

Jack had put the water pump and generator out next to the house in case it became necessary to defend the place. Of all the preparations they'd been making, this was by far the most confronting. This was the last line of defence. It was too horrible to think that things could reach this point.

But they had to be practical. If firefighters came, they would have the equipment within easy reach to help them fight the fire. But Sam knew that if her parents were here, it would be her dad who would stay to protect the house. Could she stay? If push came to shove, could she stay and defend her family's home?

She knew it was stupid to even consider it—beyond stupid. She would only put herself and everyone else in danger. And yet, how was she supposed to just leave the house to burn?

'It'll be okay,' Jack said again, hugging her once they were back in the house later.

'I don't remember ever feeling this scared.' Over the years, they'd had many floods and fires and needed to move livestock to higher ground, but there was never the underlying level of fear and uncertainty that was hovering with the threat of this fire.

'We just have to make sure we're prepared for anything. Best-case scenario, it's all overkill and we can pack everything back up and be glad we didn't have to use any of it.'

She didn't want to ask what the worst-case scenario was—she had a feeling it was better not to know.

'I wish you didn't have to go,' she said, enjoying the simple pleasure of being held. She breathed in the scent of his shirt. It smelled of laundry powder with a touch of fragrance from his deodorant, but the best bit was the warm, salty scent that was all Jack.

'I wish I didn't have to leave.'

She smiled against his shirt and pulled back a little to look up into his face. 'This is just like when we were kids and had to say goodbye. Do you remember how long it used to take?'

'I remember your dad threatening to do some physically impossible things to my anatomy.'

Sam laughed before crooning sympathetically. 'You know he wouldn't really have done any of it.'

Jack gave a wince. 'Back then, I sure as hell wasn't going to take the risk.'

'Are you sure I can't tempt you to stay for dinner?'

'You have no idea how much I want to, but I've got a meeting to get to before I head out to relieve the guys.'

'But you've got to eat,' she persisted.

'They'll feed us at the club.'

'Oh, fine then,' she sighed, and tried not to pout.

'I'll be back as soon as I can get away. I promise.'

'Okay. Go be a hero. I guess I can share you with the rest of the valley for a while.'

'I'd rather be here with you,' he said, nuzzling her neck with a smile before she playfully pushed him away.

'Hurry up and go so you can get back here faster.'

They shared a final kiss before he climbed into his car and headed up the hill. The smoke hid the rest of his journey, and a chill ran across her shoulders as the fear began to creep back over her.

'We've just spoken to Thomas,' her mother said when Sam answered her call that afternoon. 'How're things there?'

'So far it's okay. Jack's been keeping me up to date. If it gets too serious, he'll let me know.'

'That's good. Yes, Jack will know what to do. But if it does get close, I want you to leave.'

'I will. But I'm hoping it won't come to that.'

'If it does, you leave,' her father put in sternly.

'We spent today getting the safe paddock ready. Don't worry about the cattle, I'll make sure they're okay.'

'If you need help, you call your brothers. They'll know what to do,' he said. 'I've told Thomas to get out there and check everything later today.'

Sam felt a brief flare of irritation. Of course she would call for help if she needed it, but she'd just said she had everything under control. 'I'm sure Thomas has enough to do between the SES and his place. Seriously, Dad, I can handle everything here at the moment.'

'Yeah, well, it won't hurt to have someone else there to make sure.'

'So, how *is* Jack?' her mother cut in smoothly.

'He's pretty busy. He's been out with the fires for the last week or so. I don't know how they do it.'

'Poor boy,' Margaret clucked, and Sam found herself smiling. *Boy?* 'I've been worried about him over the last few years. He's not the same Jack he used to be.'

Sam was glad this wasn't a video call: she was terrible at masking her thoughts and her mother had always been able to read what she was thinking. Right now she would probably be able to see the flush that was creeping up Sam's neck. She was a grown woman with grown kids, she should be able to tell her parents that she had been seeing Jack, and yet . . . it was still too new.

'Well, I guess we've all changed over the years.'

'He didn't handle Cilia leaving very well at all. It broke his heart to lose those girls of his,' her mother continued sadly, and Sam could picture her shaking her head with a worried frown. 'I hope he's taking care of himself during all this fire business.'

'I've dropped over a few meals here and there,' Sam said, trying for a casual tone to put Margaret's mother hen instinct to rest. 'You know, because he's been over here to check on things and whatnot . . .' Sam's voice trailed off. 'Just being neighbourly,' she tacked on for good measure.

'Well, that's nice, darling. It's good to be neighbourly.'

She couldn't be sure, but she could have sworn that she detected a note of amusement in her mother's tone. Maybe it was just the connection—they were on the other side of the world, after all.

'Well, we better go. Make sure you call us if there's any news,' her mum went on.

'Day or night. Doesn't matter,' her father added briskly.

'I will. Please try to enjoy your holiday. There's enough of us here to take care of everything.' She knew that her parents would still worry, but there was literally nothing they could do that hadn't already been done, even if they were here. It was a watch-and-be-prepared situation. Sam just hoped that all this preparation would end up being for nothing and in a few days they could go back to life as normal.

Thirteen

Sam had always been organised. Once she'd had kids she'd become even more so. When she packed for a weekend away, she always included Panadol, cold medicine, band aids, and everything in between. In her car she had a snake-bite kit because, well, you just never knew when you might come across one and it paid to be prepared. So she decided, just to be safe, that she would pack the most important things into her car and store them at Alex's place until the fires were no longer a threat.

    Sam stood in her parents' lounge room and turned in a slow circle as the enormity of the situation settled on her shoulders. She needed to pack in case she had to evacuate—but pack what? The whole house held memories. She looked at the baby photos of her and her brothers on the wall, and the heirloom oval timber frame with her father's great-great-great-grandparents, the original first settlers of their family. What about the piano that was over a hundred and twenty years old? How was she supposed to move that? Worse yet—how was she supposed to leave it behind?

Thinking practically, she started with the important things: documents and photo albums, then her mother's jewellery and anything with sentimental value from the linen press, packing them all safely into a large suitcase. She filled two garbage bags with clothes for her parents, and placed the bone china into a plastic storage tub. Before she knew it, the car was full, so she set out for Alex's place in Glenview.

Alex hadn't started out a farmer. He'd spent close to fifteen years in the navy before an accident made him reassess his career and his future, and he and Thomas had come up with the partnership growing macadamia trees.

The long driveway wound its way to the property like a snake, flanked either side by rows of neatly planted macadamia trees, until it opened out onto a wide clearing. On one side, two massive sheds housed the processing and packing business, and on the other was a two-storey house and shed where her brother and his family lived.

'Hey, stranger,' Alex called as he walked towards her car. 'I was beginning to get worried about you. I haven't seen you since Mum and Dad's farewell dinner.'

Sam hugged her brother and kissed his cheek. 'Hey, yourself. I've been busy feeding cattle. I'm a farmer now, you know,' she told him with as much of a straight face as she could manage.

'Well, that makes one of us, then.' He grinned, following her around to the back of the car.

Her father and older brother still found it funny that Alex, who had always sworn he would never be a farmer, had ended up back here doing exactly that.

'And go ahead, call me a panic merchant like Thomas, but I'm not taking any chances with this stuff,' she said, opening the back door and taking out the garbage bags of clothing.

'No harm in being cautious,' Alex said, taking a plastic tub from the boot. 'I've cleared some room in the shed.' Sam followed him, and together they continued to unload her car. When they finished, Alex straightened up and dusted off his hands. 'Coming inside for a cuppa?'

Sam nodded. 'Sounds great.' As they headed towards the house, she realised how quiet it was. 'Marcie not home?' she asked, looking around the empty kitchen.

'She's in Sydney for a conference,' Alex said with a shrug. 'The kids and I are baching for the week.'

Marcie was every inch the businesswoman, managing her booming online health-food business. Sam had never really been close to her younger sister-in-law. In theory, they shared similar backgrounds—they were both businesswomen and had families, but Sam found Marcie difficult. She was very opinionated and outspoken about pretty much everything and seemed to enjoy arguing for the sake of arguing. Sam couldn't see what her brother had seen in the woman when he asked her to marry him. However, he was one of the sweetest men she knew, so there had to be something redeemable in Marcie's qualities. She loved her children and she was a good mum. So, there was that. In the grand scheme of things, it really didn't matter if Sam liked her or not—as long as her brother was happy, that was all that mattered.

'So, I hear you and Jack Cameron have been seeing a bit of each other,' Alex said, handing over a mug of coffee as he sat down across from her, causing Sam to give a small start and almost spill the contents.

'What? Where on earth did you hear that?'

She narrowed her gaze as he smirked. 'You really have been away too long if you're surprised by how fast news travels around here. I gather it's true, then?'

'He's Mum and Dad's next-door neighbour, of course I've been *seeing* him. I've been giving him a hand while he's been out fighting fires.'

'So, it's just neighbourly?'

'He's an old friend.'

'Friend with benefits,' Alex scoffed.

'I can't believe there's already gossip going around.' She and Jack had barely left the farm, except to go to the meeting the other day, but they'd hardly been all over each other or done anything to suggest they'd been, well . . . *together*. Clearly the fact that they arrived in the same car and sat side by side had been all the evidence anyone needed to jump to conclusions.

'This place'll have you married off in a couple of weeks.'

'Typical,' she muttered.

'You could do worse,' Alex said.

'Who says I need to get married to be happy?'

'All I'm saying is, you two have a second chance. You're both single again.'

'Ah, excuse me, Mr I-Had-A-Girl-In-Every-Port,' Sam said, raising her eyebrows. 'You do remember how you used to protest that single life was too good to give up for marriage? That was only a handful of years ago, wasn't it?'

'Yeah, and I've grown up.'

She watched him drop a teaspoon of sugar in his cup and stir it methodically left then right. Her younger brother was taller than Thomas and their father. He didn't have the stocky build of the Murphys, taking after their grandfather on their mother's side with his height and more reserved nature. In his younger days, he'd been a bit of a handful—always too rebellious for school. Joining the navy was the best thing he ever did: it gave him the purpose and discipline he seemed to be searching for. Once he met Marcie, the change in him had been drastic. Sam worried it may have come at the cost of who he really was, but he always swore he'd just been waiting for the right woman to come along and tame him. Sam just hoped he wasn't confusing tamed with being dominated.

'Well, I rather like being my own person at the moment, thank you very much,' she told her brother. 'So, there's no marriage plans on the horizon for me.'

They chatted about their parents and the postcards that had started to arrive, and about the kids, but Sam sensed there was something else on her brother's mind. When she looked at her watch she was surprised by how late it was getting. 'You'll have to go and pick up the kids from school soon,' she said, getting to her feet. 'I better let you go.'

'Yeah, it comes around fast,' he said, collecting their cups and placing them in the sink.

As they returned to her car, Sam looked across at her brother, fidgeting with the rubber seal in the open car door. 'What is it?'

Alex hesitated before giving an offhand shrug. 'If you're not serious about Jack, you might want to make that clear to him sooner rather than later.'

Sam frowned. 'What do you mean? Has he said something?'

'No,' Alex said quickly, shaking his head. 'It's just that . . . he's a mate, you know.' He held her gaze. 'I was here when you left. He was in a bad way. I don't want to see either of you hurt again.'

'We were kids,' Sam said, surprised by her brother's warning.

'Jack's . . .' Alex started, before giving a small sigh. 'He's one of the good guys, Sam. I don't reckon he ever really got over you leaving. I know,' he said when she opened her mouth to protest, 'it's probably none of my business, and it happened a long time ago, but I'm just saying . . . I've known him a long time. I think if you two have started something and you're not serious about it, you need to tell him.'

'Aren't you supposed to be on my side in all this—warning the guy away from your sister?'

Alex didn't smile at her teasing; instead his face became even more serious. 'Usually, but in this case you're not the one who needs protecting.'

Sam stared, speechless, at her brother's retreating back. Is that who she really was: some cold-hearted monster who left a trail of destruction behind her?

Christ almighty. She'd been eighteen years old when she'd left town, a kid. Why was her leaving something that people like her brother still felt a need to remind her about?

All through the drive home, the comment stayed with her. *Was* it serious? Could there be something between her and Jack after she left Burrumba? She didn't even know what she wanted to do when she went back to the Sunshine Coast. She still had her house, and there were the kids to consider. Yes, she was now thinking she wanted her own little farm, but she had no idea where. Did she really want to have a relationship thrown into the equation while so many of her decisions were still up in the air?

Maybe Alex had a point. If Jack was already thinking long term, she probably should talk to him. And yet, Jack was a grown man—surely he would say something to gauge where she was at before he went ahead and started making plans for the future?

Sam gave a long sigh. Wasn't life supposed to get easier as you got older? She thought the days of drama were long gone . . . apparently not.

Jack tipped his head back against the side of the truck and closed his eyes. They stung, which was nothing new—they'd been dry and itchy from all the smoke in the air for weeks—but today he was feeling it even more.

In the background, he could hear the scratchy voices over the two-way radios and quiet murmurs of the men who were taking a quick breather. They'd been at it for the past eight hours straight, all through the night, and they were barely making a dent in the monster. They had no hope of getting on top of this fire—they hadn't for close to a month now, ever since it had started deep in the inaccessible parts of the national park from that lightning strike. But they'd been managing to stay ahead of it using fire breaks and sheer bloody-mindedness. Until now. The weather was playing havoc with the whole situation. Drought had dried out the landscape, and years of neglect of the undergrowth within the parks provided an abundance of fuel that the fire was tearing through at an alarming pace, and now strong winds were upgrading an already serious situation into a disaster. It was only a matter of time before the fire broke free.

Of course, it had to be during all this that Sam would drop back into his life and turn everything upside down. He'd barely had time to process what had been happening between them, since he'd been on call and out fighting fires pretty much the whole time. But there were times, like now, when he found his mind drifting back to her. Maybe it was his brain's way of giving him a few moments of reprieve.

It almost felt too good to be true. Sometimes he worried that maybe he was dreaming and he would wake up to find that his life was once again the mundane shitshow it had been for too long to remember. He knew that over the past few years he'd become bitter—he'd thrown himself into the farm and cattle, and while it made him a bit of a recluse socially, his property had never been in better shape. He may have been a grumpy bastard with no love life, but his business was thriving.

And then Sam came home.

He pulled his mind up hastily, and that warm glow that had begun to spread across his chest stopped. Sam hadn't technically come home to stay . . . which was the slight glitch in this whole scenario. She was just back. For a bit.

It didn't seem to matter how often he reminded himself of that; his heart still managed to get ahead of him and throw up images of a future together. It was crazy. It was too soon to even consider, and part of him wasn't entirely convinced that it could ever work anyway. It hadn't before.

It was different this time, of course—he wasn't some lovesick kid with no idea. He'd toughened up considerably since then. He'd tried and failed at marriage, so he wasn't overly confident he had much to offer Sam, even if she *was* interested in that. And yet . . . when he thought of Sam, it wasn't as a brief, casual fling.

He'd wanted to bring it up but it had all happened so fast and there was never enough time. When he had managed to snag a few precious hours with her lately, he sure as hell didn't want to waste them on deep conversations that had the potential to blow up in his face.

It was probably best to just wait and see where it went before he risked opening his big mouth. In the meantime, he supposed if this damn fire had any kind of upside, it was that it was keeping him too busy to mess things up with Sam.

The next lot of weary men walked towards them, and Jack winced as he pulled himself upright. He'd been in the rural brigade ever since he was a teenager—it was just part of growing up out here. His dad had been a member, all the neighbours were members; but over the years the volunteers had grown older and the new recruits fewer. He glanced around; of the eight men before him, he was probably the youngest. The rest were in their late sixties and early seventies. There was a lifetime of experience and knowledge gathered around the makeshift campsite, but that was also an ongoing concern. Sooner or later these men wouldn't be able to continue, and what would happen to the rural communities then? It was already becoming clear that in times like these, when there were more fires than men or equipment, it was basically a case of every man, or area, for themselves.

The local lads who'd been forming their own small bands of firefighting units were doing more for themselves than the RFS could do. The red tape and bureaucracy chain of command that was beginning to impose itself on their efforts was only going to get worse once they started bringing in outside units. Resources would be funnelled into the places with the greatest populations and risk to houses, which meant the smaller communities out here, way up in the arms, North Arm, South Arm, Brown's Arm and all the other river tributary places, would be left without any Rural Fire Service support, with their fire crews made up of the families who lived and worked their properties in the area.

Jack had been lending a hand wherever he could to the farming units when he came across them—most of them he knew well. At least their presence meant these places wouldn't be completely defenceless, though they had limited equipment, relying on farm utes with plastic containers of water and repurposed tractors and earthmoving equipment to fight fires. There had been growing tension between farmers and the RFS over the past few days, with many frustrated that they weren't being given the help they needed, and Jack worried it was only going to get worse in the days to come.

Fourteen

Sam spent the morning fussing over Matey, brushing him and untangling his mane as she located his halter and dug out a lead rope. It had been a long time since he'd had any real handling done. His days of pony club and shows were long gone, and Sam smiled wistfully at the memories as she secured his halter and gave him a pat. Some days the past didn't seem all that long ago.

The sound of a vehicle approaching drew her gaze. A white four-wheel drive and horse float was making its way down her parents' long gravelled driveway, and she gave a small click of her tongue and led Matey forward.

'Thanks for doing this, Troy,' Sam said when he climbed out. 'I know there're a million other things you probably need to be doing. I did try to tell Chelsea you didn't need to do it *right now*,' she apologised.

'No worries,' Troy said, giving her a brief, shy smile before stroking the old horse's neck. 'How does he float?'

'Honestly, I have no idea. It's been years since he's left the property, but he used to be okay.' She continued to gently stroke the neck of the horse. Her parents had lent him out to a neighbour with a young girl who'd used him in gymkhanas for a good few years when Sam had left home. After that, he'd remained on the farm doing only light cattle work with her father until now. 'You've had a pretty good life, haven't you old boy?' she said affectionately.

Troy dropped the rear of the float, and Sam gave Matey one final pat. 'Okay, old man, you need to be on your best behaviour. We don't have time to muck around today.' She took up the lead rope then walked him through the stockyard gate and up to the float. As they approached, she paused to let him sniff at the ramp cautiously before giving a click of her tongue to walk on, and with only a brief hesitation, thankfully, the old horse ambled up the ramp and into the float.

'Good boy, Matey.' She beamed with a mix of relief and pride. The last thing anyone needed today was to spend precious time coaxing a reluctant horse into a float.

Sam followed Troy into town and headed for the showground. When she got there, she looked around in surprise at the crowd already gathered. It almost looked like the local show day. Cars and floats filled the saleyard, and already a lot of the stalls in the long stables were filled with horses and nervous owners.

Sam helped unload Matey and thanked Troy, before searching for someone in charge to find out where to house her horse.

Walking into the chook pavilion, she was greeted by a din of hens clucking and roosters crowing, ducks quacking and turkeys and geese gobbling and screeching in their wall of cages. Down another aisle, rows of cats blinked back at her as they took in their surroundings with unamused stares, and excited small dogs yelped for attention across the shed in another row. In between, there was an assortment of other animals, from rabbits to guinea pigs, and parrots to budgerigars, all adding to the commotion of the large shed.

As Sam moved to the rear of the building, she found the local land-services officer, who looked up from her makeshift desk and smiled. 'How can I help?'

'I called earlier about a horse. My name's Samantha . . . Murphy,' she added after a small hesitation. No one from around here knew her by her married name, and now that she was divorced and back in her home town, it felt right to be Sam Murphy once again.

'Oh. Samantha. Yes, you were talking to me. I've got your paperwork here somewhere, just a sec.' The woman flicked through a stack of forms on the desk and smiled triumphantly when she located the right one. 'You're bringing in Matey.'

'Yes, please. I'm probably overreacting, but I just don't think he's safe enough at home. He's a bit old, and I really don't want to risk him running around and getting scared at his age.'

'It's not an overreaction to be prepared. We prefer people to organise themselves and their animals early. Saves a lot of worry and stress when it's too late.' She handed Sam some paperwork to fill in and gave her a number to find on the stalls down behind the stockyards.

As Sam made her way back to the stables, she walked past several people who had set up campsites. There were tents and caravans and motorhomes parked around the centre ring where the horse events usually took place during the annual show, and she recognised a few of them as people who had already lost their homes, from further up in the arms surrounding their valley. Sam swallowed hard as she saw women holding small children in camp chairs while trying to entertain older kids. Some were hanging out washing on makeshift clotheslines while others tended to the dogs they had tied to their vans and tent poles. There was a palatable cocktail of grief, confusion and, most notably, fear in the air. It was in stark contrast to the sound of children running between tents and playing—seeing the whole thing as an unexpected camping trip. She suspected these happy children had evacuated ahead of the fire and hadn't been caught up in the frantic scramble to leave a burning house as some people here had the day before. On those faces she saw nothing but stunned disbelief and defeat.

She couldn't even imagine how she would cope with losing a house. She knew many of these people had been evacuated from areas in the thick of the fires where Jack had been working and weren't allowed back in to check on their properties. The uncertainty must be excruciating.

'It's going to be okay,' she told Matey softly as she led him to his stall. 'I know you're not used to all this, but it's only for a few days and then I'll take you home, okay?'

All around her, horses snorted and neighed and stamped their feet. Matey picked up on the environment, holding his head high and blowing little snorts through his nostrils as he investigated all the strange new scents suddenly bombarding him. Sam closed the stall door behind her and dropped in the biscuits she'd brought to feed him.

'I've got to get home and feed the others, but I'll be back later this afternoon, okay?' she said, giving him one last, lingering rub. She felt terrible as she walked away and began to rethink the whole idea of leaving him, until she remembered she still had the cattle and dogs at home to worry about. *It's only for a few days and he's safer here at the moment*, she told herself firmly, but she still sent a worried frown into the rear-view mirror as she drove through the showground gates.

The little hall up the road from her parents' farm had seen many things over the past hundred or so years. It had farewelled young men off to wars and seen generations of weddings and birthday parties within its four square walls, but today it had a sombre feel. There was tension in the air as the local farming families gathered, sitting on hard blue plastic chairs to listen to the fire chief.

The Rural Fire Service had been doing it tough. They were responsible for protecting a huge area of land, and their units were spread far too thinly to cover it all. Unease had been growing with the fires breaking containment lines on and off for the past two days, and the continued hot weather and strong winds were making the difficult task of holding it back almost impossible.

Sam searched the crowd for Jack as she walked inside, but couldn't spot him immediately, so she took a seat in the back row.

The fire chief, Derrick Bradshaw, was a chubby man in his late sixties. He raised his voice at the front of the hall, and the murmur of voices around the room stopped.

'Thank you for coming along today. I know everyone's got things to do, and I appreciate your time.'

He read out the media release of the current situation and location of the fire, which was uncomfortably close—not that anyone needed reminding, with the smoke growing thicker each day. 'As previously stated, we've got two units situated out at Blackbutt Road and Kemps Creek. They've both been backburning during the night, and there's nothing more we can do at this stage. If the wind changes direction tomorrow as predicted, I'll be honest, we'll be in trouble. I strongly urge anyone who is not prepared to stay and defend property, to leave now. Tomorrow will be too late.'

'You said you have two units out here,' a man from the back of the crowd called out. 'Why can't you send more if it's that bad?'

'We're stretched to capacity as it is. Those two units are being redeployed elsewhere later this morning. We've got fires breaking out everywhere at the moment.'

Another murmur followed that announcement.

'Which is why I'm saying this again. If you do not have the ability to safely defend your property, make your preparations to leave now. If the fire jumps that containment line, there won't be any units available to come out here and help.'

Sam stared at the man blankly.

'So, what? We're on our own?' someone else asked. 'Where's our bloody local unit?'

'I'm sorry,' Derrick said, shaking his head wearily. 'But we've got all available resources defending Burrumba at the moment. We have to protect the town.'

'So, just because we're a handful of families up here, even though we're closer to the fire danger, we don't get any priority?'

'It's nothing personal,' the captain snapped, then rubbed a hand across his sooty face. 'Look, we've got too few people and only a couple of trucks. We can't be everywhere. At the moment our orders are to protect the town and population. We've been told to advise everyone west of the township to evacuate into Burrumba if they don't have suitable equipment to stay and defend.'

'Well, thanks for nothing,' snarled a man close to Sam.

'Come on, guys, it's not Derrick's fault. He's just doing his job,' Ted Morris, a neighbour from up the road, cut in.

Sam felt for the man up the front; he was clearly not happy about delivering the news. But the farmers were on their own with an uncontrolled fire bearing down on them. People were understandably on edge.

'What about *our* crew?' a young man called out, and Sam turned, spotting Jack standing at the rear of the hall with a small group of men, dressed in various items of bushfire brigade uniform. 'You blokes should be here, defending us.'

'And usually we would be, along with every other available unit, but these aren't usual times. The whole valley is on fire,' Derrick replied with weary defeat. 'I don't make the rules. We're under the command of the RFS. We go where they say we go.'

'This is bullshit,' one of the men standing next to Jack said. 'What about you, Jack?' he continued, turning to face him. 'What if your place goes up? Or mine. Are you just gonna turn your back on that?'

Sam saw Jack's jaw clench and felt her heart lurch at the predicament he suddenly found himself in—caught between his mates and his duty.

'We're under the control of the RFS,' the fire chief repeated. 'They have a job to do. As do we all. I'd suggest that instead of standing around here debating all morning, we get back to it. My advice to you is: keep doing what you've been doing, but be prepared to get out if that containment line breaks.' He sighed bleakly. '*When* that containment line breaks.'

'This is bullshit,' another voice called.

'He's only being honest. They're doing the best they can with what they've got.' Ted tried again to be the voice of reason.

'Well, where's all the reinforcement we were promised a few days ago?' someone else asked.

'We're still waiting,' Derrick said.

Sam had read on the Rural Fire Service site that morning that there were more than one hundred fires currently burning in the state, and the majority were listed as out of control. It wasn't surprising that the extra manpower that would normally have been allocated to a fire this size in their district would be hard to find with so many other fires burning at the same time.

'I don't know about anyone else, but I don't reckon we need these guys anyway. We've been managing to protect our places for the last few days with the gear we've got between us,' another young man Sam didn't recognise piped up. 'We've been from Stockyard Road down to Piper's Crossing and haven't seen a single crew,' he added, his tone reflecting the frustration felt by many of the locals who'd been out working day and night to protect their properties.

Derrick gave another weary shrug. 'Like I said, mate, we've been pretty stretched.' Sam saw the fatigue in the older firefighter's face. 'The fact is, you've all been doing a fantastic job up here,' Derrick added, dropping his professional persona briefly and shaking his head in admiration. 'I just drove the containment line. It's farmers like you who make our life so much easier. I mean, if you hadn't put in that containment line, we'd be chasing this thing for miles, and it'd already be in Burrumba by now. I can't thank you guys enough. Really.'

'Yeah, well I can tell ya, mate,' another man spoke up from the group gathered, 'we've had maybe forty, fifty people up here working our guts out around the clock to get it done.'

'I'm so grateful to all of you,' Derrick said, and Sam heard the honest admiration in the man's voice as he swung his gaze around the group. 'I was only saying on the way up here that farmers don't get the recognition they deserve for all the help they give us. So, thank you. Please pass on my thanks to everyone who's helped. It's been a huge effort, and don't think that it's not appreciated or has gone unnoticed.'

Derrick's radio went off, and Sam watched as he frowned slightly listening to the call. 'Okay, I have to go. I'm sorry the news hasn't been better. Thank you again for everything you've been doing up here, but please do not put yourselves in danger.'

They watched him head out the door as the meeting ended. People dispersed into smaller groups, digesting the news. Sam glanced around at some of the faces—ones she'd known most of her life, usually friendly and warm, today etched with strain and uncertainty. She'd stopped and exchanged small talk with a few she knew and some new faces too. In happier times she might have celebrated the fact there were younger families moving to the district. At the moment, though, these families, like everyone else here, were probably wondering if they would still have a house by the end of the week. Not much to celebrate in that.

She walked up to Judy Howle, a long-time friend of her mother, and reached out to take her hand, squeezing it gently.

'How are you doing, Sam? Are you okay over there at your parents' place?'

'I'm fine. How are you and Mick going?'

'You know Mick,' Judy laughed lightly, shaking her head. The couple were two of the most generous people in the valley—always willing to lend a hand to friends and neighbours, always smiling. Mick would be out with the local farmers doing what he could, despite the fact he had his own property to worry about.

These people were farmers, used to handling hard times, but this was something altogether different. This was a monster slowly creeping up on them and it had the potential to wipe out everything in its path.

Judy said goodbye and the group broke up, many of the men walking away shaking their heads and muttering in angry tones as they went.

Sam watched as Jack glanced up and spotted her. He said something quickly to the man he was talking to before walking towards her. 'Hi,' he said and reached out a hand as he drew closer. She grasped his firmly in her own and managed a grateful smile. 'We're about to head back out.'

'I heard. Are you okay?' she asked, searching his tired, bloodshot eyes.

'Yeah. Just pissed off at the whole situation.'

'I can imagine. It wasn't fair of them to put you on the spot like that, Jack.'

'They're right, though. We *do* belong here, helping our own. But everyone's in the same boat. Over the ridge, up the road . . . people we all know, about to lose their livelihoods and property, and it's not even our call about who we turn our backs on and who we help.'

'Just do what you can,' she said, giving his hand a squeeze. 'That's all you can do.'

He gave her a smile that didn't quite reach his eyes. He looked so damn exhausted. 'I gotta go,' he said as men started to climb up into their truck.

'Be careful,' she said and, without thinking, reached up and kissed him.

'What happened to keeping things quiet?' he asked with a slightly raised eyebrow when they broke apart.

'I don't care anymore,' she said simply.

He held her gaze for a moment, then lowered his head and kissed her once more. It was brief, but deeper, and anyone looking on would be left in no doubt that he was making a statement. 'For luck,' he said after pulling away and taking a step backwards, before turning and jogging back to the truck.

She watched until it drove out of sight. It was funny how all the uncertainty she'd had about their future seemed to dissolve in that one instant. Right now, sending him off into whatever awaited him out there, she knew it was pointless to deny how much she cared about him—had always cared about him.

Back inside, the hall-committee women were already busy making sandwiches and packing food boxes to deliver to the men and women working on the front line—farmers and rural firefighters alike. Families who'd started to leave their properties had been drifting in steadily today, and the committee were busy feeding these people too. It was only the first stop for most of them. The showground at Burrumba was the designated evacuation site, but for many, heading straight there seemed like a final defeat. The hall was a gathering place that helped people find the strength to make that last break and leave the area for the showground.

Most were women and children and grandparents. The men were all staying behind to defend properties and help neighbours. Sam spent the rest of the day circulating the hall with food and tried to help out with babies and small children to give their stressed mothers a few minutes' reprieve. The worry and uncertainty in the air were palpable. Would they return to find their homes gone? Would animals they couldn't bring with them survive? Would their loved ones come back to them safe? All justifiable and real concerns for which no one had any answers.

Fifteen

The next day after feeding Matey, Sam pulled up outside the supermarket. As she walked up the aisles she passed groups of people talking over trolleys, all wearing grim expressions.

'I heard Carmel and Peter Jenkins lost their home,' she overheard as she walked past two older women, and she felt her breath catch a little in her chest. She'd gone to school with their daughter, Sharon.

'That's six houses I've heard of today, gone,' another voice floated across the aisles as Sam placed a packet of biscuits into her basket.

'Matt said the rural fire boys they don't think they'll be able to hold it back much longer. Once it crossed the ridge last night, they say there's nothing stopping it from coming through town.'

'Through town? Surely not,' another woman exclaimed in a shocked voice.

'Look what happened last week down the coast. It burnt all the way to the beach. Right through the main street.'

'But surely it won't get that bad here.'

'I don't know, that's just what Matt heard.'

'Sam? Are you all right?'

Samantha snapped her gaze up to find Peter standing beside her, watching her curiously. She realised she'd been staring at the shelves, side-tracked by what she was overhearing. 'Oh, hi. Yeah, I'm fine.'

'You okay up at your place?'

'Yeah, we're fine at the moment. Well, better than some, I guess.'

'It's pretty sad. We've had people coming in all morning with some horrific stories. But most of the fire damage has been up further than you.'

'Yeah.' Sam waved a hand through the air with an offhand shrug. 'It's still a long way from me.'

'Well, I better keep going. It's crazy around here today. Stay safe.'

'Yeah,' she said as Peter walked off. 'You too.'

The fire could be heading into town? The thought echoed through her mind. She'd watched the news report of people standing on a beach, an orange glow in the sky as flames burnt through the buildings in the main street behind them. It didn't seem possible, and yet it had happened. But before it reached the coast, it had to go through the farms and the smaller towns like Burrumba. A shiver of dread ran through Sam as she gathered the remaining items on her list, making sure she had the essentials: matches, bread, long-life milk, fruit and packet noodles, as well as dog food.

She was grateful the girls weren't with her. For now, they were both safe up north, and she just hoped it stayed that way. It seemed impossible, but looking at the fire map on the app they'd been encouraged to download, it looked like the whole of Australia was on fire.

She made her way to the checkout, without stopping to look sideways. She didn't want to overhear any more rumours or bump into anyone she knew. She already had too much to process without any more unsettling news.

The next morning, Sam carried her box of sandwiches into the CWA hall in town and handed them over to Mavis Brown, another long-time friend of her mum.

'Thank you, Sam, these will be a big help.'

'That's okay. What else can I do?' Sam asked, looking around at the small hall and seeing a group of women busily packing food into plastic bags.

'We're making up snack packs for the firefighters to take out with them. You could help with those if you like.' Sam knew from Jack that units were sent into places that were a long way from town and getting back for meals was often not feasible, so these food parcels were a welcome sight.

She sat at the table and looked over the list of items to place inside the bags. She looked up and smiled when Chelsea sat down beside her.

'How are you holding up?' Chelsea asked, placing more food on the table.

'Not too bad. I've had a few sleepless nights, but better than a lot of people around here. Every day I'm hearing of more people we know who've lost houses and livestock. It's just terrible.'

Chelsea shook her head sadly. 'Doesn't help that every man and his dog has an opinion on why it's happening. Every conversation always ends with someone blaming someone else. None of it's going to put these fires out.'

'Nope,' Sam agreed. She placed another completed bag in the basket on the floor and started a new one, happy at least to be doing something useful. 'Will you guys evacuate?'

'There's no real need at the moment. Troy and his father have been out with the neighbours making fire breaks and keeping on top of any spot fires. They'll stay and defend, if it comes to that.'

'But what about you?' Sam asked. 'You're so far out, what if the roads get blocked? You'll be stuck out there.'

Chelsea gave a small lift of her shoulder. 'No point borrowing trouble. We'll deal with that if it happens. Besides, we don't have much choice—the cows have to be milked twice a day, so someone has to stay.'

Like just about everyone in the valley, the Grahams lived on a property close to the national park that covered a lot of country. As calmly as her friend tried to play down the danger, Sam knew that the fire was behind them and inching closer each day. Despite the efforts of everyone out there keeping a watchful eye, if the conditions changed for the worse, there would be no holding it back.

'Just be careful,' Sam said earnestly.

'We will. We've been through this before, and Troy and his dad are well prepared.'

Sam wished she felt as self-assured as her friend. It had been a long time since she'd been home during bushfire season, but she remembered the years the fires had been particularly bad. They had never been this much of a threat to the whole community, though. She couldn't remember a time when the air was so thick with smoke that the schools closed. And she surely would have recalled if half the district had been issued with evacuation orders and others had lost their homes.

She worried that Chelsea's attitude was a little too relaxed. But maybe she'd just been away too long. Understandably, most farmers didn't like to think they were succumbing to media-driven panic, but fires were racing through places with barely any warning when the wind decided to change. Sam was worried that some of the hardier, old-time farming families weren't taking the threat as seriously as they should.

'How're things with Jack?' Chelsea asked, lowering her voice amid the other conversations around the table.

'Hard to say, really. It's not exactly an ideal situation to start a . . .'

'Hot and sordid romp of mindless sex?' Chelsea supplied, with a touch too much glee for Sam's liking. At Sam's unimpressed raised eyebrow, Chelsea cackled. 'Oh, come on, he's still got bad boy written all over him, even after all these years.'

'Is your husband even aware of what a shameless hussy you really are, beneath that wholesome maternal image you hide behind?' Sam asked.

'How do you think we ended up with five kids,' Chelsea shot back, wiggling her eyebrows.

It was hard to picture easy-going, quiet Troy as some kind of sex machine, and quite frankly, now that she had, Sam was wishing very much that she had not.

'You never used to be this much of a prude,' Chelsea said with a disgruntled cluck of her tongue. 'Okay, so at least tell me, do you see it going somewhere? After all this?'

Sam dropped another completed snack pack into the basket as she considered the question. 'I honestly don't know. Since I've been home, I keep having all these crazy ideas about what I could do, but then I wonder if once I go back north, maybe I'll just settle back into life up there?' She always had a dose of homesickness whenever she left Burrumba to return to the Sunshine Coast, but once she was back and into the thick of it all with kids and school and work, life just always seemed to go on. This time though, it was different. She wasn't going back to all that. She had no business, the house was empty. There was nothing to keep her there.

'Or maybe you won't,' Chelsea countered. 'The Sunshine Coast may have a lot of things, but it doesn't have Jack Cameron,' she said with triumphant smugness as she reached for more items to pack.

And that was the hell of it, Sam knew. What was life going to be like without Jack in it?

Sixteen

'Hello, Sam, this is Enid Murry.'

Sam frowned in concern. 'Hello, Mrs Murry. Is everything okay?' The older woman's voice sounded frailer than she remembered.

'I'm just calling to let you know that Jeff and I are about to leave to go to our daughter's. I know you're over there looking after your mum and dad's place, and I just wanted to make sure you were all right. I think you should head into town too, dear.'

The call had scared Sam more than she cared to admit. If the Murrys, with their sixty years of farming experience in the area, were conceding that it was too dangerous to stay, then things must be bad. She thanked Enid and promised to get herself ready to leave.

After seeing the number of people who had evacuated at the showground, Sam made the decision to at least start preparing the animals in her care. Her father wouldn't consider chooks and a cat as overly important priorities, but she knew her mother would be devastated if something happened and they were left to fend for themselves. The chooks were caught and caged easily enough; even Mr Buttons, although unhappy about being stuffed in a cat carrier and complaining quite loudly about it, didn't really put up much of a fight. The guinea fowl were a whole different matter.

Sam tried herding them into their coop, but for stupid animals they suddenly developed remarkably insightful skills for avoiding capture. Of course, they could never find the doorway when she wanted them to find it, but they sure as hell found it when they wanted to escape. In the end, Sam gave up. 'Sorry, Mum,' she muttered as she trudged back to the house to get her car keys. 'I tried.'

Arriving at the showground with her noisy brood, Sam felt a little better; at least she'd managed to do something constructive to safeguard what she could. During the booking-in process, Sam overheard quite a few conversations. As usual, news was circulating quickly. The wind had picked up and the sky had grown quite dark. For a moment, Sam had been hopeful that it meant rain and relief from the fires, but then she realised it was caused by smoke. She'd had to wear a mask when working outside—it wasn't comfortable, but it made breathing a little easier. The smoke was getting thicker and hovered in the air like clouds on an overcast day, blocking any sunlight from shining through.

There was an eeriness in the lurking threat.

Sam wasted no time getting back to the farm. Each time she went into town she feared the road would be shut, as many in the district now were, and she would be unable to get home. She still had dogs and livestock to attend to, both her own and Jack's, and the thought of not being able to reach them was very unsettling. She made it home without any trouble, but her uneasiness remained. She hadn't seen Jack since the meeting the day before. He'd decided to sleep when and where he could, unable to leave due to how limited their resources were now. He'd assured her he was safe, and checked in as often as possible, but she found herself worrying as the smoke grew thicker.

Sam tied a scarf around her mouth and nose as she climbed up on the back of the ute to throw feed out to her father's cattle. Thomas and Alex had come over the day before and helped her move them into the safe paddock, which had been eaten down over the past few months. Thanks to the drought, the good paddocks didn't have much more feed in them than this one, but it was the barest and that made it the safest place for the cattle in a fire. If the fire came through, she would open the two other gates to allow them free access to run, but at least they would be in the safest part of the farm here. She checked the float was still working in the trough—filling automatically as the water level dropped—and ran her gaze around the fences to make sure they were all still okay. Her nerves felt stretched like an elastic band. There was no escaping the thought of fire and destruction: it was on the news, it was on her phone with constant updates of where the fire was, and it was in every single conversation she had with anyone in town. Her every waking thought now was *fire*.

Smoke was a relentless part of life. Sam hadn't seen blue sky in over a week now. And the continual stress over animals and their safety was beginning to take its toll. She'd let a phone call from the girls ring out earlier, simply because she couldn't bring herself to put on a bright, cheerful voice again, to reassure them everything was okay.

The day before, she had taken Jack's dogs and Tasmin's horse, Snowy, into the showground and had been feeding and visiting them along with Matey every time she went in. Jack was almost never at home now to take care of them, and it was one less thing he had to worry about.

Sam had thought it had been busy at the showground earlier, but it was nothing compared to now. Extra dog cages had been built for animals still coming in, and makeshift round yards erected for livestock out the back. It was like a show day on steroids, with every kind of animal imaginable being housed in one place.

The number of caravans and tents had also increased—a sad testament to how many families had been displaced. It was becoming harder to dismiss. Sooner or later, Sam feared, she would be one of these people—forced to leave the house and seek shelter elsewhere. It made her feel ill to think about it. Most of the people here lived higher up the range, and everyone had been evacuated from that area now. The next lot of evacuations, if the fire continued on its current path, would include the road the Murphy property was on.

Brook and Kenzie had suggested she come home, but the thought of leaving while so many others couldn't felt wrong. Then, there was Jack. She had no idea where to start with that. Everything was happening so fast, and with no time to talk about it. Whatever this was between them, it would have to wait until they dealt with the current disaster.

After feeding his cattle, Sam waited on the front verandah of Jack's place. He'd texted to tell her he was heading home to grab some equipment. She knew he wouldn't have long, but she didn't intend to miss an opportunity to see him.

She watched him unfold himself stiffly from the driver's seat of a borrowed fire vehicle, and head up the path towards her. His face and uniform were streaked with soot; his ash-covered boots were filthy, and his eyes bloodshot and red-rimmed.

They didn't speak, just held each other tightly for a few moments before Jack pulled away, protesting about getting her dirty.

'I don't care,' she said, holding him tighter.

'I can't stay long, they're waiting for the generator. I just needed to see you.' His voice sounded husky and raw, no doubt due to yelling over the sound of fire and engines pumping, not to mention the smoke. She wished she could make him lie down and rest. She knew that was impossible—he was just one of many who were dead on their feet but unable to stop working.

'I thought you might be hungry,' she said, bending down to pick up the soft-sided esky she'd brought over, big enough to hold a few sandwiches and a drink. 'Do you want to sit and eat?'

'Nah, I have to get back. I'll eat it in the car, though. Thank you,' he said, kissing her gently then resting his forehead against hers. 'I'm not sure how I would have coped over these last few weeks without you helping out.'

'I'm sure you would have.'

'I guess so, but it wouldn't have been as fun,' he said, winking, before sobering. 'I think you should head into town, Sam.'

Her breath caught.

'I'd feel better if I knew you were with someone.'

'I'm okay. I've got everything packed, and the car's ready to go. We haven't been given any evacuation orders yet. I'd rather stay as long as I can.' There was no feed in the paddock she had put her father's cattle in, and if she went into town too early and the roads shut, the animals would be left without food. She saw his frown deepen, and gently rubbed her fingertips over the lines that had formed between his eyebrows. 'I promise I won't put myself in danger. If they evacuate us, I'll go. I've got plenty of people checking on me. You just concentrate on keeping yourself safe.' The last thing she wanted was for him to be worrying about her when he should be focusing on his job.

'Okay, but keep your phone on you, and keep checking the updates.'

'I will,' she promised, then felt her fingers tighten in his shirt as he went to move away.

'I gotta go, Sam.'

For one terrifying moment she felt a chill of foreboding run down her spine. She knew it was stupid. She was simply jumpy, as was everyone at the moment, but more than anything she just wished Jack could stay with her. Carefully, she released her grip and summoned a wobbly smile. 'Please be careful.'

'Always,' he said, kissing her once more before stepping away.

She handed him the esky and nodded as he waved. She hugged herself tightly as she watched the car slip into the smoke haze, shielding the rest of the driveway from sight. 'Stay safe,' she whispered.

Sam wiped her brow as she went inside. She was hot and thirsty. It was scorching outside, and as she filled a glass with water and looked out the kitchen window, she saw that the wind had begun to pick up. The branches in the trees were waving like drunken sailors, and that horrible, dreaded feeling filled her once more. *Bloody wind.* It fanned the flames and helped move the fire, and it was the last thing they needed.

The forecast of strong winds and hot days for at least a week had everyone on edge. Like everyone else in town, Sam was glued to the weather announcements. They needed rain, desperately.

A message pinged on Sam's phone, her heart sinking as she saw the sender: New South Wales Rural Fire Service.

Fire—Burrumba—seek shelter as the fire approaches.

Within moments, her brother's name came up on her phone and she answered quickly.

'Did you just get the fire warning?' Thomas asked, without bothering with a greeting.

'Yeah.'

'As far as I can tell, it's still above you. Can you see anything?'

'It's still just a lot of smoke. Jack hasn't called with an update yet.'

'I think you better get out. I just heard the highway's shut north and south, so you won't be able to get down to Alex's.'

Another announcement pinged, and she pulled the phone away from her ear to check it. 'Hang on, I just got another one.' She put Thomas on loudspeaker and read the message out.

> Long Yard Road warning. Leave now towards Burrumba. An emergency warning has been issued for the Long Yard Road fire at 2.26pm. The RFS says the fire has breached containment lines and is burning towards Burrumba. If you're near Long Yard Road, Marrabellam Creek or Saddleback Ridge, seek shelter as the fire approaches. Protect yourself from the heat of the fire.

'That's it. Just go,' Thomas said when she'd finished.

'Where's Jo?' she asked.

'She went to stay with Alison and the kids in Glenview last night. But you're in its path, so you better get out now while you can. If the road into town gets cut off, you won't be able to get out even if you want to.'

She knew he was right—her head was agreeing completely, but her heart was torn. It just felt wrong to abandon the place. Wasn't she the one who'd been harping on about 'better to be safe than sorry' when she'd taken Matey to the showground? It turns out, it was a lot easier to be level headed when you weren't in the middle of a crisis.

'Go to the showground, it's safer than where you are. Who knows which way the bloody thing's gonna go.'

'Yeah. Okay. I'll call you later. You be careful.'

'I will. You too.'

The smoke was getting so thick she couldn't even see the paddock beyond the chook pen anymore.

When her phone rang again and she saw Jack's name on the screen, she knew what he was going to say.

'It's time to leave, Sam.'

The words echoed loudly in her head.

'Where are you?' she asked.

'Just up past the McCally place. It's broken the containment line we put in.'

The McCally property was only a couple of kilometres up the road.

'You need to go,' he said. 'It's not safe anymore. The wind's changing constantly and we can't predict which way it's going to send the fire. It could turn at any moment and if it does, it's going to run straight down the ridge towards both our places.'

That shocked her out of her momentary stupor. 'Okay. I'm going. I'll go down and turn on the sprinklers first, then I'll head into the showground.' She pulled on her boots, the phone pressed between her ear and shoulder.

'Forget about the cattle and sprinklers. Just go, Sam.'

'I'm not leaving the cattle out there without water. I'm already on my way down now,' she said, heading outside.

'Fine, turn the sprinklers on and then get into town,' Jack snapped. She could tell from his tense tone that he was under a lot of stress, but there was no way she was leaving her father's cattle to fend for themselves completely. 'Be careful, Sam,' he added, then hung up before she could say the same to him.

She was grateful that Jack had helped her set up the irrigation pipes and had run her through the process of turning them on. She looked around and tried to calm her racing thoughts. She just hoped that she remembered everything, and that there was enough water left in the shallow creek to pump up.

She dragged out another load of hay bales and wrestled them into the ute. If the roads were cut off after she left, who knew how long it would be until the authorities would allow them back home to feed the animals. The process was taking a lot longer than she had anticipated, but she pushed away her growing fear as she opened the ute door and slid into the driver's seat, her dad's two dogs squashed in beside her. The dogs, usually full of energy, were subdued, picking up on the danger around them.

She opened the last of the gates after throwing out the hay and ran back to the ute, wiping tears as she went. Seated behind the wheel again, she fumbled with the ignition and had to force herself to stop and take a breath. Her heart raced as fast as her mind as she tried to think of everything she should do before she left. But there was nothing left to do—everything that could be done, had been done, and now it was just up to the wind to decide which direction it felt like blowing the ferocious beast of a fire. Sam tried to slow her breathing but heard it come out in a shaky breath. They had been building up to this for days but she never really thought it would happen. It was getting darker by the minute and the smoke was making it almost impossible to see ahead of her. Thankfully, she could pretty much make the trip home blindfolded, which wasn't much of an exaggeration this time, and she managed to get back to the house at a crawl.

As she parked the ute she suddenly remembered the guinea fowl. 'Shit.'

With a resigned sigh, she ran for the chook yard, hoping beyond hope that they had somehow put themselves to bed so they would be contained in the coop and easier to catch. Sticking her head inside the pen, she swore loudly. They hadn't. *Of course they hadn't.* That would have made life so much easier for everyone but no, these guinea fowl thrived on making life complicated. Every goddamn time. 'Bloody guinea fowl!' she yelled, turning in a circle to search for any sign of them.

There, high up in the gum tree, swaying unsteadily as they perched on limbs in the heavy wind, sat a dozen of the stupidest creatures God had ever created. Suddenly, all the stress of Sam's day unravelled inside her. 'Stay here and die, then, you ungrateful little bastards!' she yelled, ending on a loud sob. It was too much. She'd been trying so hard to keep everything safe, but she felt helpless. The cattle were too big to move anywhere, and she hated that all she could do for them was leave them in a paddock with the hope that it wouldn't burn, and now the stupid guinea fowl were stuck up a bloody tree and refusing to come down. There wasn't any more time, she knew she had to go, and with one last look at the squabbling brats, she shook her head and ran back to the ute.

She glanced at her car and quickly dismissed the idea of taking it. Her dad's ute was far more practical, and though she had a brief moment of regret over leaving her car behind, she had too much else to worry about. Wind whipped the loose tendrils of hair around her face and she wiped them away impatiently, then stared at her hand. It was covered in black dust. Ash. She glanced down at the ground, and her alarm skyrocketed. Burnt leaves and ash fluttered down from the sky like a strange new form of rain, heavier than it had been for the past few days.

She turned on the garden hose and wet the outside of the house, and left the soaker hose on in the yard to spray its fine mist along the side of the house that she guessed the fire would approach from. It felt incredibly inadequate, but it was all she could do.

A police vehicle was heading down the driveway just as she finished, and she ran over to it before it stopped.

'You need to evacuate right now,' the officer said through his window.

'I'm on my way,' Sam assured him, and he gave a brief nod.

'Do you know if any of your neighbours have already left?'

'Next door is empty. Jack's out with the fires. The elderly couple on the other side are away at their daughter's place, but I'm not sure about anyone else nearby.'

'Okay, thanks for that. You make sure you leave right now.'

'I will,' she promised, and ran back inside the house to grab the last of her things, then knew she couldn't put it off any longer. Walking out the door, she gently closed it behind her and paused, closing her eyes. 'You'll be fine, old girl,' she said firmly.

Walking away from the house she'd grown up in was the hardest thing she'd done in a very long time. She opened the door of the ute and both dogs jumped inside, tongues hanging out, looking at her expectantly. 'We're going on a bit of an adventure, guys,' she said, hoping it sounded reassuring, but fearing it didn't.

She started the car and headed up the driveway. The sky had turned an eerie orange, and instantly the memory of those terrified people on the news, huddled together on a beach, flashed through Sam's mind. The smoke was still thick, but not as bad as it had been on the flats just before. Flashing lights ahead made her heart rate spike as two RFS fire trucks raced past, heading the way she'd just come. Relief rushed through her body at the sight of them. *Thank God for these men and women*, she thought. Just seeing them made her feel safer.

'Please let them keep our place safe,' she whispered as she clutched the steering wheel tight and blinked back tears.

Seventeen

Now Jack knew that Sam was out safely, he could better focus on his job. The instant things began to turn hairy, all he could think about was that she would be trapped if she stayed and he might not be able to hold this fire back.

Jack and his crew had positioned the truck in front of the old McCally house in order to protect the property. They were kept busy with small spot fires starting in the grass paddocks surrounding the house, as embers flew through the air and lit the dry, drought-ravaged pasture that hadn't seen rain for far too long. Normally these paddocks would be lush and green, but not anymore—now they were perfect tinder boxes, ready to ignite.

The wind refused to ease, blowing the treetops in a wild, violent dance. The red glow of the fire lit up the sky in a menacing reminder that it was moving ever closer—biding its time until it could break out in a massive charge. The wind carried the heat and smoke across the paddocks, hitting Jack and his crew in their faces. Their masks did little to help, and Jack put his arm up to try to deflect some of the heat. There was an eeriness to a bushfire: entering it was like stepping into a bubble. Above, the sun was out, but the fire ground was an alien world. The smoke blanketed the sun and darkness descended—the thrum of diesel pumps echoed all around and the flash of blue and red lights from the truck was the only way Jack could fix himself to his location.

They were only a few kilometres from his place and they'd been fighting a losing battle. His radio went off again, and he ignored it once more.

'Jack, you should go,' Laurie Johnson said from beside him as he heard the radio. 'They're looking for you.'

'I'm not leaving.'

'There's nothing much else we can do here, mate.'

He knew his neighbour was right, but he couldn't turn his back on his own place, even if it was now seriously under threat. He'd been on a break—forced at that—when he'd overheard the call about the fire breaking the lines at the McCallys' property. Two days earlier, at the meeting up at the hall, he'd wondered what he would do if he were faced with this decision. Would he obey a command to go where he was told? Or would he fight for his own place if it were under threat? Maybe if he hadn't heard the radio chatter, and maybe if he hadn't been away from the front line, he might have stayed with his unit, but hearing it and knowing there were no resources spare and that the men he lived alongside would be the only ones up there fighting—the decision wasn't really a hard one.

Officially, he was AWOL. He'd radioed in to tell them his location and he did feel bad that the rest of his unit were stuck back across the valley, but he couldn't leave these men to defend his property and theirs, on their own.

He knew he would be in a world of shit after all this was over, but he didn't care. He had bigger problems to deal with. Namely, the huge fire storm that was blowing its way towards him right now.

He'd never got used to the sound of fire. Despite being around it for weeks on end, the roar of it still chilled him to the bone. Anyone who didn't think fire was a living, breathing entity had clearly never been caught up in one. He'd had more than a few close calls—times he'd thought he was going to die; trapped and separated from his unit. And he'd seen what hell would surely look like if it had a face: a hollow-eyed, vengeful predator with an insatiable appetite for everything in its path.

The roar was growing louder, and suddenly, above them on the ridge, he saw it.

'Pull back! Pull back!' Jack shouted at the men around him as they all stopped to stare at the red inferno that was devouring the ridge line.

Men scrambled into vehicles and withdrew from the position they'd been valiantly trying to hold all day.

Embers had been travelling well ahead of the main fire front, and spot fires had broken out in the trees. As the fire broke over the ridge, the embers fell like fireworks all around them. Despite it being mid-afternoon, it looked like midnight—smoke choked out any hope of daylight above, and Jack stared out the windscreen as the headlights bounced along the track, moving their line back to the next property . . . his.

When they arrived at his place, Jack barely waited for the ute to come to a standstill before he was out and moving at speed to the group of men hovering around a small tanker truck. He felt a mixture of relief and dread as he approached. 'What are you guys doing here? Did headquarters have a change of heart?'

'Not exactly. We heard over the radio the fire broke the ridge. Stuff 'em. You guys need help just as much as anyone else out there.'

Jack had a brief moment of hesitation—it was one thing that he'd gone AWOL, it was another entirely when the rest of the squad did a runner with a truck. But the fact was, the powers that be had a completely different agenda to the blokes on the ground. They were dictated to by statistics, whereas out here, Jack could see the faces of the people in his small community, and they were struggling right now. Fuck it. He would deal with the bureaucracy later—if there was a later. They were all in very real danger. The wind had picked up as predicted, and everywhere they looked was red. On the ridge above them, it flowed down like a stream of lava, relentlessly onward.

In the background he heard men yelling, calling for more hose, more water. But nothing was going to hold this beast back. The wind was changing direction, whipping the fire into a frenzy. Embers flew overhead in a spectacular display of sparks, lighting up the dark sky like a New Year's Eve celebration.

It was moving too fast.

Until now, Jack hadn't been focusing on the fact that this was *his* family property. He couldn't. Every property was important. They risked their lives to save every house, every property, and it was always hard to walk away when the situation intensified to a point where there was no possible way they could save it. But now it was his home, and it was killing him inside.

As the men around him clambered back into their trucks, the fire seemed to almost rear up before them in defiance, like a wild beast standing on its hind legs, ready for a fight.

The truck he'd jumped into after directing the other vehicles to move roared into reverse then swung out onto the road. They had no chance of holding the line here, but they might be able to stop it moving further.

They were headed for the Murphy place. The rest of the McCally boys were still there, down at the paddock near the creek with their bulldozer and tractors, steadily working to cut a fire break between the creek on this side of the bank and the fire across at his place. They'd been working there for most of the afternoon, pushing over trees and grading the top soil back to bare dirt in a wide path, in an effort to keep any kind of flammable material from catching alight from the embers falling ahead of the fire.

'The road's blocked,' one of the guys in the vehicle ahead announced over the radio.

'We'll have to take the fire trail,' Jack yelled over the noise. The track was regularly used and Jack often moved stock along it, but with so much smoke around it was slow going once they located it.

Everywhere he looked, trees were on fire. Jack kept his eyes peeled for falling timber. Some of the trees in this area were massive—growing seventy metres or more—and when they crashed, they could take out a vehicle in a single swipe. Up ahead, a spray of red and yellow sparks flew high into the air, and two of the utes ahead slammed on their brakes. Jack swore savagely when he saw the tree fall across the track, blocking their escape. He immediately grabbed the radio handset, checking in with the other men in their convoy, learning that two others had got through safely before the tree came down. His relief that no one had been hurt was short-lived, though, as he realised the predicament they were now in.

'We have to find another way out,' Laurie said beside him as he turned their vehicle around.

'There's a bike track at the bottom of our place that loops around Jack's and onto Old Stockyard Flat,' said a younger voice over the radio, and Jack realised it was Brayden, one of the McCally boys who'd been among the farmer crew fighting the fire. He was in the ute in front that narrowly missed being hit by the falling tree.

Because Brayden was now stuck at the rear, as the vehicles all did their best to make U-turns on the narrow track, he was forced to give directions from the back of the convoy, which left Jack and Laurie in the front searching for the landmarks the kid was giving them to look for.

Eventually, they managed to find the rough dirt track as they retraced their path. Behind them, the ridge was now completely alight, and the fire was moving downhill rapidly. Embers cascaded down around them, sticks and branches bouncing off the vehicles. The heat inside the car was almost unbearable. Trees on either side of the track were alight, and they feared that at any moment another one could fall. With visibility down to only a few metres, progress was painfully slow and all around them the roar of fire bellowed and raged like a wounded beast.

The track was precariously steep, better suited to horseback than four-wheel drives or trucks. If they survived this, it would be a miracle. In the rear-view mirror, a fierce red glow lit up the hillside behind them and trees burst into flames as embers flew on the savage wind. Jack looked back through the windscreen after checking on the vehicle behind them, turning just in time to see the road before them falling away, and his warning to stop came too late as the vehicle lost a wheel over the side of the mountain and began to slide.

Eighteen

Sam drove through the showground gates and made her way to the makeshift office to register as an evacuee. She was drained. Now that the adrenalin had worn off, it was becoming harder to keep moving forward. The trip into town had been nerve-racking as she fought to keep the ute on the road as strong winds battered against it. Roadblocks were in place with weary SES workers waving her through. She watched the rear-view mirror with a heavy heart as they replaced the 'Road Closed' signs behind her.

She checked her phone once more, not expecting but hoping there might be some update from Jack. Then she messaged her daughters and her brothers to let them know where she was and that she was fine, but it was all done on autopilot; she was feeling numb and disorientated. *What now?* Without the adrenalin coursing through her veins, she found her hands were a little shaky.

She parked the ute in a space with a tree and a bit of a grassed area, and got the dogs out, tying them up to ensure they didn't wander off to explore their new surroundings or get into any fights with the multitude of other displaced farm dogs. After setting out their food and water bowls, Sam went off in search of a coffee.

'Hello, Samantha,' said the kind woman behind the window of the canteen area. Sam didn't recognise her, but she looked around the same age as her mum. 'I saw you drive past a minute ago.' The gentle sympathy behind the words was enough to release a fresh sting of tears from Sam's eyes. 'Oh, sweetheart, it's all right,' the older woman clucked. 'It's better to be in here and safe. That's the most important thing.'

Sam managed a weak smile and blinked back the threat of more tears. She just wanted to get her coffee and slink back to the car so she could close her eyes and forget about what all this meant, at least for a few minutes.

'Here you go, darling, a nice hot cuppa and a sandwich,' the woman said, passing over the Styrofoam cup and a wrapped package. Sam wasn't hungry—she actually felt a bit queasy at the thought of food, but she knew all too well that any protest would only spark a debate on the importance of making sure you were eating. She had found herself uttering the same words over the years. When in doubt—eat something. If someone was sad—feed them. Food was supposed to equal comfort, but there was nothing that could comfort her at the moment.

Sam took the coffee and sandwich back to the car and sat down with the dogs. They sniffed at the plastic and she unwrapped the food and fed it to them with a small smile. They needed the comfort more than she did right now. She rubbed their heads gently, wondering how their little doggy minds were processing all this. There were so many new sights and sounds and smells; she imagined it would be kind of like canine heaven. A headache was beginning to form at her temples; she tipped her head back against the tree trunk behind her and closed her eyes. Maybe when she opened them she would discover this was all a really bad dream.

Sam heard Tess whimper, and opened her eyes to find the dogs huddled on either side of her. 'What's wrong, girl?' she murmured, rubbing her head before noticing that a few people had gathered and were looking at something in the opposite direction. Sam stood up and turned to face the ridges in the distance. She felt her breath catch. The sky was orange. She checked her watch: it was barely five in the afternoon. It looked like she'd woken up on some strange new planet.

'That doesn't look good,' a man close by commented as he slowed down on his way to the amenities.

'No. It doesn't,' Sam agreed hesitantly.

'I pity those poor bastards out there fighting it,' he said before walking away.

Sam felt her heart stop momentarily.

Jack.

She had no idea where he was or what he was doing, but she was fairly sure he was out there in the middle of it all. She just wished she knew he was okay.

Her phone rang and for a moment her hopes soared, until she saw the number. Sam took a deep, steadying breath before answering. 'Hi, Dad.'

'Are you okay? It's all over the damn news here. We turned the telly on and there it was—Burrumba. *On the flamin' UK news!*' her dad said, sounding as frantic as her father was ever likely to get.

'I'm fine. We had to evacuate, but it's just a precaution. The cows are in the middle pasture and the irrigation system's on. I've got the dogs, and I hosed down the house and filled the gutters before I left. But I'm sure it's just a case of better to be safe than sorry,' she said, then to her horror she found she couldn't speak through her tears.

'Oh, darling,' her mum's voice joined the conversation.

'I don't care about the bloody house or the cattle,' her dad said firmly. 'I'm just glad you're safe.'

'I'm sorry, Dad. I did everything I could. I just don't know if I did enough.'

'Rubbish,' Henry said, and the gruff emotion in his voice only made the tears fall faster. 'We know you did your best. No one could do any more than what you've done. Besides, you've got my two best mates there with you, that's all I can ask.'

'I'll keep them safe,' Sam promised. 'Even Mr Buttons is here,' she added, smiling a little when she heard his derisive grunt at the news and a small sniffle from her mother.

'I'll go back as soon as Jack calls to say it's safe. I'm sure it'll only be a couple of hours.'

'You just make sure you listen to Jack, okay? Don't go taking any risks,' her father told her sternly.

'We can replace the house—we can't replace you,' her mother added.

'I know. I'll let you know when I hear any more news.'

She said goodbye and disconnected the call, biting her lip as it threatened to tremble once more. She knew they'd be worried, being on the other side of the world and unable to do anything. She felt exactly the same and she was right here.

Sam pulled her T-shirt away from her chest—the hot summer air made her clothing cling uncomfortably to her skin. She called Chelsea and listened to the phone ring out again. They had another fire approaching from the other direction; it had been tormenting them for the past few days but Sam had heard that it was getting serious and most residents on their road had been told to evacuate today.

Sam knew that Troy would stay to protect the property—they had the right gear and were as prepared as possible—but hearing the stories of how some people from higher up the range had barely managed to outrun the fire earlier, she knew no one could afford to take the threat lightly and she was worried for her friends.

It was getting dark, and the hot, relentless wind blew through the trees nearby in ruthless gusts. Sam could feel the heat against her skin and a dry sweat dotting her forehead. The sky, which had been an orange glow earlier, was now blood red and black, dotted with burnt gum leaves steadily falling from the sky—an unnerving reminder of what was happening only a few kilometres away. It was still afternoon, and yet it looked like night.

Sam made a quick call to the girls to reassure them she was fine, before they saw it on the news.

'We got your text. Why are you staying at the showground?' Brook asked.

'They're evacuating people from around Nan and Pop's place,' Sam said calmly.

'Evacuating?'

'It's okay, it's just a precaution.'

'Mum, are you sure you're all right?' Kenzie asked, sounding worried.

'I promise I'm fine. I just wanted to let you know that I'm not at the farm and I'm okay. I'll check in again a bit later when I find out what's going on, but don't worry if you can't reach me. There's been a lot of trouble with reception. I think some phone towers have been damaged.'

'We love you, Mum. Let us know what's happening,' Kenzie said, still sounding concerned but at least mollified for now knowing that Sam was safe.

A couple camping nearby had stopped to tell her that dinner was being put on by a few of the local clubs in the exhibition hall. Socialising was the last thing she felt like doing, but she needed to find out if anyone else had more information. She gathered up her towel and a change of clothes and headed for the showers. She stank of smoke and sweat and probably a healthy dose of fear, and the cool water went a long way to reviving her waning spirits. By the time she was ready to head across to the hall, she felt a little more in control of herself.

There were already people gathered when she walked inside. Long tables had been set up and people were chatting as they sat and ate. Sam joined the line, accepting a plastic plate from a volunteer and smiling her thanks. She recognised many faces in the hall, but no one she knew well. Again, she thought about Chelsea. By the time she reached the window where women and men were busily serving up food, Sam realised she was starving. The roast meat and vegetables looked like a feast, and she carefully manoeuvred her way across to an empty seat at a table and sat down to eat.

'You're Henry Murphy's girl, aren't you?' a man from across the table asked.

Sam glanced up and smiled as she recognised Ted Glover and his wife, Elsie, who owned the property behind her parents. 'Yes,' she said, 'I'm Sam.'

'I don't even remember the last time I saw you. You were probably a teenager,' Ted said.

Her parents hadn't really had much to do with the Glovers; they were neighbours but not close friends. Sam suspected it had something to do with a fallout over boundary fencing once upon a time.

'That *was* a long time ago,' Sam said with a wry grin.

'Your mum and dad still away?' Ted asked.

'Yeah,' she said, slicing open a baked potato and feeling the heavy weight of guilt fall back on her shoulders once more.

'Don't like our chances of finding much left when we head back,' the older man continued with a shake of his head.

'Now, Ted,' Elsie cut in briskly, 'we don't know anything for sure. There's no point assuming the worst.'

'We saw it roaring across the ridge before we left. It was heading straight for us. Nothing was gonna stop that.'

'But you haven't had any news? Heard anything since you left?' Sam asked, striving to remain calm after the old man's pessimistic comments.

'No, dear, no one's had any updates. We don't know anything for certain yet,' Elsie said, looking pointedly at her husband.

'The power's gone out across most of the valley,' another woman nearby chipped in. 'That's the main reason we came in here. We can't do much to fight the fire without power to pump the water tank, and we don't have a generator.'

'And where's your property?' Sam asked.

'Out past Yoval's Road.'

That was only a few kilometres from Chelsea's place. Maybe that's why she hadn't been able to get in contact with her.

'The road out there was shut not long after we came through. I'm glad we left before that happened.'

'The road's closed?' Sam asked, as her momentary relief was again cut short.

'Yep. They're not letting anyone in, and the fire had crossed the road in at least two different places we could see, so it's most likely unpassable higher up.'

Sam swore silently. That meant that even if Chelsea wanted to leave, she couldn't.

'I heard someone say that the fire chief was going to give an update a bit later on. Maybe they'll be able to shed some more light on what's going on,' the woman said.

Sam hadn't heard from Jack or her brother and was growing more frustrated by the minute. Whatever information she was getting was delayed. By now, everything could have changed. The constant worry about Jack and Chelsea was taking its toll. Sam's head throbbed, and she was sick and tired of the bloody smoke. What she wanted was answers—to know the people she loved were all safe. But no one had answers, and everyone was stuck here in the strange nothingness. All she could do was stay put and wait. But for how much longer?

Nineteen

Sam looked out at the bustling showground. It was amazing, really. Despite all the chaos and uncertainty happening around them, life was continuing with a normal kind of routine. Meals were provided by a team of volunteers. Animals were being cared for through community organisations. And all around her, there were offers of help that provided great comfort, despite the fact no one actually knew anything for certain. Newcomers brought news about which properties were still standing, but the majority of people wouldn't know anything for some time yet. The not knowing was probably the worst.

Sam looked over as a group walked into the hall: one man in the familiar Rural Fire Service uniform, along with a man in a National Parks uniform and another man she didn't recognise. They shook hands with the president of the Rotary Club, who called out to the room.

'Ladies and gentlemen, if I could have your attention, please. I have with me Mick Benson, the public liaison officer who's been sent along tonight to give us an update on the fire situation and hopefully give us a little bit more information.'

Mick, a short man with a quiet authority about him, stepped forward and greeted the crowd. 'I know a lot of you have been here for a number of days now, and it must be incredibly frustrating, but as this fire is constantly changing, relaying up-to-date information has been extremely challenging. At this stage we have two out-of-control fires burning on two fronts surrounding our town. The Rural Fire Service has every available man and woman out there in the field fighting as we speak. We are doing everything we can to protect as many properties as possible, but this fire is unlike anything we've seen. It's relentless, and the weather conditions are only adding to the danger. Tomorrow's forecast has placed our valley into the catastrophic category. I'm not saying this to scare everyone, I'm saying it because that's what it is. Temperatures are set to soar and we're expecting strong winds. It's the perfect conditions for an already huge fire to turn, well . . . catastrophic,' he said, shaking his head helplessly. 'We're expecting more out-of-area assistance crews to arrive later tonight to relieve our local crews where possible, which is going to be a huge relief.'

'When do you expect we'll be able to get back to our homes?' someone asked from the back of the hall.

'I sympathise with your frustration. But as I said, we're expecting a massive day tomorrow and we have no idea how much damage will occur, or even how widespread it'll be.

There's a high probability it could reach the outskirts of town if it continues on its current trajectory,' he said, and an anxious murmur followed. 'So,' he continued, raising his voice, 'you can understand that it's near impossible to allow people access to places that are currently unstable due to ongoing fire threat.'

'Well, can you give us any info on houses that have been lost?' This time it was Ted who spoke up.

'Unfortunately not. There's no way to assess damage at this stage. Conditions have been too unstable to allow our volunteers back into those areas.'

A general murmur of unrest followed and Mick raised his voice again to speak. 'I do understand your frustration,' he repeated. 'But there's no way to establish which homes have been lost. We need to get through tomorrow first, and then reassess where we're at after that.'

He quickly handed the meeting over to the National Parks representative and backed away from the microphone.

There was a quick rundown of the estimated damage to the local national park and the effect it had had on wildlife numbers, which was far too depressing to even begin to process, before the men thanked the audience and left the hall.

'Well, that was a fat lot of good. They basically told us nothing,' Ted grumbled.

'I think they've got their hands a bit full at the moment,' Sam said, getting to her feet. Yes, it was frustrating, but everyone was doing the best they could. The fires were still burning and the danger was far from over. They couldn't deal with the aftermath while they were in the middle of the disaster.

Sam said goodnight to the others at her table and made her way outside. It was still a stinking hot evening, and the air was filled with smoke, but it was a relief to be out of the hall.

She walked across the centre ring to the stables to check on Matey and smiled as she passed the other horse owners who'd made their own little community, camping in their horse floats near their animals.

Tomorrow she would move her own temporary campsite down here. It made sense to be closer to Matey for feeding. But she was too tired to do it tonight.

Horses nickered as she walked down the centre of the stables, eager heads popping over the stall gates hopefully, looking for a friendly owner's face and a treat. When she reached Matey's stall, though, he wasn't standing there eager to greet her.

She quickened her pace for the last few steps and opened the gate, finding to her dismay that Matey was lying down at the back of the stall. Feeling her stomach drop, she sank to her knees beside him and ran her hands over his head. 'What's up, big guy, huh?' He wasn't just resting as she'd been hoping: she could tell immediately that something was wrong.

The big horse gave a low nicker and a small grunt before he attempted to get to his feet. Under the best of circumstances, it took Matey a considerable amount of time to get up once he was down, due to his age and arthritis, and she hated watching him struggle, but this time, he couldn't get up at all.

'Oh no,' Sam muttered, standing up and watching her old horse in despair. 'I'll be back, old fella,' she said, letting herself out of the stall and walking quickly back up the centre of the stables. She was sure she'd seen the local vet's car parked at the pavilion earlier, and now prayed it was still there. By the time she'd run back across the centre ring towards the barking dogs and noisy fowl, she was out of breath. Luckily, the car was still there, and she ran inside, frantically searching the aisles of caged animals for the veterinarian.

'I'm sorry to interrupt,' she said after the vet and another man finished talking, 'but my horse . . .' Her words stopped and she found her throat had closed up as tears began to fall. *No, no, no*, she told herself frantically. *Hold it together.* However, once the tears started, they wouldn't stop. 'I'm sorry,' she managed, drawing in a large breath to get herself under control.

'It's okay,' the vet said, and his deep soothing tone had the instant effect of calming her down. 'Where's your horse?'

'Down in the stables. He can't get up. He's really old. I think it's colic.'

'Let's go and take a look,' he said, putting a hand on Sam's elbow and steering her out towards his vehicle. He held the door open for her to climb in, then shut it behind her. Sam didn't even remember the short ride around the outside of the grounds, or whether he asked her any questions, but as soon as the car pulled up, she was out of the seat and heading back towards Matey's stall.

Two women were deep in conversation in front of his stall, and looked up when Sam came closer. 'Oh, there you are. We were just trying to work out who to call. We heard your old boy and came over to check on him. But I see you've got the vet,' the older of the women said, stepping back to allow the vet inside the stall.

'Yes. Thank you,' Sam said, trying for a smile but too worried to manage more than a wince.

She hovered at the stall door as the vet ran his hands over Matey and listened to his heart and gut. Sam tried to read his face but couldn't. He'd worn the same carefully masked expression when she'd been talking to him earlier. 'I'll give him a sedative to help with his pain for now,' he said, digging through the bag at his feet and preparing the syringe.

When he stood up to face her, though, her hopes of good news faded. 'He's got extreme abdominal pain,' he said gravely.

'So, it *is* colic?' she asked tentatively, hoping to be wrong.

'Yep,' he said, nodding.

Fear clutched at her insides. Colic was horrible and dangerous for any horse, but in one of Matey's age, it was very, very bad indeed.

'We can get him up and try walking him around, but I feel I have to tell you, I think it's just prolonging his agony. He's struggling to get to his feet, and even if he does, there's no guarantee he'll be able to stay up and dislodge anything. There's no sounds at all coming from his gut. Added to his high heart rate, I think we're looking at an abdominal distension, which would take surgery to treat.'

For an instant, Sam's eyes lit up, until she saw the vet shake his head at her slowly. 'Matey and I are old friends,' he said, gently rubbing the horse's neck. 'This isn't his first call-out for a case of colic.' He gave a regretful tilt of his mouth. 'We've treated a few less severe bouts on and off over the past couple of years, but this time it's far worse and in my experience, even with surgery, at his age, there's no way he'd survive.'

Sam wanted to cover her ears and close her eyes. She didn't want to understand what the vet was telling her and yet, hearing Matey's painful grunts and groans, she couldn't ignore it. He was in pain and he was dying.

Christ. Hadn't she dealt with enough for one day? Now this? She'd been trying to prepare herself for this day for years, but she'd never really believed it would actually happen. Now, here, right this minute . . . she wasn't prepared at all.

'I don't want him to be in pain,' she managed, turning her rapidly filling eyes away from the vet and onto the horse.

'It won't take long, but once the sedative takes effect, we'll need to get him up so we can move him outside.' He didn't have to explain the reasons why. He was being practical. Getting a deceased horse out of a stall inside a stable would be quite difficult, and traumatic for the rest of the animals and the owners to witness. Sam felt sick thinking about the aftermath. She would need to call someone to take him away, but who, and where would they take him? The town was currently dealing with the threat of an uncontrollable bushfire. She wanted Jack, but she pushed her pointless pining aside. She couldn't start thinking about Jack right now or she'd never be able to get through this without collapsing into a blubbering mess, and that wouldn't do anyone any good—least of all her darling old Matey.

As she sat with Matey out behind the stables in the dark, her tears eventually dried up as she continued to stroke his big face. The vet packed away his equipment and quietly spoke on his phone before coming back to sink to his haunches beside her.

'I've made all the arrangements to have Matey moved out of here. Unfortunately, they won't be able to take him back to your parents' property. But I've taken care of it. He was a top old fella. I'm sorry I couldn't give you a better outcome tonight,' he said sadly.

'Thank you for everything. It all just happened so fast. I wasn't expecting this.'

'No, we never do. Your dad's a good bloke, been a loyal client for a long time. I'm happy to help. If you want to stay with Matey until they get here, that's fine, but it's probably a good idea not to hang around when they start to move him.'

Sam didn't want to think about that side of things. Matey was gone and couldn't feel anything anymore, but still . . . In the end she waited for the truck to arrive and gave her trusted old mate one last pat before she left.

Sam had felt exhausted earlier, but now she was emotionally wrecked. She climbed into her swag and cried herself to sleep, too tired to care about anything anymore.

Twenty

Sam didn't sleep much, despite her exhaustion. Each time she woke up she remembered the events of the day before and went back over everything. She gave up trying to sleep and at first light sat outside with the dogs, who seemed to have no problem sleeping in unfamiliar surroundings.

She looked down at her phone with a sigh. She'd hoped to hear from Jack and Chelsea, but neither had called. She knew if Jack wasn't busy or sleeping that he would have contacted her, so there was no point trying to call him, and yet she itched to do so. Chelsea, on the other hand, hadn't called because she probably couldn't.

Sam scrolled through Facebook, shocked at the images that were coming through her newsfeed. It seemed like the entire country was on fire. How was that even possible? Whole towns had been wiped out—streets and neighbourhoods flattened into unrecognisable piles of twisted metal. Firefighters had narrowly escaped horrific fire storms inside their trucks, and some had not survived. Sam felt tears trickle down her face as she watched the interviews reporting the death of another young father who'd died volunteering to keep his community safe.

Then she paused as she came across a friend's post that mentioned missing locals. It was frustratingly brief. Just a one-sentence post saying, *'Praying they're found safe.'*

Sam ran through the comments, but at this hour of the morning there were very few. Equally frustrating was the fact that clearly everyone else knew what was happening, without anyone actually saying what *it* was. She didn't recognise the name from the post, but she hoped that whoever it was, was okay.

When she took the dogs around the outskirts of the showground to let them run, her thoughts returned to Matey and she wiped away the tears that escaped. But before she could think about it too much, her phone rang and she quickly pulled it from her pocket. The name on her screen wasn't one she'd been expecting.

'Thomas? Hi.'

'Hey, kiddo. How are you hanging in there?'

'I'm okay . . . Actually, I'm not really.'

'I heard about poor old Matey,' he said quietly.

'What? How?'

'My neighbour's wife is staying at the showground with her horses.'

'Oh.' Of course. She should have known news would travel even during a bushfire.

'Listen, I'm on my way up there now with the SES, but there's something you probably need to know. It's about Jack . . .' Her brother paused uncertainly. 'He's missing.'

Sam took a moment to process what she'd just heard. 'What?'

'He was in a convoy of three vehicles. They lost radio contact with them last night and there's been no contact made since.'

Sam struggled to understand what was happening through a brain fog that had suddenly descended.

'Their last known position was somewhere on Long Yard Road. The main road was blocked, so they were going to cut through on an old fire trail.'

'Then they know where to start looking,' Sam said, hearing the slight shake in her tone.

'Sam, the fire ripped right through there. We sent a chopper up at first light, and there's nothing left either side of the road for miles.'

This can't be happening.

'Well, surely they'd spot a vehicle if it was there,' she said, though her lips felt numb as she spoke the words.

'There was a lot of debris scattered along it, but visibility made it almost impossible to identify anything for sure.'

'So, that proves nothing. They could have turned back and gone a different way.'

Thomas went quiet on the other end, and Sam felt her heart lurch. 'It's possible, but I think you should prepare yourself just in case, sis.'

'Is there anyone out there looking now?'

'We've got everyone available searching. I'm turning into the showground now to meet up with some other volunteers. I'll see you in a few minutes.'

It didn't make sense: how hard could it be to find three vehicles? Surely they'd stick out like a sore thumb?

Sam tied the dogs back up, her fingers clumsy and her brain numb. *Jack, missing?* It couldn't be right. Maybe they were just out of reception somewhere . . . it was possible . . . more than possible; towers were down all over the place. There was no way she was going to assume the worst, not yet. She couldn't. She wouldn't.

She saw the big four-wheel drive pull up from across the grounds and jogged over to meet her brother. By the time she reached him, a small group was gathered around a map spread out on the bonnet of his vehicle.

As she listened to the briefing she realised the extent of the situation. In total, seven men were missing in three vehicles, and she watched as her brother issued orders, dividing up the areas on the map to the SES volunteers present. When everyone had their areas, they picked up their day packs and headed off.

'When do we go out?' Sam asked, staring after the last lot to drive away.

'We don't. This is the command point.'

'I need to go out and look for them,' Sam said, frowning at her older brother.

'You're not trained to go out and search, Sam. You'd only get in the way. Besides, most of the search area is still an active fire.'

'Have you heard any news about Mum and Dad's place?'

'Nothing official, but it's not good news up there. I've heard that at least five places around them have been lost. Including the Cameron property,' he said softly.

Oh God, no. Jack's place—gone? Sam felt herself deflate further. Up until now she'd stubbornly believed their houses would be safe, but if Jack's place was gone, then all of a sudden it was a very real possibility that her parents' was too.

When would this nightmare end? The reality of Jack and the other men going missing was finally sinking in. Sam stared down at her phone and blinked back tears.

Damn it, Jack. Call.

Jack groaned as he gingerly opened his eyes and blinked against the bright torch light shining in his face.

'Jack? Jack! You hear me?'

'Yeah, I hear you,' Jack muttered as he struggled to shake off the dizziness that threatened to drag him back into the dark. 'I'm okay.' He wasn't—not really. He had no idea what had happened, but the fact that young Brayden sounded so frantic meant it had been something bad. He closed his eyes, and it all came flooding back.

He was inside the cabin of the ute, and it was on its side.

'Laurie?' he said, opening his eyes again and turning his head, groaning when the movement hurt.

'I'm fine, mate,' he heard from some point behind the young face he saw looking at him in concern.

Thank Christ for that.

The last thing he remembered was the tyre dropping over the edge ... He closed his eyes against the memory of the heart-stopping moment that followed.

Slowly, he started to move his limbs. First his toes and then his feet. He wriggled his fingers and tested his arms and legs before breathing a sigh of relief. His hands went to the seat belt and he searched for the clasp.

'Whoa. Easy,' Brayden said, reaching his hand in to steady Jack's movements through the smashed side window. 'We can't get the door open, so we'll have to get you out through the front.' He was handed a shirt to cover his face, every muscle protesting against the slightest movement, and then he heard a thump and the sound of glass smashing and falling across his lap and chest. The metal creaked and groaned as Jack crawled out of the vehicle, sometimes in unison with Jack himself. It took some doing, but eventually after releasing the seat belt they were able to carefully extract him from the wreckage.

'I'm okay,' he said when they made him sit down again.

'Scared the crap out of me, mate,' Laurie said, shaking his head and running a hand over his bald head. Jack noticed a small trickle of dried blood across his forehead.

'Feeling's pretty mutual,' Jack said drolly. He glanced up the side of the ridge they'd just been driving along and double-checked all his body parts once more. How the hell had they survived? Thankfully, they weren't as high up as he'd first feared, but still, to roll a vehicle at night in the middle of a raging bushfire and come out relatively unscathed was pretty damn lucky in anyone's books.

The trees on the top of the gully were still alight, illuminating the pre-dawn sky, but the fire storm that had been following them had swept straight across the top of the ridge, missing the narrow gully below.

Jack glanced around and saw the other vehicles nearby, and was relieved everyone seemed to be accounted for. 'What happened?'

'When we saw you go over the edge, we floored it down the track. The fire was breathing down our neck, so we didn't have time to stop and get out to see if you two were okay. I thought we were all goners,' Brayden said, giving a nervous chuckle. 'We saw the gully and just headed in here. There was nowhere else to go. Then we saw the ute, and Laurie was already out. Jesus, I thought we were gonna find you both mangled for sure.'

'You sound disappointed,' Laurie joked weakly.

'Nah, mate. Relieved. I really didn't feel like finding two dead bodies today.'

'Can't say I blame you,' Jack agreed. 'So, it went straight over us?'

'Yep. Couldn't believe it either. I was crappin' myself.'

Jack was kind of relieved he'd still been out cold when the fire passed over. He gave a small shudder at how close they must have come to death, not once, driving over the side of a mountain edge, but twice, narrowly missing being caught up in the fire that had been chasing them.

'Do we have any contact with anyone? Do they know where we are?'

'Nah, nothing,' one of the other young McCallys said. 'Can't get any reception or radio. Might be the gully blocking it.'

'We should get moving. It'll be daylight soon. I don't want them sending people out here looking for us. It's too dangerous with all this falling timber and spot fires ready to flare back up at any minute,' Jack said wearily.

They climbed into the remaining vehicles and slowly picked their way along the gully and back out onto what was left of the fire trail. All around them were blackened trees and burning stumps. It looked like the aftermath of a war zone.

Jack cursed as his aching shoulder throbbed insistently, and distracted himself from the pain by thinking about Sam. She would be beside herself by now. He'd been too busy trying to keep them all alive last night to think about much else, but he recalled fleeting thoughts of Sam and how pissed off she was going to be if he didn't make it out of this alive. Come to think of it, he wouldn't have been too damn pleased either. The sound of that fire as it bore down on them still sent a shiver of fear through him. That had been too close for comfort.

On the side of the road lay bloated bodies of dead wildlife—kangaroos, a few deer, possums—their blackened remains twisted into grotesque forms. Jack could only imagine the terror of their final moments. In the paddocks, some still alight with spot fires, were the carcasses of cattle and livestock where they had been trapped in the fire's path. He felt his gut clench at the thought of his own cattle and what had happened to them.

'Christ, would you look at that,' Laurie murmured, drawing Jack's gaze to the other side window. They were passing a long dirt driveway that led up to what had once been a house but was now a smouldering pile of tin and metal. The remains of two vehicles and an old bus sat in the driveway—now just burnt-out shells.

Jack knew the owners—a hard-working battler who, despite living on minimum wage, managed to build anything he and his family needed from scrap iron and recycled materials. He was a good bloke, always happy to lend a hand to anyone who needed it. Now, it would be him depending on help from others, Jack thought sadly. There was going to be a lot of help needed in the coming months, even years, around here, to try to put their community back together again after all this. Although he wondered how many people would stay around and rebuild. Where the hell would they even start?

'Stop,' Jack said as a movement beside the road caught his eye. He pushed open the door and eased himself out, walking slowly to the deep drainage trench at the side of the road. A small wallaby thrashed about but quickly stilled as the exertion took up too much of its energy. Its fur was singed and its paws burnt as it lay there, seemingly resigned to its fate. Its breathing sounded laboured as it watched Jack approach. Jack bent down, taking off his jacket to gently scoop the animal out of the ditch. Surprisingly, it didn't struggle—it was probably in shock from its burns, Jack thought as he carried it back to the car.

'Don't think it's gonna make it,' Brayden announced, eyeing the tiny head that poked out from Jack's coat. 'Probably better to knock it on the head now. Put it out of its misery.'

Under normal circumstances, Jack would agree with the kid. He was a farmer—practical, with no particular love for wallabies and kangaroos, who could eat through a paddock of feed with devastating results. During the drought they competed with livestock for feed, and their populations had exploded over recent years. But that was before. Now, all Jack saw was another victim of the fire. 'I reckon if this little fella was tough enough to survive last night on his own, he deserves a shot at getting better.'

After seeing so much devastation, he couldn't bring himself to witness another death right now.

By the time daylight broke, they had just found sealed road once more and it brought them out on the other side of the range. 'Hang in there, little mate. Not long now,' Jack murmured. 'We're almost home.'

Twenty-one

Sam jumped as Thomas's radio crackled to life.

'Search command post, this is SES South-West One. We have located the seven missing persons.'

Relief instantly spilled over Sam at the words, until she saw Thomas turn away slightly, as though shielding her from the radio. 'SES South-West One, can I have a report on their condition, please.'

One glance at the tense set of her brother's shoulders and the air was sucked from her lungs. She'd been so eager for them to be found, she hadn't considered the possibility that there could still be a devastating outcome. Instinctively, Sam grabbed Thomas's shirt sleeve.

'Dehydrated and a few minor injuries, over.'

Sam felt the fierce burn of tears force their way out as she sagged against the side of the car. He was alive.

'They're okay,' Thomas said, his words coming out in a long breath as he turned back to her, hugging her tightly with one arm, still holding the radio in his other hand. 'They've found him.'

Sam didn't trust her voice, couldn't even summon the strength to find it, but she nodded quickly and tried to smile. Jack was okay.

Thomas left her briefly to make a few phone calls and when he came back it was to tell her that Jack and a few others were being taken straight to hospital to be checked over.

'I'll meet them there,' she said, already moving towards her campsite.

The dogs met her with their usual excitement, eagerly waiting for her command to do something. They weren't used to being away from the property this long and were probably confused by the events going on around them. She took a minute to sit with them, one under each arm, and was thankful for their presence although her heart ached for Matey, to whom she would normally turn for comfort. So much had happened in the past twenty-four hours, and now was not the time to fall apart, she decided, taking a slow, calming breath and wiping her eyes. With one final pat of the dogs, she got up to feed them and made sure they had water before climbing into her dad's old ute to head for the hospital.

When Sam arrived she found she wasn't the only one waiting for more news. She recognised the McCallys, a large family who lived on the other side of Jack's place. Janet McCally had a husband and two sons missing, as well as a nephew, and she sat in the emergency waiting room looking far calmer than Sam felt.

After what seemed an eternity, the women were told they could come through. Sam found herself hanging back as the others filed past eagerly. Now that she was here, she felt a little awkward. She'd just assumed she should come to see him, but she had no real claim to be here. She wasn't family and she wasn't officially a significant other. But who else was going to be here for him?

As she walked beside the row of curtains, she smiled and nodded at the soot-covered men who sat on examination beds in various stages of undress, some coughing and others looking like they just wanted to sleep. She was beginning to wonder whether Jack had already been released, when she found him at the very end.

Immediately, Sam forgot her initial jitters when she saw the cut above his eye and the bruising. His arms and hands were black from the soot and grime of the fire, and his shoulders were slumped. Exhaustion radiated from every pore of his body. But he was here. And he was safe.

It took her a moment to gather herself, before she stepped into the curtained cubicle and crossed to sit on the bed.

'I'm okay,' he said before she opened her mouth to ask. 'Just a bit banged up.'

'I can see that.' She blinked quickly and cleared her throat. She was not going to allow herself to fall apart this time. She was a strong, independent . . .

'Don't cry, Sam. I promise, I'm fine.'

Damn it. Sam wiped at the stupid tears escaping. 'Sorry. I'm not as tough as I was hoping to be. It's been a particularly shit twenty-four hours.'

'I know,' he said gently, running a hand up her arm.

Catching his hand in hers, she stared down at it for a moment, distracted by the multitude of cuts and calluses covering it. They were working hands that had been fighting to save this entire community for weeks on end and, just like the man they belonged to, they were tough and unassuming.

'I was worried about you yesterday,' she said quietly, 'and all last night.'

'I was worried about *you* until I knew you'd headed into town. It was one of the hairiest situations I've been in for a long time.' He said it lightly enough, but when she looked up she could see his eyes were solemn.

'Have the doctors finished checking you over?' she asked. All she wanted to do was get out of this place and go home . . . the thought stopped her. *Home?* Was there even a home to go back to?

'Pretty much. They wanted me to hang around and make sure I don't have a concussion. I told them I don't, but you know doctors.'

'Yeah, they insist on doing all these annoying things because they have nothing else to do,' she said sarcastically.

From the end of the room, Sam heard a low murmur of voices and then the sound of soft crying. She swapped a concerned glance with Jack moments before two RFS-dressed men, fresh from the field if the condition of their clothing was anything to go by, came to the entrance of the makeshift doorway.

Jack reached out across Sam to shake hands with both men—she suspected they all belonged to the same unit.

'Hey Jack, glad to see you in one piece,' the younger of the two men said, and nodded at Sam in greeting.

'I'll go back out to the waiting room,' Sam said, making to move from the edge of the bed, but Jack held her back.

'No, it's all right. Stay.'

The two men seemed to shuffle a little, and Sam's concern grew. They weren't here just to catch up with a teammate.

'We, ah, wanted to come up here and tell everyone in person . . .' the older man said, holding Jack's gaze firmly, if not reluctantly. 'The McCallys lost their place,' he continued quietly, and Sam recognised the tone; it was the same one she'd heard moments before, further down the room. 'Your place, as well as the B&B upriver, Terry Derkin's and the Swains' are gone too, mate. I'm really sorry. We just thought we'd let you guys know.'

Sam felt a little light-headed—Thomas had told her unofficially that the Cameron property had been lost, but it hadn't really registered, what with Jack going missing. She looked across at Jack, but he didn't seem to be as shocked as she was feeling. She saw him nod and she squeezed his hand tighter.

'And the Murphys'?' Jack asked gruffly and Sam felt her heart stop, her eyes flying across to the two men.

'It's okay. One shed has some pretty major damage, but the house is fine.'

She felt the breath she hadn't realised she'd been holding rush out. *Oh, thank God.*

It took a moment to realise the men were still talking but it was only to tell Jack they were needed for a meeting later that day.

The house is fine. The words echoed through her head as she wiped at the tears that flowed unchecked down her face.

When Jack said goodbye to his teammates, her relief was suddenly replaced by despair once more. Jack's house hadn't survived. She looked over at him now and read the weariness on his face. 'I'm so sorry, Jack.'

'I already knew it was gone,' he said quietly. 'When we got there yesterday it was right in the path. There was no stopping it.'

Sam had no words. She leaned across and kissed his forehead gently, and he closed his eyes, resting his head against hers. 'I'm so bloody tired, Sam.'

'I know.' So was she, but he had to be dead on his feet. They had all been fighting this relentless fire for so long now. She wasn't sure how these men had managed to keep going day after day.

The wind had changed direction in the early hours of the morning, driving the fire line away from its original path into town, but the destruction it had already caused to many of the families on the outskirts of town was beyond comprehension. And the fire continued to burn.

Jack just wanted to sleep. They'd put him in this hospital bed while they'd stitched up a few cuts from the crash, and then made him stay under observation. All he wanted was a proper bed and a few weeks of sleep. He was getting too old for this shit. He would have smiled to himself as he thought about young McCally if last night and the early morning hadn't been such a shit fight. The kid reminded him of himself not so long ago. He'd been fighting fires since he was sixteen, alongside his old man and most of the neighbours. Back then he'd felt indestructible. Not anymore.

Dying had never really crossed his mind, but it was different this time. Yesterday, he'd actually thought maybe they weren't going to make it out, and the thought had terrified him. He would never get to see his girls grow up and find partners and have children. And then there was Sam. He'd just found her again. The fact he survived was reason enough to make him realise how precious life really was. He'd made a decision while lying in this hospital bed. He wasn't going to continue living the way he had been—merely existing day to day, working and burying himself in the farm. He was going to make his life count.

For a moment he'd forgotten about the house. Then it hit him again. He'd been trying not to think about it—he couldn't afford to yesterday, he'd had too much to do just to keep them all alive, but now there was nowhere to hide. It was gone.

He'd never been one for sentimentality. He was proud of his heritage—the farm and all the hard work generations of Cameron men had put into the land he now owned—but he'd never really cared much about *things*. He didn't understand people having attachments to objects. There'd been heirlooms and old stuff stored inside the old house for generations, and his mum had packed it all up and taken it with her when she moved. His sister was more into the whole family history and old stuff than he ever was, and now, more than ever, he was glad she had been, because it would have all been lost.

It was the house he would miss. He'd grown up inside its walls. Still, he'd spent more time on the outside of it, and though he still had the land, it didn't take away the pain of losing the homestead.

He felt Sam gently stroke his head and he held her hand a little tighter. He'd never dared dream of having her back in his life again. Well, he may have *dreamed* about it over the years, but he never truly believed it was possible. Now that it was happening, he still sometimes couldn't quite believe it. He woke up every day with a terrible feeling that one day it would all be gone again.

The truth was, it *could* all just disappear. He'd been avoiding bringing up the conversation about what happened after her parents came home. There hadn't really been time to talk about it with him out fighting fires almost every waking hour lately . . . but the thought weighed heavily on his mind now.

There was no doubt they had something again, but was it enough to base a future on? And for that matter, what kind of future could he offer her? He didn't even have a house. He swore silently as the reality of his situation began to sink in. What the hell was he going to do now?

Twenty-two

As they walked across the carpark towards her car, Sam watched Jack carefully. He was walking slower than usual and she caught him wincing now and again when he moved, but considering what he'd been through overnight, he was doing remarkably well.

'I called Thomas while you were talking to the doctor,' she said, starting the car but not moving. 'We can stay at his place until we figure out . . .' She hesitated briefly. 'He said we're welcome to stay there as long as we need to,' she said, realising she had no real idea where else to go. 'I've got some of your clothes in the back,' she continued. 'The ones you packed. You can have a hot shower and a sleep once we get to Thomas's. But I need to go and pick up Dad's dogs from the showground first. Do you want to bring your two with us as well?' she asked.

Jack shook his head. 'Nah, they'll only be in the way over there. Best to keep them where they are until we know what we're doing. They can keep old Matey company,' he said with a tired smile.

In all the commotion, she hadn't had time to tell Jack, but now, hearing Matey's name so unexpectedly, Sam could only stare at Jack, unable to hide her devastation.

'Sam? What's wrong?'

'Matey passed away last night,' she finally managed, proud of herself for not crying. She'd done too much of that yesterday. Maybe there were no more tears left.

'Well, shit,' he said, sounding gutted. 'I'm sorry, Sam. I don't know what to say.'

She shook her head. 'Colic got him. The vet was there, though, so he didn't suffer.'

'He had a pretty damn charmed life, that horse,' Jack said quietly, and despite her best efforts a single, warm tear escaped from the corner of her eye. She was glad Jack seemed to sense she couldn't talk about it yet and dropped the subject. Maybe in a few days she'd be ready, but not right now.

'Thank you for everything you've done, Sam,' Jack said after a moment, and she glanced over at him.

'I haven't really done much.'

'You've been keeping my place going all this time. You've been looking out for me, feeding me, you're taking care of me now with a place to stay. I'm not sure what I would have done without you.'

'You would have managed. You have lots of people around who'd have stepped in and helped out.'

'Maybe. But they're not you.'

Sam smiled, something she hadn't done for what felt like a long time. 'I'm glad I was here to help.'

As hard as these past few weeks had been, she wouldn't have wished to be anywhere else. She felt a wave of emotion threatening to drown her once again and pushed it away. Now was not the time to start dealing with all that. There were too many other things hanging over their heads. For starters, they were both effectively homeless. It was going to be days before they could even start to assess the amount of damage at their properties. No, limbo land was not the place to start talking about these feelings and a possible future when neither of them had any clue where they were going from here.

'Thanks, Tom,' Sam said, hugging her brother once they arrived at his house and unloaded their dad's dogs. 'I wasn't looking forward to another night in the swag.'

'No worries, plenty of room here.'

The weather conditions had eased considerably since the night before and the fire had slowed down. It was now past her parents' property, but there were smaller fires breaking out from trees still alight and flare-ups were a constant headache for the firefighters who remained out there. Her brother's property was safe to go to, now that the main roads were back open, and the horrific conditions of yesterday's events, for now at least, seemed to have passed.

Jack was told not to go back out for a few days and ordered to rest, but clearly the doctor didn't know Jack too well—the man didn't even know the concept of *rest*.

He'd gone to the meeting with the Rural Fire Service and was there for longer than she'd expected.

'How was it?' Sam ventured when they sat down at the kitchen table afterwards.

'About as fun as a kick to the head,' Jack grunted, staring at the coffee cup he cradled in his hand. 'The big guns had a bit to say about us going AWOL. They weren't exactly thrilled by the whole thing.'

She figured that was probably a gross understatement. He might be a volunteer, but he and his crew were expected to be as disciplined as any military unit while working.

'Did you get in trouble?'

She watched him shrug and knew he was trying to pretend that whatever happened hadn't hurt as much as it clearly had.

'They demoted me, there was a bit of yelling, but nothing I can't handle.'

'What?! Are they crazy? After everything you've done over the years? Everything you've sacrificed lately? How *dare* they demote you,' Sam seethed.

'It's not a huge deal,' Jack dismissed calmly. 'It's not worth getting riled up about,' he added, shrugging and finally looking up from his mug.

'Oh, I'm more than riled up,' she snapped. 'I take it loyalty doesn't count anymore? I expected more from people around here.'

'It wasn't them—the bigwigs from headquarters just happened to be in town with the media circus. They weren't too impressed with us absconding with an RFS tanker,' he said with a twist of his lips. 'Apparently they were a bit concerned they could have lost a hundred-and-fifty-thousand-dollar vehicle.'

'But that wasn't your call. The other guys made that decision. How come you were the one who copped the blame?'

'Cause I was the one who was supposed to be in charge. Besides, if they hadn't been there, we would have certainly lost even more properties and probably our lives.'

'But it's not fair you shoulder all the blame.'

'I'll gladly take the fall for that result. I couldn't give a shit about rank or whatever else they want to strip away. I do this to keep everyone safe. They can shove all their glory and their badges and uniforms. I just did what I've been trained to do—fight fires.'

At his words, Sam lost a little of her indignation. Never had she felt more pride for someone than right at this very moment. There wouldn't be a single farmer or firefighter around here who wouldn't happily stand up for Jack over his actions, and she doubted the Rural Fire Service would risk the public backlash if it took things any further. This community would stand behind one of its own if it came to a fight. But there was nothing really to be gained by protesting or making a fuss. There were so many bigger issues at hand to think about, and Jack had already sacrificed so much. He and every other local out there fighting were heroes, and there was nothing anyone could do to take that away.

Thomas was out with the SES manning roadblocks and helping clear roads, so it was only the two of them home for dinner that evening. They'd both slept for a solid two hours in the afternoon and Sam had carefully slid out from under Jack's arm, leaving him to continue sleeping.

She'd missed that part of being in a relationship. The intimacy. Not sex ... well, maybe that too, but more the little things like being held close and holding hands as you fell asleep. An arm across the back of your chair and snuggling up on the lounge together. As she threw together a pasta dish, she thought about this new relationship she and Jack found themselves in. Some of it felt familiar—their bodies remembered each other and fitted back together like a jigsaw finding a missing piece—and yet there was so much that was new. He was a man now, not the eighteen-year-old she remembered. He had a past of his own: kids and memories that didn't include her. Just as she did.

They talked about their kids often, but they'd never really talked about what it might mean if this thing was to become permanent.

She would have two new children in her life. They were teenagers and lived with their mother, but they would still be part of their lives. Sam didn't dislike the idea, but it was something that definitely made her stop and think. How would her girls feel about a new man in their lives and two more sisters? This thing between Sam and Jack was bigger than just the two of them—nothing like it had been when they were teenagers. This time they both came as a set of three.

Sam hadn't yet brought up the idea of moving down here with Brook and Kenzie, but in her heart, the decision was pretty much already made. Sifting through her thoughts now, she knew the road ahead wasn't going to be easy.

Her phone pinged and she reached for it as she stirred in the sauce, relief flooding through her as she saw a text message from Chelsea.

> Hey. Just seen all the missed calls and texts. We've been without power, and reception has been dodgy as. We're all fine. Cattle are safe. Talk as soon as we've finished milking. Xx

Sam let out a long breath of relief.

This was the most frustrating thing about the whole situation—the realisation that without technology, they may as well be living back in the nineteenth century. A few miles out of town felt like hundreds when you couldn't communicate.

As if on cue, her phone rang with a video call from her girls. She swiped to accept and plastered a smile on her face as she waited for the call to connect.

'Hi, Mum,' Brook and Kenzie chorused, making her actually smile. God, she missed those faces so much.

'Hi, my babies,' she crooned and saw them both roll their eyes. 'Everything okay?'

'That's what we were calling to ask you. Any more news?'

'Everything's much better now.' She tried her best to sound calm and positive. She couldn't mention Matey; that was something she would tell them in person.

'Is the farm okay?'

'Yes, Nan and Pop's farm is safe. I can't go back yet, they're not letting anyone home until the fires are under control.

There's lots of falling trees and debris along the roads, so I'm staying at Uncle Thomas's until I can go back.'

As she finished talking, she noticed both girls' eyes had widened considerably and she frowned, moments before she heard Jack's voice.

'You should have woken me up earlier,' he was saying, and she turned around to see him stretching as he gave a wide yawn, standing in the kitchen behind her. He'd pulled his jeans on, but the top button hadn't been done up and he was bare chested . . . on camera. In front of her daughters.

He dropped his arms from his stretch and saw her horrified glance before switching his attention to the phone propped up on the kitchen bench before her.

'Oh, shit,' he muttered.

Oh, shit indeed, Sam thought, biting the inside of her lip anxiously before turning back to the phone. She gave a weak smile before clearing her throat. 'Ah, girls, this is Jack.'

In the video box on her screen she saw him lift a hand in greeting, before backing out of the kitchen. 'I'll, ah . . . just go put on . . . a shirt,' he mumbled before disappearing, leaving her to deal with the awkward silence that followed.

'So . . .' she said on a long breath. 'Is everything okay up there with you two?'

'Mother . . .' Brook said, drawing it out with a narrowed glare. 'Who was that?'

'Jack,' Sam said with a shrug.

'Why is there a half-naked man with you, at Uncle Thomas's place?' Brook continued.

'Jack's your grandparents' neighbour. He's staying here too. The road's closed, so we . . . I mean . . . no one can get out of town,' she said, stumbling through the explanation.

'And he's walking around like *that*?'

'He's an old friend, actually.'

'Mum, are you *sleeping* with that guy?' Brook asked, sounding somewhat shocked by the thought.

'Brook!' Kenzie snapped at her younger sister.

'What? It's a reasonable question.'

'Ah.' Sam felt herself getting flustered. How had this happened? Why was she suddenly being interrogated by her children? It was supposed to be the other way around, wasn't it?

'Mum, it's fine. It's none of our business,' Kenzie said pointedly to her sister.

'Of course it is!' Brook shot back. 'She's our mother.'

'Look, it's been a really stressful few days. How about I call you back tomorrow after I've had time to . . .'

'Come up with a reasonable explanation?' Brook suggested.

'Sleep, I was going to say,' Sam snapped, then gave a small sigh. 'I'm sorry, girls, it really has been a long few days. I'll call you tomorrow and we can talk about everything then, okay?'

'It's fine, Mum, seriously. You don't have to explain anything. We just wanted to make sure you were okay,' Kenzie said.

'Clearly she's more *okay* than we expected,' Brook added, crossing her arms and sending her a look that she'd most likely picked up from her mother over the years.

'Night, Mum,' Kenzie said, disconnecting the call before her younger sister could say any more on the subject.

Sam shut her eyes and groaned. That was not at all how she'd been planning to broach the subject of Jack.

'Jesus, Sam, I'm really sorry about that,' Jack said when he ventured back into the kitchen.

'It's okay. No harm done.'

'I didn't know you were on the phone. Are they okay?'

'They're fine. I don't think they've really thought much about their mum having sleepovers.'

'I hear you. It's like they think we're old or something,' he said with a small grunt.

'We *are* old,' she replied.

'We're not *that* old,' he corrected, sliding his arms around her. 'I can't believe we spent two hours in bed and actually slept,' he said, kissing the side of her neck.

'You needed it,' she told him as sternly as she could while he was doing delicious things to the side of her neck with his mouth.

'Well, now I need something else a lot more,' he said, leading her from the kitchen back to the bedroom, where dinner was pushed to the back of her mind.

Twenty-three

'Do you think the kids will be okay with it?' Jack asked later as he held Sam's hand in his and admired the dainty way her fingers stretched around his much larger ones. Next to her, he'd always felt like a big, clumsy bull. He'd been frightened of breaking her. Turned out she was the one who'd broken him.

'With us?' she asked, turning her head on the pillow to look at him. 'Brook might need some adjustment time, but Kenzie seemed pretty okay with it.'

'Probably wasn't the best way to meet them.' He cringed at the memory. He'd been thinking about the whole meet-the-kids thing, on and off, and the thought made him break out in a cold sweat. It was like meeting her parents for the first time as a pimple-faced kid—only worse. He wasn't sure if Sam was really okay with it or if she was just trying to make him feel better. He knew if the roles had been reversed and she'd been the one to walk out of his bedroom half naked in front of his girls . . . for a moment he'd almost forgotten. He no longer *had* a bedroom. The first decent stretch of sleep he'd had in weeks and having Sam here had momentarily delayed his thoughts from returning back to brutal reality. His stomach dropped and that horrible empty feeling returned.

He'd left the meeting earlier with the desire to hit something. He and the rest of the boys had been dragged over the coals for their stunt with the truck. He didn't mention that he hadn't been in on it—they were a team after all: one in, all in—so, he'd copped the arse-chewing over that along with his team. But when it came to deserting his post, he'd been less inclined to keep his mouth shut. As volunteers, they couldn't be ordered to stay in the field. They always did, of course, because the unwritten rule of firefighting was that you were there to fight and protect the community. In this case, though, he hadn't been deserting his post in order to try to save his own place. He heard the desperation and the determination of his neighbours on the radio. He knew they were out there fighting not only for their properties, but for their lives. There was no way he could stay where he was, where they had men and assets in place, and leave his neighbours to fight out there alone.

Those men would have most certainly perished yesterday if the truck hadn't arrived when it did. They hadn't been able to save properties, but they had saved lives.

It would have been a slightly uncomfortable conversation for the fire service to have with the media had it come out that they'd denied assistance to residents who had then died as a result. They had shut down the discussions fairly quickly after that, but Jack had no doubt there would be more about the matter brought up at a later date. That was okay. He had bigger concerns at the moment.

'How are you doing?'

Jack looked up at Sam's gentle tone and opened his mouth to say the usual, 'Yeah, okay,' but then he stopped. He didn't want to hide from her.

'Honestly, I have no idea.' He saw her eyes soften and felt his throat tighten. 'I don't think it's sunk in yet. I mean, I know what to expect. I've seen enough burnt-out homes to last a lifetime, but I don't know, I can't see *my* house like that. It just doesn't feel real. At least it won't until I see it, and see how much damage there is to the rest of the place, I guess.'

'When do you think they'll start letting people back in?'

'All depends on how fast they get control of the spot fires. Maybe a few more days.'

'Well, at least we're lucky enough to have a real bed until we figure out where to go. There's so many people still stuck up at the showground in tents with nothing.'

'Yeah,' he agreed with a sigh. After seeing the damage the fire had done over the past few days and the number of homes lost, he knew there would be a lot of people in the same boat as him—wondering where the hell they went from here.

Sam braced herself as they turned into the driveway of the Cameron property. She'd been telling herself over and over to be strong for Jack, but the first glimpses of burnt patches around her parents' property as they'd driven past had immediately shaken her resolve and now, seeing the remains of the mailbox on the front fence brought an instant sting to her eyes.

She saw Jack's grip on the steering wheel tighten, but she couldn't bring herself to look at him. As they slowly drove along the driveway, now a black avenue of scorched gum trees, Jack eventually pulled the car to a stop and for a long moment neither of them spoke as they stared through the windscreen.

It was gone.

Where once the Cameron family home had stood, was a twisted, flattened, smouldering mess of iron and ash. Not a single wall was standing. Only a column of bricks, where the original fireplace had been built, remained.

Sam felt nauseous as she stared, speechless, at the sight before her.

Jack opened his door and the action sounded loud after the heavy silence inside the car. It took a moment for Sam to regain her senses and scramble out from her side to join him. A strong, foul smell of burnt plastic mixed with smoke instantly assaulted her. As she picked her way carefully through the grey, powdery ash and blackened debris on the ground to follow Jack, she struggled to identify where they were. Everything looked different. This should be the front of the house and yet nothing remained to identify it. As she reached Jack's side, she gently took his hand in hers and for a while they simply stood side by side and took in the devastation around them. She saw Jack's shoulders shake, and she turned to hold him. A low, mournful sound reverberated against her chest, something between a sob and a groan, and Sam tightened her hold on him and wished she could absorb the anguish and sorrow she could feel rolling through his body. Her own tears ran like a torrent. This was more than just a house burnt to the ground. This building had been a home. It had raised generations of a family within it. Memories filled its very walls—walls that no longer existed. It was a death they were looking upon. The death of something irreplaceable. Buildings could be replaced, but not history.

After a long while, Jack slowly straightened and wiped his arm across his face, turning away from her. She knew he needed some time alone, but she also knew there was no way she was going to be far away. She let him walk through the burnt-out remains of the structure, watching him listlessly poke things with his boot as he made his way through the rubble.

Sam gazed tiredly at the scene before her. Two of the three large sheds were completely destroyed—they were now piles of twisted and mangled metal, destroying with them machinery and equipment that had taken years to accumulate. The third shed still stood, singed and blackened, but had lost its roof and most of its contents, as had a smaller shed off to the side.

Jack's mother's beautiful garden was gone. Sam blinked back warm tears as she turned in a circle, trying to locate the hydrangea bushes that had stood against the fence line of the house yard. She crossed to where sheets of tin, maybe part of the roof, had fallen. She crouched to look underneath, and for the briefest moment her heart rose as she spotted a faint hint of green among the surrounding black. Pulling away the tin, she uncovered a limp-but-alive hydrangea plant.

A fresh lot of tears started once again as she bowed her head in a mix of anguish and relief. She didn't know why this one small plant surviving when so much else had perished meant so much to her, but it did.

She lifted her head when two strong hands rested on her shoulders. She stood up and his hands slid down her arms to her waist as he pulled her back against him.

She wanted to say something, but there were no words. Nothing racing through her mind would help if it were voiced out loud, and she was having trouble connecting the destruction she was seeing with any sense.

'I knew it was gone,' Jack finally said, 'when we had to pull back. But I guess part of me was hoping we'd get back here today and find it'd somehow miraculously survived. Pretty stupid.'

'It's not stupid. It's human,' she said softly. So often in the aftermath of the fires, houses *had* survived seemingly impossible odds—somehow spared from the flames when everything else around had burnt to the ground. 'I'm so sorry, Jack.'

Sam felt him let out an unsteady breath behind her and she turned in his arms. She looked up into his sad eyes, and placed a palm against his cheek before reaching up to kiss him tenderly. As distressing as it was to stand among the ash and ruin of this place, it was the grief she saw in Jack's eyes that shattered her heart.

Sam was a mix of emotions as they turned into her parents' driveway. From the top of the hill she could see the stark reminder of how close danger had come. The tree line along the creek was now a streak of burnt remains standing guard over the dry banks of the creek bed. At the bottom of the hill stood the house. Safe and whole, so very different from Jack's. What stroke of luck had turned that wind before it had the chance to sweep through as it had all the properties beyond? She was so grateful there was a house to come home to, and yet she felt guilty for that moment of utter relief with Jack sitting beside her.

They drove down the driveway and Sam searched for any sign of the cattle. From the top of the hill you could see almost the entire property, except for one part that was tucked behind the last little ridge. With no sign of the cattle so far, she was hoping that's where they would be.

Loading the ute with some hay, they stopped to close gates and turn off the irrigation system as they made their way through the property. There were paddocks with some fire damage, most likely the result of spot fires from embers that flew ahead of the main fire storm, but compared to the damage over at Jack's place, it was minimal. Sam held her breath as they cut through the gully. *Please let them be here*, she thought silently. She closed her eyes in gratitude as she saw the first shapes moving towards them.

'Oh, thank God,' she said on an unsteady breath.

Jack put his hand over hers and gave it a squeeze. 'All safe and sound,' he said.

Spotting the ute and knowing that it usually meant feed, the cattle began to run towards them as they threw out the hay.

'Should we go and search for yours now?' she asked once she'd taken a few photos to send to her dad to put his mind at ease.

'No need. Ivan up the road said he'd already found a few in the national park. I'd say they're all up that way.'

'The national park? But how are you going to get them back?'

'Not just mine,' Jack said with a grimace. 'With everyone's fences down, there's livestock scattered everywhere. We'll have to try to organise a bit of a muster, but there's not much we can do until we sort out the fencing to keep them all in once we manage to find them and get them back.'

'What a mess,' Sam groaned. The enormity of the damage wasn't just limited to the houses lost. The kilometres of fencing that had been destroyed were almost as distressing. As Jack said, finding lost livestock was one thing; being in a position to hold them once they were found was something else. How did you contain your livestock when all your fencing was gone? It seemed a near-impossible task to replace it all.

'It'll be okay,' he said, surprising her from her worries.

'I just feel so terrible. You lost so much,' she said.

'It's just the way it is. Complaining won't fix it, and there's a lot of people worse off than me out there. At least I have insurance. It can all be put back, it's just going to take a long time to get everything sorted.'

She saw him smile a little, despite the anxiety and grief etched on his strong face, and her heart swelled with love and pride. For an instant it didn't click what she'd admitted to herself.

'I would have hated to see your mum and dad lose everything at their age,' Jack said.

It hurt to even think about. So, she didn't. She was still distracted by her earlier thoughts. There was no turning back now that she'd admitted to herself how she truly felt about Jack. Deep down she knew this wasn't some holiday fling—it could never be with the history they shared—but ignoring that fact because the consequences were too hard to figure out only worked . . . until it didn't anymore.

She was going to have to tell her kids she was moving.

Logically, she knew the girls were old enough to handle the news. They were out living their own lives. And yet, motherly guilt never seemed to go away. The same old arguments ran through her mind. What if she was too far away to help them when they needed her? Why did she feel as though she would be abandoning them? She knew their father wouldn't think twice about it if he suddenly had a desire to move away. But that was the difference between them: she had never put her own happiness before the kids when they'd been little. But what about now they were grown . . . well, almost grown . . . grown enough? She looked around and realised she couldn't imagine leaving all this behind her to return to her old life. She'd felt a reconnection to her community; it was more than just Jack. It was this whole valley she'd missed.

It was time to come home.

Twenty-four

It was a strange new world over the next few days. Everyone Jack spoke to wore the same battle-fatigued expression, like they'd just gone through a war that had destroyed everything. The once tall, beautiful gum trees that surrounded farms and roadsides were now forests of tall, black sticks, smoke still spewing from inside them like giant chimney stacks.

Jack kicked at a burnt-out fence post and dropped his head. All his fencing was gone. His stock were missing and there was no feed for them if they turned up alive somewhere anyway. He'd lost all his hay in the shed and there was nothing left in the paddocks. Each day seemed to reveal a new disaster. All his dad's machinery was gone. His tools were all melted inside what was left of his main work shed. He'd allowed himself to break down just the once but he felt like he could do it over and over again. The enormity of what he faced was just too much to deal with. But crying wouldn't fix anything. It was going to take hard work—and lots of it. He just didn't know where to start when he stood here and looked out over the destruction before him. He'd lost everything.

His gaze drifted back to where the house had once stood and he let out a short, decisive sigh. A place to live was probably the first thing he needed to sort out. He'd been staying at Sam's place, but that wasn't going to work long term. Her parents were due back in a couple of weeks and he wasn't sure how they'd feel about him living with their daughter right under their noses. It just didn't feel right.

Of all the things that had survived, his mother's old craft shed was probably the least useful thing he could wish for, and yet there it was, relatively unscathed, though blackened and filthy. His father had built it for her as a place to sew, after years of listening to her complain about having to work on the kitchen table and the fact she had to pack it all away before every meal time.

It was a smaller version of the other tin sheds around the place, but it was big enough for a bed and a bit of furniture and it had wiring and plumbing . . . or at least it did before the water tank melted. But that could be fixed. It wasn't a great solution, but it was a place to start.

'I brought morning tea,' Sam said, accepting the kiss Jack offered as she walked into the small shed. 'Wow, it's really taking shape,' she said, smiling as she looked around. When he'd first told her about his idea for fixing up his mum's old craft shed, she'd been a little doubtful. But seeing what he'd done with it, she was quickly changing her mind.

Before, it had housed a long bench along one wall and a big table in the centre, with a small sink up one end, and a tiny room with an old toilet and a couple of storage cupboards up the other. He'd taken out the toilet wall and made the area larger, putting in a shower stall to create a small bathroom.

'This was such a clever idea,' she said, handing him a meat pie after he dusted off his hands.

'It'll do for a while.'

'You know, this would make an awesome Airbnb down the track. You could make a nice little income renting it out to tourists looking for a farm-stay experience.'

'First I've got to get the farm part up and running again,' he said dryly, before taking a bite of his pie.

'Yeah, there's a bit to do before that. But if anyone can do it, it's you,' she said, watching with horrified amusement as he finished the pie in only a few bites.

Before she could comment, a car pulling up drew her attention through the doorway and she spotted her younger brother, Alex, heading towards them.

'Damn. I thought if I left it long enough you'd have this thing finished by the time I got here,' Alex said, stepping inside to shake Jack's hand and kiss Sam's cheek.

'Nah, I was waiting for you to turn up so you could show me how it's done.' Jack shrugged.

'I thought I was supervising?'

'Fat chance,' Jack said with a grin, handing him a sheet of paper.

'What's this?' Alex frowned, then groaned. 'Aw man, seriously? You never said anything about a flat-pack kitchen.'

'Really? Must have slipped my mind.' Jack's grin widened.

'It's okay, Alex. If it's too tricky for you, I can do it,' Sam said, patting his shoulder.

'Yeah, right. I've seen you building flat packs. A certain bookcase comes to mind.'

'What? I'll have you know it's still going strong to this day.'

'Uh-huh, so long as you don't walk past it too close at speed.'

'Well, you're not *supposed* to touch a bookcase,' she told him with a slight sniff.

'Especially one that doesn't have all the screws in it.'

'I told you, they were leftovers. They do that in case you lose some.'

She saw Alex roll his eyes at Jack and nod sarcastically. 'Sure they do. It's okay, I think I've got this.'

'Great. Well, I see this place is in safe hands with the two of you, so I might leave you to it,' she said, walking across to Jack.

'Where are you off to?' he asked, wrapping his hands around her waist.

'I said I'd go in and help sort out donations at the RSL for a bit. They've been inundated.'

'Oh, okay. That's a good idea.'

She smiled at his hesitant tone. They'd pretty much been joined at the hip over the past few days and it did feel strange to be leaving him, but when Alex had called to say he was coming out to give Jack a hand renovating, she thought a bit of male bonding might be what Jack needed. She knew he could talk to her, but there was a lot to be said for some time alone with a good mate to help him feel normal again.

'I'll only be a couple of hours,' she promised, kissing him gently before sending a look towards her brother.

'I'll take care of him,' Alex teased, but gave her a reassuring wink as she walked past.

'That's kind of what I'm afraid of,' she threw over her shoulder.

Jack hammered the final piece of gyprock into place and stood back to admire the job. It wasn't much, but it was a big step towards creating something stable in his recently unstable world.

'Looking good,' Alex said, breaking into Jack's thoughts and drawing his gaze across the room to where the kitchen was now taking shape.

'Lucky you managed to figure out that flat pack or you'd never live it down with your sister.'

'Tell me about it. Nothing like a bit of pressure to inspire confidence.'

Jack took the other end of the bench and lifted it up to sit on top of the base cabinets Alex had managed to assemble, then helped screw it in place.

'Thanks for coming out today, mate. I really appreciate it.'

'No worries. Happy to help. How are you doing with everything?'

'Yeah, you know.' Jack shrugged. 'Doing my best to stay positive.'

'That's good.'

'It'd be a hell of a lot harder if Sam wasn't here.'

'I'm really glad you two are hitting it off again. Is it official?'

'I dunno. I think everything kind of happened in such a weird way that we haven't really been able to put a label on it. Has she said anything to you about it?' He hoped he sounded offhand but he wasn't sure he managed it.

'You know Sam. She doesn't talk much about what's going on. I can say, though, that this is probably the happiest I've seen her in a long while. I think if you want to find out where she's at, you'll just have to ask her straight up.'

'Yeah,' Jack sighed irritably. He'd always handled everything head on, but this thing with Sam wasn't just any old thing. This mattered.

The two men worked side by side for the remainder of the afternoon and when they'd finished, Jack couldn't help but shake his head at what they'd managed to accomplish.

'Thanks, mate,' he said again as he handed Alex a beer from the esky. 'Next job on the list is finding a fridge to keep the beer cold,' he muttered as he downed most of the cool-ish bottle to quench his thirst.

'I've got an old fridge in the shed and a bed to bring over as soon as you have room for it,' Alex said. 'I'll have a hunt around and see what else is there too, if you want. It's all been sitting there since Marcie and I moved up here.'

'That'd be great. Just to tide me over for a bit until everything's sorted out.' Jack tried not to let despondency settle in, as it tended to do whenever he let his thoughts stray to his immediate future. Once, he had his life pretty much mapped out. He had a house, vehicles, a property, some money in the bank. He wasn't a millionaire, nor would he ever be, not by a long shot, but he'd been comfortable and he had a good life. Now, he had nothing. Well, not *nothing*. He had a ute and he had his land and his dogs; he had the foundations to rebuild his life. It was just going to take some time to do it.

Later, after Alex left, Jack reached for his phone and called his girls. He'd let them know he was okay through the worst of the fires, and had given them the basics about the loss of the house, but until now he hadn't been able to bring himself to talk about it in detail. They'd cried when he broke the news, and he'd tried to stay positive, but he'd ended the call saying he'd been called back out and had to go. The truth was, it was still too raw to talk about. The conversation with his mother was worse. Hearing the tears in her voice and the quiet sobs, he'd felt guilt rack his insides. He knew it wasn't his fault, but that knowledge did nothing to ease the torment.

'Hey,' he said as Bianca's face came up on the screen, dragging him away from his thoughts.

'Hi, Dad.' He waited as she called out to her sister. 'Dad's on the phone!' she yelled, before returning her attention to the phone.

'How're things going down there?' he asked, and it was nice to have some kind of normality descend as he listened to Bianca filling him in on her social life and her latest dramas with friends.

'Hi, Dad,' Tasmin said, bounding into the room to flop onto her sister's bed.

'How are you, princess?' he asked, his weary old heart filling with a surge of love as he soaked in the faces of the two most precious things in the world to him. It put everything instantly in perspective once more. He had his daughters. They were safe, and nothing else compared to that.

'Daddy? Where are we going to sleep when we come to visit?' Tasmin asked innocently.

'I've been busy making Granny's old craft room into a house for us.' He switched the phone camera around so he could take them on a virtual tour of the shed. 'It'll be a bit cramped for a while, but I've got a loan of a caravan I can sleep in when you guys are here, and you two can sleep inside. It's got a shower and a new toilet, and check out the new kitchen,' he said, slowly panning the camera around and smiling at the oohs and ahhs he heard on the other end of the phone.

'That looks so cool,' Tasmin said, her eyes wide. 'When can we come up?'

'As soon as everything settles down here a bit more.' There were still fires burning, and the last thing he wanted was to bring the girls up when there was a chance things could flare up once more.

'Where's Snowy?' Tasmin asked. 'Can I see him?'

'He's over at the Murphy place,' Jack said. 'We've got no fences or feed for him here at the moment. But I'll take a photo tomorrow and send it to you, okay?'

'Okay,' she said, sounding a bit disappointed, but then she immediately lit up as she told him all about the new cat they were getting. Jack took that one on the chin—his ex-wife never missed an opportunity to rub in the fact he'd never allowed cats at the farm, and now they had about five of them. He was pretty sure she only did it because he no longer had any say in it. Maybe he was just being petty, but it seemed a bit over the top to have that many cats in a townhouse. *Not my monkey, not my circus*, he repeated to himself firmly. Good old Paul, the guy Cilia left him for—he must be a freaking saint.

Jack decided the time had come to man up. Alex was right—if he wanted to know what was going on in Sam's head, he had to ask her.

The next day, he waited as Sam made her way across from the car to where he was standing in front of the shed.

'Okay, I'm here. What's the big surprise?' she asked, smiling expectantly at him.

'Close your eyes,' he told her, then watched as she obeyed with only the slightest hesitation. He took her hand and carefully led her up the step and into the shed. 'Okay, you can open your eyes now.'

Her little gasp of pleasure sent a riot of warm feelings through him as she took in the darkened space, lit only by candles he'd placed all around the room. In the centre, he'd set a small round table for two with a scattering of rose petals.

'It's beautiful, Jack,' Sam breathed. 'And you made dinner?'

'I did . . . cooked in my brand-new kitchen. And I borrowed the fridge and table from Alex. But don't get too excited, it's only spag bol. I wasn't game to try the oven out on a roast yet.'

'It smells delicious,' she said, gliding into his arms. 'You've done an amazing job with the place. I'd never imagined it could turn out like this.'

Her praise touched him. 'Yeah. It came up pretty well.'

'So, we're celebrating the completion of the shed renovation,' she said with a nod. 'Where's the wine?'

'Coming right up,' he said, leaving her to cross the very short distance to the kitchen. Handing her a wine as she sat at the bench, he touched his glass to hers, holding her gaze. 'To new beginnings,' he said and watched as her eyes seemed to soften. He still wasn't sure he wanted to rock the boat in case it tipped, but he needed to know where this thing was going. It seemed important to have something concrete, something dependable amid so much uncertainty.

'Sam, I wanted to . . .' He paused, searching for the right words. 'I was hoping that maybe you . . .' He groaned silently; this wasn't how he'd practised it in his head. 'What I'm trying to say is . . .'

'I love you, Jack,' she cut in quietly, stunning him. Then she carefully placed her wine glass on the bench. 'When I thought I'd lost you, I had a brief glimpse of what life without you would mean . . . and it was no life.'

Jack set his own glass down and stepped closer, taking her hands in his. 'I was scared out there, Sam,' he admitted softly. 'I thought that was it.' He paused, closing his eyes briefly as the roar of fire and the heat played through his mind once more. 'I realised I hadn't even told you how I felt.' His eyes roamed her face, the one that he'd held firmly in his mind as the truck had rolled over the edge of that bloody cliff. 'I love you, Sam. I don't think I ever really stopped.'

Sam searched his eyes. 'Me either.'

'I know we haven't really talked about the future, but maybe now it's time we did. Do you think you could see yourself staying on here?'

Her gentle smile suddenly gave him hope. 'I could. In fact, I've been wanting to talk to you about it. I'm planning to sell my house so I can buy my own little farm around here somewhere. Just big enough to keep a couple of horses, but somewhere of my own.'

'You are?'

'I realised I don't want to go back up there and leave all this . . . *you*, behind. Even without factoring you into the equation, I've really loved being back here and I think it's time for a change.'

'So, you're not going back?'

'Well, I have to go back for a while. I need to put my house on the market and pack. And I still have to break it to the girls,' she said with a wince.

'How do you think they'll take it?'

'I'm not sure. I think Kenzie will understand. Brook will probably be less thrilled about the idea. But I'm sure they'll both be okay with it by the time the house sells. What about your girls?' she asked.

'They'll be fine,' he assured her. 'They handled their mother moving in with someone else.' He honestly couldn't see how this would be anything they'd get too worked up about.

'I wish I had your confidence.'

'Maybe you'll be surprised,' he suggested lightly. 'I just hope your house sells fast,' he added, pulling her to him. 'I can't seem to imagine you not being here anymore.'

'I know.' She rested her head against his chest. 'I don't want to leave either.'

'So, don't. Rent out your house and work it all out later.'

'I'd still need to go up there and pack. Let's not talk about all that right now,' she said, changing the subject. 'I want to taste this amazing spaghetti bolognaise you've talked up so much.'

'Well, it *is* my specialty,' he admitted. She was right, he didn't want to think about her leaving either. He wanted to enjoy the night and savour the fact they'd finally got around to admitting out loud how they felt. As he served their meal, he couldn't suppress the grin he felt settling on his face. Sam loved him and he loved her. Somehow, despite all the pain of the past few days, this one thought soothed his raw, broken heart and he could see a way forward more clearly than ever before. Then, something amazing happened.

'Do you hear that?' Sam asked, pausing as she was about to take some spaghetti from her fork.

He stopped chewing to listen, his eyes widening, as loud drops hit the roof above them.

'It's raining!' Sam said. 'Come on!' She dragged him outside.

It was only sprinkling, barely more than a few spits, but it was *rain*. More than they'd had in the past eighteen months. The smell was unmistakable as the dry, cracked earth greedily soaked it up. Maybe it was a sign that everything was finally starting to fall into place.

As they went to bed that night, listening to the splatter of raindrops on the tin roof above them, Jack fell asleep for the first time in what seemed like forever without a heavy heart; without worrying about what was to come. It wasn't going to be easy, but with Sam beside him, he knew he could do anything.

Twenty-five

Sam opened the chook-pen gate, carrying a bucket of feed. 'Here guinea, guinea, guinea,' she called as she walked around the yard, searching. A small part of her—a very small part—had been feeling bad about leaving them behind, but when she'd returned home and hadn't found them in the tree where she'd last seen them, she'd begun to worry about having to tell her mother, so she did what any guilt-racked daughter would do: she went in search of guinea fowl for sale and bought twelve more of the stupid little feathered freaks. She'd had high hopes that these ones would be a lot smarter than the original batch.

Unfortunately, it seemed this second lot were just as daft.

Sam had kept them locked in their pen to get used to their new home, but on the second day, when she opened the door to feed them, they suddenly decided to act as one hysterical mob, crashing and bumping into the walls and swooping at her head, then somehow during the whole fiasco they managed to push open the door on the other side of the cage and escape. So now Sam had a dozen rebel guinea fowl who refused to go into their cage and who for the most part just hid under the bushes.

With an irritated sigh, she tossed the feed on the ground, checked the water and left them to it.

Sam had been busy cleaning her parents' house, ready for their return. So much had happened in the time since she'd first arrived. It seemed like a lifetime ago.

Tomorrow she'd pick them up from the airport. Then next week Sam would drive back to the Sunshine Coast. Despite the fact she knew she was coming back, it still felt like saying goodbye.

She had quickly got used to the life she and Jack had set up for themselves: the cosy dinners, the nights curled up on the lounge, talking about the day and making plans. Even though they'd spoken about her going back to put her house on the market, she couldn't shake the horrible empty sensation that filled her each time she thought of leaving.

As a welcome distraction, Chelsea arrived. 'I come bearing morning tea,' she announced cheerily, depositing a Tupperware container on the kitchen bench.

'I'm going to miss all these unexpected calories,' Sam sighed.

'I can't believe you're going home already. How did six weeks go so fast?'

'A lot's happened,' Sam agreed, and the women shared a long look. *So much* had happened. The fires, now finally being contained, were still a long way from being put out. The few rain showers in the last few days had barely wet the topsoil and were certainly not enough to drench the still smouldering trees around the district. There were daily flare-ups that required immediate attention; any one of them had the potential to reignite the remaining unburnt fuel load in the area. Until they had a proper 'rain event', the drought still had a firm grip on the landscape and it would take months before any feed grew from the dry earth, once it did finally rain.

'So, what's the plan?' Chelsea demanded, taking a seat at the bench and opening the lid of the plastic container as Sam put the kettle on.

The mouth-watering aroma of freshly baked apple slice wafted between them. 'I'll head back up the coast on the weekend, see the girls and then get started on listing the house for sale.'

'Excellent. Are you excited?' Chelsea asked, tilting her head slightly.

'I am,' Sam said with a smile, then bobbed her head as Chelsea held her gaze. 'It's a bit daunting,' she added. 'I'm not sure how the girls will take it, and then there's the whole packing-up thing and selling and finding a place to buy.' So many of the places nearby had been burnt or had some kind of damage, and Sam wondered how that might affect what was available.

'I knew you'd been stressing. You sounded far too chirpy last night when I called.'

Sam gave her a lopsided grin. So, that explained the unannounced visit. 'I'm fine.'

'Of course you are,' Chelsea said, blithely brushing off her reply as she took out two pieces of the slice and put them on the plate Sam handed her. 'But it's a lot to process and I knew you'd start overthinking the whole thing.'

There were certain times when having someone know you so well was kind of a pain. But on the other hand, it was also nice to know she had a friend who understood.

'There's so much to do,' Sam said.

'There is. But you just take it one day at a time.'

'What if the house sells fast?'

'Wouldn't that be a good thing?'

'Well, yes, but it means I'd need to figure out where I'm moving to and I haven't found anything listed that's really suitable.'

'So, you move in with your parents . . . or Jack, until you do.'

'I can't move in with Jack.'

'Why not?'

'Well, because . . . I don't know. I want my own place.' Somehow, she knew if she moved in with Jack she'd more than likely never move out.

'I don't see what the big deal is. You two *are* together, aren't you?'

'Well, yeah, but it's all still new and it's hardly been a normal start to a relationship. Besides, I want a chance to buy my own place and have whatever animals I want and not have to feel like I need to ask permission from someone.'

'Oh God,' Chelsea said, rolling her eyes. 'You're going to turn into one of those Old McDonald women, aren't you?

Buying alpacas and goats and every other ridiculous farm animal known to humankind.'

'Maybe,' Sam agreed, grinning at her friend. And this was exactly why she wanted her own property. She didn't want to be a real farmer like Chelsea and the rest of her family. She wanted a hobby farm where she could just enjoy her space and animals without having to defend each purchase based on what profit it could make or what job it could do on the farm. 'And you know what? If I do, I won't have to answer to anyone else about doing it.'

'Okay, fair enough,' Chelsea replied with a smile.

As images of horses and miniature cattle flickered through her mind, Sam's excitement was reignited.

'I guess it just feels as though you and Jack have been together longer than you really have.'

It was true, it felt that way even to Sam. Maybe it was because of their history. Or maybe it was just that the past few weeks and everything they'd been through had forged a deeper connection. Traumatic situations had a habit of bonding people. 'There's also the fact we have to take into account each other's kids. I mean, we come as a job lot nowadays. I don't want to rush into anything without giving them time to get used to the idea.'

'How have his girls taken it?' Chelsea asked, taking a bite of her apple slice.

'Hard to say, really. Everything's been pretty upsetting. They lost the home they grew up in, and there's no room for them to stay here if they wanted to come and visit, so it's been a bit hard to actually meet them face to face. We thought it was better not to rush anything.'

'So they don't know about you and Jack?' Chelsea asked, lifting an eyebrow.

'Not really.'

'Is that weird?'

Sam shrugged. 'I mean, it would be under normal circumstances,' she said carefully. In truth it did worry her, but she also knew that it wasn't exactly a run-of-the-mill situation. 'But Jack's been fighting fires for months and hadn't been able to talk to the kids as often as he used to, and then the fire swept through and he's been swamped with insurance and fencing and renovating the shed to live in and dealing with the stress that goes along with all that. It's just been too much to try to introduce a new relationship to his kids on FaceTime at the moment.' She reached for another piece of slice. 'We figured there'd be plenty of time once I move back to do it properly.'

'Yeah, I'd imagine it would be hard for them. They're close to their dad and loved the farm. What's Jack going to do when they visit? The shed isn't very big.'

'He was pretty worried about it. But Mum and Dad have given him the caravan to use for extra beds, so that should be okay.'

'Let's just hope things get back to normal sooner rather than later,' Chelsea said with a soft shake of her head.

'Amen,' Sam agreed, taking a sip of her coffee. Though it was hard to remember what normal felt like.

Twenty-six

Sam stood by the large glass window of the airport with her two brothers and sister-in-law Joanne, watching people disembark. It had seemed to take forever for the plane to land and roll to a stop on the tarmac. She saw kids and young mums being pulled into tight embraces of grandparents in the arrivals area, and happy faces and tears from others who were flowing through the door in a sea of people. One young couple arrived home to family and friends looking tanned and relaxed, clearly returning from a honeymoon, and Sam smiled at the reunion.

Her attention was drawn to the doorway as a couple came through, and immediately a rush of affection washed through her and she felt her eyes sting a little. You were never too old to miss your mum and dad. She waited for her brothers to hug her parents before she stepped forward and held them tightly. It felt like a lifetime since she'd sent them off on their trip.

'I'm so glad you're home,' Sam said, pulling away.

'Not as glad as I am,' her father muttered. 'I can't wait to sleep in my own flamin' bed after all this time.'

'Back to his old self,' her mother said, rolling her eyes.

'I hope you still managed to have a great time, despite all this,' Sam said, waving her hand in the air.

'We did,' her mother said with a long sigh. 'Oh, Rome was so lovely. And France!' She sighed again. 'Just beautiful. It was everything I'd ever imagined it would be.'

'I'm so glad,' Sam said, squeezing her mum's hand as they waited at the baggage carousel.

Sam and Joanne stayed with her mother as the men moved to claim the luggage that had just begun to appear, listening to her mum chat about the trip. She didn't stop until they'd reached the car, where Sam and her parents said goodbye to the others. But as they made their way home, the mood in the car gradually began to change. The smoke still lingered, although it was not as thick or as choking as it had been. The closer they got to the Murphys' property, the more evidence of what had taken place began to emerge. It started out with just the odd blackened tree here and there, until eventually, up ahead, a whole burnt-out ridge appeared.

She heard her father's low, murmured curse as he took in the charred landscape, and her mother gave a small gasp.

There was no conversation for the remainder of the trip from town to the farm.

'I knew what to expect,' her dad said quietly once they pulled in at the top of the driveway and looked down over the surrounding valley, 'but it still takes my breath away.'

'It shocks me each time I see it, too,' Sam said, letting out a long exhale.

'There's just so much destruction,' her mother said from behind the trembling fingers covering her mouth.

'I can't believe the house and sheds are still standing,' her dad muttered, shaking his head as he stared at the buildings at the bottom of the long driveway ahead. 'Those poor bastards on the other side of the creek,' he added, glancing over towards Jack's place, and Sam's heart plummeted once more.

'How *is* Jack?' her mother asked.

'He's doing okay,' Sam said honestly. 'It's been really hard, and there's so much to do, but it's incredible how he's set his mind to putting everything back together again.'

'He's a hard worker, that boy,' her mum said, nodding. 'Always has been.'

'You could do worse than Jack Cameron,' her father said gruffly, surprising Sam.

'I'm sure you could,' she hedged.

'Oh, come on, Sam, we've been on the other side of the world—not on another planet. We've heard all about how you two have become inseparable.'

'It was the boys, wasn't it?' Sam muttered, narrowing her eyes as she imagined all the kinds of painful retribution she was going to dish out to her brothers.

'So, there *is* something going on?' her dad asked slowly, then looked at her mother. 'You were right.'

'What?'

Hang on a minute . . . did I just get hoodwinked by my own father?

Her mother gave her a self-satisfied smile as she nodded calmly in agreement. 'I told you.'

'Told him what?' Sam frowned, feeling as though she were a fifteen-year-old back in front of her parents.

'That you and Jack were back together again.'

'We're not . . . that is, we're trying to . . .' Sam gave an irritated huff. 'There's a lot to sort out,' she finished, giving up trying to explain the situation.

'I can imagine,' her mother soothed.

'I'm actually heading back home on the weekend, to look at putting my house on the market,' Sam said, wincing slightly as she waited for her parents' reaction.

'Oh,' her mother said, with a surprised blink. 'Well, that *is* big news.'

'I'd already decided I wanted to move back down here, before Jack and all this,' Sam said, waving a hand in the air vaguely. 'I miss not having horses, and I didn't realise how much I missed having family around, and Chelsea. I'd like to buy a small place with a couple of acres somewhere nearby.'

'Sounds like a good idea to me. Can't believe it took you this long to figure it out, though.' Her dad shrugged.

Sam felt the tension in her shoulders relax a little. *Well, that went better than expected.*

'You better call Jack and get him over here,' her dad went on brusquely. 'Apparently we have a few things to discuss.'

Oh dear God no. 'Dad, he's a grown man. You don't need to pull the grumpy-father routine.'

'I'm not pulling anything. Neighbour or no neighbour, if he's interested in my daughter, he needs to hear a few things.'

Sam shot an exasperated glance over at her mother, who only laughed and shook her head. 'Do you honestly see your father saying anything to scare off Jack? He was heartbroken you two broke up in the first place,' her mother said.

Sam looked back at her father and blinked uncertainly. She'd never really considered how the break-up with Jack had affected her parents. Back then she'd only ever thought of them as rule makers and constant chaperones who were always getting in the way of her teenage hormones. As grumpy and foreboding as her father had been back then towards Jack, she knew that he at least respected his family, and over the years the two men had become great mates—the way neighbours around here did; always there to lend a hand and look out for each other.

'I'll give him a call once you unpack,' Sam said, putting the car back in gear and heading down the driveway.

'Mum, you don't have to make scones,' Sam said as she walked into the kitchen.

'Rubbish. What else are we going to have for afternoon tea? Jack loves my scones. It doesn't take long to whip them up. Besides, I've missed my kitchen. Pass me the milk out of the fridge, will you, darling?' her mum said as she threw ingredients into a mixing bowl without measuring. Sam couldn't help but smile. There was something comforting about sitting at the bench, just as she had as a child, watching her mother—and her grandmother before her—make a batch of scones.

'Your father and I are really happy for you and Jack, you know,' her mum said, watching her as she rubbed the butter and flour between her fingers.

'Thanks, Mum. It just kind of happened. I wasn't expecting it.'

'Good things always happen when you least expect them,' her mum recited her favourite motto with a wry grin.

'It was very true this time,' Sam agreed. 'I'm kind of sad it took this long to find him again, though. All those years we wasted.'

'Timing is everything. You both had your own paths to walk before you met up again at the perfect point in time.'

Maybe fate knew what it was doing, after all. Any earlier than this and Sam would never have had the opportunity to move back home—not with the kids still in school. It just wouldn't have worked. Now, she and Jack were both free to make the choices they wanted to make. She smiled. *Timing.*

They chatted about her brothers and Chelsea, and Sam filled her mother in on all the different ways she had witnessed the community pull together over the last few weeks. She felt calm as she watched her mother's hands mix and knead, gliding across the dough as she cut it into rounds and arranged them on a baking tray.

They set out cups and plates along with jam and cream, and had the table outside on the verandah all ready when Jack arrived.

Sam saw her father walk out of the shed and the two men shook hands and exchanged greetings, followed by a brief moment of conversation. Before Sam could head out and put a stop to whatever overbearing fatherly warnings her dad was delivering, he slapped a hand on Jack's shoulder and the pair headed amicably up the path towards the house.

'Hey,' Sam said, eyeing Jack carefully. 'Everything all right?' She sent a swift glance between the two men.

'Everything's fine.' Jack grinned, bending down to kiss her as her father moved on ahead. 'Your dad just reminded me about the chat we had when I was sixteen.'

'Which was?' she asked, hitching an eyebrow. 'You never told me what he said back then.'

'And I'm not telling you now. Suffice to say, your old man can still scare the crap out of me.'

'Oh, for goodness sake,' she muttered as they walked up to the verandah. 'We're supposed to be adults,' she reminded him.

'Exactly. And I've grown very attached to all my parts over the years.'

Thankfully, neither of her parents brought up their relationship again, and Sam eventually allowed herself to let out a calming breath. They looked at photos from her parents' trip, and Sam found herself envious of all the places they'd been over the past six weeks. It was hard to imagine that while they had been climbing the Eiffel Tower, she and Jack were fleeing a fire storm.

Jack and her father discussed his plans for rebuilding and restocking his place, and Sam gave her mum a gentle smile as she caught her dabbing at her eyes when Jack spoke about losing the house. Once more she found herself overcome by her own emotions as she tried to imagine how this homecoming for her parents would have been so very different had they lost this place.

Conversation turned to less emotional topics, and soon the men were caught up in farm talk.

'I can't wait to see all my girls,' her mother said as she sipped her coffee and glanced out towards the chook pen. 'I've missed them. Did they give you much trouble?'

Sam plastered a wide smile on her face and shook her head. 'Nope. They were perfect angels,' she lied.

'Even my guineas?' her mum asked, lifting an eyebrow curiously.

'Yep.' The little idiots had probably aged Sam a good ten years since arriving, and she knew she wouldn't miss that particular job once she left.

'Shall we go out and take a look?'

Sam ignored Jack's knowing grin as they rose from their seats. 'Sure,' Sam said, carefully masking a moment of panic. *Just relax. The replacements look identical.* There was no way her mother would suspect a thing.

Sam waited as her mum opened the gate and walked inside the yard; a loud chorus of squabbling started up at their arrival.

'I've missed watching their antics,' her mum said as a movement in the bushes was shortly followed by the appearance of the fat-bodied little weirdos. They ran out in single file, heading towards something that had obviously caught their eye.

'Ten, eleven, twelve,' her mother counted them off, and Sam let out a relieved sigh. *Good. All accounted for.* 'Oh . . .'

Sam lost her momentary cockiness at her mother's gasp. 'Thirteen . . . fourteen . . . fifteen, sixteen, seventeen, eighteen.' She felt her mother's confused gaze on her but was too busy taking over the count to return her look.

Twenty-two, twenty-three . . . twenty-four. What the actual hell?

'We seem to have acquired a few ring-ins,' her mum said with a confused titter.

Bloody guinea fowl. They've bloody well come back.

'Ah, so there was *one* tiny issue,' Sam was forced to admit guiltily. 'I kind of lost them after the fires, but I didn't want to upset you while you were away, so I, ah . . . replaced them. But apparently they're back now.'

'I see.' Her mum's dry response was tempered by her crooked smile. 'Well, you can never have too many guineas,' she said, shrugging.

That was clearly a matter of opinion, but Sam was glad her mother was at least taking it in her stride.

With one last dirty look at the traitorous fowl, Sam left her mother to wander around and get reacquainted with her feathered friends. At least looking after them was one job she would no longer have to do. And good riddance.

Twenty-seven

The next couple of days were hard. Gone was the routine that Jack and Sam had established when it had just been the two of them. Sam felt torn—she wanted to be with Jack, but she hadn't spent an entire night with him since her parents returned home.

'I hate sneaking around like this,' Jack said as they lay side by side in his bed late in the afternoon.

'I know,' Sam sighed miserably.

'I'm sure your parents are aware that we've been sleeping together.'

'I'm sure they are,' Sam said uneasily, hating that even as a grown-up she couldn't imagine having a conversation with her parents about having her boyfriend stay the night. 'But I really don't feel comfortable flaunting it right under their noses. Alex and Marcie slept in separate beds here at Christmastime even when they'd been living together for months. It just takes Mum and Dad time to get their heads around it.'

'Time's going too fast. You'll be gone in a couple of days,' Jack said, breathing out a long sigh into her hair.

'I know. I can't believe how quickly this week's flown by,' she said, leaning up on her elbows to look at him.

'I can't even imagine this place without you around anymore,' he said softly.

'You're saying it like this is goodbye forever,' she said with slightly nervous enthusiasm.

'Lately, just one day without you here feels like I haven't seen you forever. I'm going soft in my old age,' he added ruefully.

'Oh, I don't know,' she said, wiggling her eyebrows suggestively.

'I'm going to miss you,' he said after a reluctant groan.

'I'll miss you too. But my real-estate friend seems pretty positive. She said she couldn't see it taking more than a couple of months at the longest. So, that's not so bad, and we can always visit in between.'

'A lot can happen in a couple of months,' he said quietly.

The seriousness of his tone made her forehead crease slightly. 'What do you think might happen?'

She watched him give a small shrug. 'I'm just saying, life has a habit of throwing a spanner in the works sometimes.'

'Well, unless it takes a lot longer to sell than I'm expecting, I don't really think there'd be too much that could change our plans. I can't wait to find my perfect little property and have horses again.'

He smiled and seemed to shake off his low mood, pulling her in close. But long after the conversation, a niggling doubt remained. What if things *did* change once she left?

Jack hated being pessimistic. He never used to be, but life had taught him a few harsh lessons in his time, and he and Sam didn't have a great track record when it came to goodbyes. At least this time she would actually give him one, unlike the last time when she'd just up and left him without a word.

Though technically, that wasn't true. They did have words, and it was those words that had made her run as far away from him as she could get.

They'd been lying down at the creek, hand in hand as they stared up at the fluffy white clouds above, and Jack had started to talk about their future. They were about to finish school and he thought their whole lives were about to unfold before them. He'd been excited by the prospect.

But somewhere along the way—unbeknownst to him—Sam's idea of the future had begun to look very different from his. They'd never really spoken about what would happen after they finished school. Sam hadn't had any burning desire to go on to study at university like Chelsea. She and Jack had been perfectly happy living in each other's pockets and were head over heels in love—but in the space of a few weeks, something had changed.

Chelsea left for university to become a teacher and Sam started to talk about travelling.

'But I've got this place to run—Dad needs me here,' Jack had said, confused by her unexpected suggestion that they take off and head north to look for work.

'You're eighteen,' she'd said. 'You have your whole life ahead of you. Don't you want to go off on an adventure before you settle down here and become our parents?'

'Farming's always been my life,' he'd said slowly. 'I don't know how to do anything else.'

'You could learn. I mean, we could even find farm work—fruit picking, anything, really. But let's just get out of here?'

'I can't leave, Sam,' he'd told her, frowning in disbelief. She was serious, he realised, when she continued to look at him as though he'd hurt her feelings. 'I thought this was what you wanted?'

'To end up like our parents?' she'd replied sceptically.

'What's wrong with that?'

'Nothing—later on, but not right now.'

He'd wanted to keep pushing the conversation but he was too scared. He had no idea what she wanted from him. He'd never imagined his life anywhere but right here, and her bombshell had really thrown him. Could he live somewhere else? Do something other than farming? His answer had been an automatic no, until he realised that he'd always assumed Sam would be right here beside him. Without Sam, the life he'd imagined no longer existed.

He'd decided to think on it for a few days before he talked to her about it again, but in the end he didn't have a few more days—Sam had obviously decided he'd made his choice and she was gone two days later.

That had happened when she'd been young and spontaneous. Things were different this time, but he couldn't shake the feeling that if he said goodbye to her again, it would be the end of this thing they'd only just rediscovered. She sounded so sure of her plan, but a part of him worried that once she got back up the coast with her girls and all the glitz and glamour and ocean views, she would realise how lacking Burrumba really was—especially now with everything burnt and desolate and dry.

Both her brothers and their wives had come over for Sunday lunch. It was nice to have the family together; it reminded her of old times when she and Andrew used to visit and everyone came around. Although nowadays all the kids had grown up and left home, other than Alex's kids who were all much younger. She missed her girls even more at the thought.

'I never thought I'd see that again,' her mother said from beside her.

'See what?'

Her mother nodded towards the men gathered on the verandah, talking earnestly. 'Jack. He always did fit in so nicely.'

Unlike Andrew, was the unspoken message. It was true. Maybe once, she would have taken offence on her husband's behalf, but those days were long gone. Looking back, it was always such hard work whenever they came to visit. She would spend her time making sure everyone was comfortable, or explaining why Andrew was out on his phone conducting business at all hours. It had never been easy like this.

'Well, he has more in common with Dad and the boys,' Sam pointed out.

'Are you really going to sell up and move back, then?' Joanne asked, wiping the last of the bowls they'd just washed up.

'Yep. That's the plan,' Sam said nervously. 'I haven't told the kids yet, though . . . I'm not really sure they'll approve.'

Jo made a low throaty sound. 'Kids,' she said, shrugging. 'I still run after my lot like they're a bunch of kindergarten kids. Thomas is always groaning about it.'

'But they all cope living away from home, don't they?' Sam asked, hearing the hopeful tone in her voice and wishing she was a lot more certain she was doing the right thing.

'Of course they do,' Jo chuckled. 'Wouldn't even know we were missing, most of the time—only when they suddenly need something.' She shrugged. 'But it's hard to turn off the mum instinct. When they call, I usually go running.'

'We never ran after you lot once you left home,' Sam's mother put in, using the no-nonsense tone Sam remembered so well growing up. 'And look how you all turned out.'

'They'll be fine,' Jo said reassuringly. 'It's not *that* far away.'

'Yeah. I'm sure they will be.' Sam smiled bravely. She just wasn't looking forward to telling them.

'What are you going to do now you've sold the business?' Marcie asked. 'I mean, you're too young to retire.'

'I'm not really sure.' Originally, she had planned to use the time down here to work out her future—but that was before she found Jack and the whole world seemed to catch on fire.

'Maybe you could open another shop, here?' her mum supplied.

'Maybe,' Sam said hesitantly. But did she really want another homewares boutique? And would it really be suitable for this area? She didn't think so. The Sunshine Coast was a niche area and her shop had cornered the right market, which was why it had been so successful. But up here, it was a whole different demographic.

'You should look at online businesses. That's the only way to go now, in my opinion,' Marcie said, holding Sam's gaze expectantly.

'Well, like I said, I really haven't thought that much on it yet. I'll have to do some research.'

'It's not something you should just jump into.'

No kidding.

'I'm sure Sam knows what she's doing. She's run a successful business before,' Jo informed her younger sister-in-law. Jo could be honest to a fault and was one of those people whose face could never hide her true feelings—which happened a lot around Marcie.

'Research *is* very important,' Sam said, trying to stop what she knew was coming. Marcie always seemed to provoke Jo, who was not the kind of person who would let a passing comment slide.

'And *I* run a successful online nutrition business, so I think I know what *I'm* talking about, Joanne.'

'Maybe she doesn't want to run an online business.'

'Well, if she thinks opening some old bricks-and-mortar shopfront is going to make any money nowadays, she'll be in for a rude shock.'

'This is Burrumba,' Jo reminded her. 'People still like to buy things from a shop.'

'It's outdated and narrow-minded.'

'Well,' Sam cut in, 'like I said, I haven't actually decided what I'll do yet. Maybe I'll just grow my own vegetables and live off the grid for a while,' she joked, but quickly schooled her face into a semblance of seriousness when Marcie glared at her. 'I think I'll go and see if any of the men want tea or coffee,' Sam said, sliding off her chair to hurry outside.

Not for the first time, she wondered what her brother saw in Marcie. Alex was so laidback and Marcie . . . wasn't. In fact, she was the exact opposite of laidback. Still, it wasn't like Sam could talk—she'd married Andrew and he'd stuck out like a sore thumb around here too.

Her thoughts were interrupted as she stood by the door and watched Jack for a moment, sitting there among her family. It made her smile watching him as he talked to her brothers and father. She was lucky to have so many good men in her life.

Her conversation with Jo and Marcie did get her thinking, though. What was she going to do long term? It was all very well to sell up and buy her farm, but she really hadn't thought any further than that. She wasn't desperate for an income; she'd done very well out of the sale of her business, and her house would sell for far more than the value of anything down here, so she could afford to take her time to work out what she wanted to do. It was just a little unsettling to realise she had no idea what that was.

'Think of it as a blank canvas,' Jack said later that night. 'You can do whatever you want to do.'

'Maybe I could be a cattle farmer like you,' she said, grinning.

'I have no doubt you could do whatever you set your mind to,' he replied, kissing her nose.

'On second thought, I think we already have too many cattle farmers in the family.'

'Well, whatever you decide, you'll be great at it.'

'I don't want to leave tomorrow,' she said, suddenly feeling the weight of reality crushing her as they sat together outside under a blanket of stars.

'So, don't,' he said, and when she looked at him, she saw he was watching her intently. 'I'm serious, Sam. Just stay.'

'I have to get the house ready to put on the market.'

'Pay someone to do it.'

'I have to see my kids,' she said.

She heard his long sigh before he gave a reluctant grunt of acceptance. 'Yeah. I know. I just . . . I don't know what I'll do without you here.'

'It won't be for long.'

'What if you change your mind?'

'I won't,' she said. Her answers reminded her of talking to her girls when they were little, trying to reassure them about something that scared them. 'I'm coming back.'

'I know it's stupid,' Jack said, toying with a strand of her hair. 'But I keep remembering how it felt last time you left.'

She'd been angry at him when he'd brought up the past when she'd first returned—she couldn't understand why he'd been so upset over something that had happened when they were kids, but she understood now. She wasn't proud of her eighteen-year-old self—but she'd been just that: an eighteen-year-old, running away from a future that suddenly terrified her.

'I'm sorry I did things that way, back then,' she said after a while. 'I didn't know how to tell you how I was feeling.'

'Which was?'

'Trapped.' She shrugged. 'I felt as though my entire life had been mapped out for me. I had no idea what I wanted to do. Chelsea always knew she wanted to be a teacher, you always knew you wanted to be a farmer—and I had no clue what I wanted to be. I knew I loved you, but I also knew that I couldn't just stay and get married and have a tribe of babies. I would have ended up resenting you, and everything here. I wanted passion in my life. Adventure.'

'And you had that . . . with Andrew,' Jack said, without bothering to hide the bitterness in his tone.

'I had that by heading off with no real idea what I wanted or where I was going. I felt free of expectations . . . of what everyone here wanted me to do.'

'So, *I* was holding you back from life. Taking your freedom?' he pushed.

Sam shook her head. 'I was *eighteen*,' she stressed. She could see that it hurt him to hear it. 'Look, I know I went about it in a truly selfish and heartless way back then. I hurt Mum and Dad too, but they forgave me. Don't you think it's time you did too?'

He ran a hand through his short hair and tipped his head back wearily. 'I know it's stupid to still be cut up about it—I get we were young. I *have* forgiven you,' he said, looking over at her solemnly. 'I guess I'm just worried that you'll get back up there and realise I'm not what you want . . . again.'

'It was never that you weren't what I wanted,' she told him. 'I begged you to come with me.'

'Yeah, I know, and I couldn't.' He sighed.

'Couldn't you have, though?' Sam persisted. 'Okay, I know farming was what you always wanted to do, but you could have taken a couple of months away from this place and at least tried something new.'

He went to open his mouth but shut it again quickly. 'Yeah, maybe you're right. Do you think that would have changed anything, though? Would you have come back here if I tried it but still wanted to come home afterwards?'

Sam considered the question but gave a small, sad smile before shaking her head. 'Probably not.' Once she'd had a taste of freedom and fun, parties and island life, she'd never considered coming back to Burrumba. Not until now.

'So, I guess things worked out the way they were supposed to,' he said.

'I think no matter how we played it—either way, I would have broken your heart.'

'Yeah, well . . . I survived,' he said in an attempt to shrug it off.

'Fate's giving us a second chance now, though,' she said, reaching for his hand and lowering her voice. 'I promise I'm coming back to you.'

When he held her gaze she saw the anxious shadow fade a little and a smile started to turn up the corners of his mouth. 'Promise?'

'I swear.'

She could have spent the night with him, and she would have if they'd been alone, but part of her knew that if she did, she may not be strong enough to leave the next morning. So, instead, they stayed out like they had when they were teenagers, sitting close together on the front verandah swing seat, delaying their goodbye.

She couldn't bear to say it tomorrow before she drove away. The thought took her back to the last time she'd left home. She hated that she'd been such a coward then, but that had been different. She'd known that if she told Jack she was leaving, he would talk her out of it—or worse, he'd have gone with her, only to have it ruin his relationship with his father and kill his own dreams of a future, of farming. He would have eventually resented her, and they would have both ended up miserable.

This time, she was still worried he would talk her out of leaving, but it was something she needed to do. She had to tie up all her loose ends and make sure her children were okay with it before she started a new chapter.

There were tears when she drove away the next morning. Lots of them. She looked back in her rear-view mirror, saw the burnt remains of the ridge disappearing and felt the pull on her heart. *I'll be back*, she whispered, swallowing hard against the lump that had formed in her throat. *I promise.*

Twenty-eight

For a long time, Sam sat in her car in the driveway, staring at the house. She'd been so happy when she'd first bought it—it had felt like home. Her fresh start. Her new beginning. As she sat here now, she remembered that rush of emotion and how proud she'd felt, pulling up here the day she officially got her keys from the real-estate agent.

It seemed like a lifetime ago.

Once inside, Sam put her handbag on the hallway table and began to open windows and doors to let in some fresh air. The house had a strange, stuffy smell and she frowned a little as she tried to work out why. As she walked into the kitchen, she soon discovered the reason.

In the sink sat a stack of used, unwashed cups and plates, along with a frypan left to soak on the stovetop—a thin layer of fat crusting over the top.

The bin, full of glass bottles and empty alcohol cans, hadn't been emptied, and crumbs were scattered across the countertop on a chopping board where someone had made a sandwich.

Sam let out an annoyed huff, knowing exactly who that someone was.

Brook had messaged a few days earlier to say she'd been staying at the house while she caught up with some old friends. Obviously, it hadn't crossed her mind to clean up after herself before she left.

Sam's phone beeped as she was wrestling the garbage bag out of the bin to take outside, and she saw Jack's name come up on the screen.

'Hi. Just seeing how the drive went. Are you home yet?'

'Yep, I'm home,' she said dryly.

'What's wrong?'

'Nothing. Everything's exactly the same here,' she said. She knew she probably had no one to blame but herself for her younger daughter's inability to pick up after herself. After all, Sam had pretty much followed the kids around their whole lives cleaning up their messes. 'I miss you,' she said, pulling out a chair to sit down.

'I miss you too. When are you coming back?'

Sam laughed at his impatient tone. 'I only left this morning,' she pointed out.

'I know, and that's been too long.'

'I'll call the real-estate agent tomorrow and arrange for someone to come out and look at the house and tell me what they think.'

'Sounds good. Have you seen the girls?'

'I stopped in and saw Kenzie on my way through the Gold Coast, but it was only for a quick coffee. She had to get to work. But they'll both be here on the weekend for a longer visit, I can't wait. I've really missed them.'

'I bet. I'm glad you'll get to spend some time with them. But I still miss you.'

'I know and I miss you, but hopefully there'll be some good news about the house.'

They chatted for a bit longer, and when she finally hung up, Sam couldn't deny the flood of homesickness that followed. If she'd had any doubts about her decision to move, that pretty much reassured her that she was doing the right thing.

Getting back to her feet, she picked up the bag of rubbish and headed outside to the wheelie bin. Getting this house cleaned up was the first thing on her to-do list. At least it took her mind off missing Jack for a little while.

'I'm so glad you're home,' Kenzie said, hugging her tightly. 'We missed you.'

'I missed you too,' Sam said, realising just how true it was.

She led the way out onto the back deck, overlooking the Balinese-style tropical garden oasis she'd spent months creating. She poured them each a glass of wine as they sat down.

'This is nice, Mum,' Brook said, taking in the plate of cheese and biscuits and chopped raw vegetables. 'It's like a party.'

'Well, it sort of is. And I've got dinner all planned,' she added, thinking how surprised they would be when they saw the dining table all decked out with crystal and her grandmother's good bone-china dinner set and their favourite things to eat. She wasn't really buttering them up for her announcement, she told herself.

'Oh. Sorry, Mum, I've already got plans,' Brook said. She sent her older sister a frown. 'What? I didn't know we were having dinner.'

'Well, we're home for the weekend,' Kenzie pointed out.

'And we usually go out and visit friends while we're back.'

'It's all right,' Sam cut in before an argument broke out. 'It was just a last-minute thing I decided to do.'

'If it's important, I can cancel,' Brook offered with only the smallest hint of annoyance.

'It's not important, so to speak,' Sam hedged, then figured maybe drawing it out over dinner was simply delaying the inevitable. May as well get it over and done with now. 'I just wanted to tell you both something.'

'Oh no,' Brook said, staring at her mother.

'What?' Sam asked warily.

'Your new boyfriend is moving in.'

'What? No,' Sam said, shaking her head.

'I knew it was more than some mid-life crisis one-night stand,' Brook continued, nodding at her sister. 'I told you.'

'Mid-life . . .' *What the hell?*

'Would you shut up and let Mum talk,' Kenzie snapped.

'It's not about Jack,' Sam continued hesitantly. 'It's about me. And the house. I've decided to put it on the market.'

Both girls stared at her.

'Why? What's wrong with it?' Brook asked slowly.

'Nothing. What I mean is, I've been thinking ever since I went back down to Burrumba, that I'd really like to buy a little farm of my own . . . have a horse and some chooks.' *Not guinea fowl.* 'I've really missed living out of town.'

'You want to buy a farm . . . where?'

'I was thinking back down in New South Wales. Near Nan and Pop.' She saw both girls' eyes widen in alarm. 'Well, they're getting older, and it would be nice to be closer to give them a hand in case they need me.'

'*We* need you,' Brook said bluntly.

'Well, yes, of course, but you've both moved out now and you're away on the Gold Coast . . .'

'But we still come back . . .'

'Yes, I know . . .'

'And what are we supposed to do when *we* need you? It's so far to drive all the way down there.'

'I know it seems like a big step—'

'This is about that man, isn't it? He's the real reason you're moving. You want to be down there with him,' Brook said, standing to move to the railing, crossing her arms.

'No, it's not about that. I was considering the move before I met Jack again.'

'I can't believe this. You're just going to abandon us. For some guy.'

'I'm not abandoning you! You still have your father up here, and it's only five or so hours to get down to Burrumba. You could come down over the holidays. I can come up to the Gold Coast.'

'So, it's all been decided, then?' Brook demanded, throwing her arms in the air.

'Well, more or less . . .' Sam tried not to squirm in her seat. 'I wanted to tell you two first, and then put the house on the market. It's not going to happen overnight. It could take ages to sell.'

'I can't believe you're doing this,' Brook pouted.

'Brook,' Kenzie said sternly.

'And what? You're happy about it? You should be even more upset than I am—'

'Enough,' Kenzie snapped, and glared at her younger sister. 'Just give it a break.'

Sam eyed the two girls, slightly puzzled by the sudden tension between them. 'I know it must be a bit of a shock. I probably should have let you know how I was feeling before, but I didn't even really understand just how unsettled I was until I went back down there. It took me by surprise too.'

'It's okay, Mum. Maybe we just all need some time to let it sink in a bit,' Kenzie said with a weak smile.

'I'm going out. I can't even . . .' Brook announced, flapping a hand in front of her face theatrically, which would have looked funny if Sam wasn't frustrated that her daughter was behaving like a spoilt brat and that her plan for a nice evening had fallen apart.

After the front door shut, Kenzie walked over to hug her. 'I'm glad you're home, Mum. Don't worry about Brooky, she'll come around. You know how she is, always has to sprinkle everything with drama.'

'Is there something else bothering you?' Sam asked, pulling back to eye her eldest daughter curiously. Kenzie had always been the quiet one—the steady, reliable peacemaker. Sometimes to her own detriment. With a younger sister who had such a dominant personality, it was easy to overlook the quieter, self-sufficient sibling. 'You look tired.'

'It's been a really tough year and waiting for my results to come out has got me a little bit stressed.'

'It won't be long now, and I'm sure you don't have anything to worry about where your results are concerned. You've put in the hard work. It'll be fine. I hope you're not coming down with something,' Sam said, touching Kenzie's face to gauge her temperature.

'Actually, if you don't mind, I might have some dinner a bit later? I think I'll just have an early night.'

'Okay,' Sam nodded and managed a smile. 'I'll come up in a minute and bring you a hot Milo.'

'Thanks, Mum,' Kenzie said with a genuine smile.

As Sam watched her leave, she felt the last of her composure slip away. That had not gone at all the way she'd hoped. She'd expected a bit of surprise and maybe stunned silence, but not the anti-Jack protest she'd received from Brook. The more Sam thought about it, the more indignant she felt. It was fine for their father to find a woman half his age and start a new life, but the thought of her having a man in her life now, after all this time, was some kind of betrayal?

Maybe if she hadn't been racked with guilt these past few weeks thinking about moving away—and so caught off guard by Brook's outburst—she might have been able to defend herself. Packing away the table she'd set only a few hours earlier, she let the methodical movements calm her. Kenzie was right, they all just needed some time apart to let the news sink in so they could discuss it calmly. Surely they would come around.

Twenty-nine

'How did it go?' Jack asked later that night when she called him.

'Not great.'

'Really?'

Jack heard Sam let out a frustrated sigh on the other end of the phone and could picture that little frown she wore when something bothered her. 'I think it just took them both by surprise. I probably should have dropped some hints about the possibility earlier so they wouldn't feel so sideswiped.'

'Then if they didn't like the idea, you would have been arguing with them over the phone and feeling bad about it while you were down here,' he pointed out logically.

'I guess so. I'm just a bit disappointed that Brook was so against the idea. I'm not sure Kenzie was thrilled by the prospect either, but as usual she was trying to be the rational one.'

'Maybe just give it a few days.' He wished he was there with her so he could hold her and help soothe away her stress.

'What about you? How did your girls take it?' They'd agreed that it was time to start preparing his daughters in case her house sold faster than they expected.

'I, ah, still haven't had a chance to bring it up.'

'Oh.' There'd only been a slight pause before she'd answered, but it had sounded deafeningly long.

'I've been busy fencing and haven't been able to catch them for a chat.'

'That's okay. There's no real rush.'

'I'll tell them next time I call.'

'I don't know why I'm feeling so anxious.'

'Me either.'

'I guess because it's not just about you and me. It's bigger than the two of us.'

'Yeah. I guess so,' he said. He was feeling down because he'd just found out that the girls weren't coming for Christmas. It wasn't a total surprise—after all, it wasn't like there was a house to come back to, but he'd been planning a campout and had hoped it would still be fun, but apparently the kids didn't think so. Or, rather, Cilia didn't. 'It will be too traumatic for them to see the place the way it is at the moment,' she'd said in her text. He now planned on driving down later instead, to drop off their presents and catch up with them—but it wouldn't be the same. It never was when he went down there.

'It's only a few weeks until Christmas, and I'll be down. We'll sort everything out then,' Sam said and he heard the determination she'd forced into her tone. She was right. His Christmas plans may not be turning out as he'd hoped, but at least he would see Sam soon. He felt his mood lighten a little at the thought. Thank God for Sam. This year, Christmas would have been pretty bloody dismal without her—*especially* this year. Christ, he hated even thinking about how he would have handled any of this without Sam in his life right now. The thought unsettled him more than he cared to admit.

He dropped the post he'd been wrestling into the hole and rested his arms across it, wiping his brow as he looked back at the morning's work. The freshly dug holes of his new fence line stood out like dark ant nests just before the rain, earth piled up in a high mound beside the holes, down the hillside and beyond. If there had to be a silver lining in all this, it was that at least now he could put in the new paddocks he'd been wanting to—but hadn't had a good enough reason to change before. His old man and his grandfather before him had designed the paddock layout decades ago and although it had served its purpose back then, it was time to upgrade and make a few changes in line with how Jack did things today.

He looked up when Alex came to a stop beside him. He grinned as his mate took off the leather work gloves he'd been wearing, slapping them against his thigh to shake the dirt off. 'Bet you're wishing you hadn't got out of the navy now. Didn't have to work so hard back then.'

'Nah, bit of fresh air and exercise was just what I needed,' Alex shot back as he picked up a bottle of water and drank deeply.

'Thanks again, mate. I wanted to get a head start on the fencing.'

'All good. You still got BlazeAid coming out?'

The volunteer organisation had recently arrived in town and were in the process of working their way through the lengthy number of requests for help to replace fencing in the district. 'Yeah, your sister dragged me along to sign up the other day. They might be a while, though. There's hardly a decent-standing fence in the whole district.'

'I'm glad Sam made you register. There's no shame in asking for help. Especially now.'

'Yeah, I know. It's just not something I'd normally do.'

'There's nothing normal about what this valley's just gone through. People want to help.' Alex screwed the lid back on his bottle and dropped it to the ground. 'How are things going with you two, anyway?'

Jack thought back to the conversation he'd had last night with Sam about the kids.

'*We're* doing okay. It's just working it out with the kids.'

He didn't think his girls would take it too badly. They'd been okay with their mother and Paul getting together. He worried about Sam's girls, though. He hated hearing her so down about it.

'Which ones are you having trouble with?' Alex asked.

'I haven't told mine yet.'

'How come?' his friend asked, taking a seat on the esky after pulling out two packs of sandwiches for lunch and tossing one to Jack.

'I haven't really had the chance.'

'Haven't had the chance or haven't *taken* the chance?'

'I've been a bit busy, in case you haven't noticed,' Jack said, feeling a little defensive. It was an important conversation—he needed it to happen at the right time and place.

'Well,' Alex said, taking a bite of his chicken sandwich, 'I reckon her girls will come around. They're good kids. Probably just a bit of a shock to them. Sam's a bloody good mum but they've just been a little . . .' He paused, choosing his words carefully. 'Sheltered. Their father kind of spoils them, but I think Sam's managed to counteract it with a bit more of a level head. They'll come good.'

'I hope so.' Deep down Jack knew Alex was right. It was just a knee-jerk reaction and in time they would get used to the idea, but it made him nervous nevertheless. What if they didn't come around and it changed Sam's mind about moving back?

He knew he was being a tad melodramatic, but loneliness could do that to a bloke. Christ, he missed her. He just wanted their life to get started. He looked around at the progress he'd made but realised there was still a very long way to go. He had nothing to offer her even if she did come back right now, and the thought only depressed him further. He'd been using the promise of a future home to drive himself harder, yet there wasn't a lot to show for it. Sure, he was at least now starting the fencing, but he still didn't have a house and that didn't look like it would be changing anytime soon.

He wasn't alone there. Red tape was holding everyone up. Health inspectors, council inspectors and insurance inspectors all had to come by and submit their reports before anything could move forward. And then there was the clean-up—removal of toxic waste and old building scrap materials. Team's of people, and the equipment needed to organise the massive undertaking, had to be sourced before they could start work, and the number of properties affected meant the waiting list was incredibly long. It was going to be months before they reached Jack's place and there was nothing he could do about it except wait. Wait and work.

Now that he had some fencing in place, he and his neighbours would try to muster as many lost stock as they could find in the national park. He just hoped they managed to track down the majority of them. He'd spent too many years and too much money breeding his stock to have to start again—but chances were he was going to have to. His thoughts went back to the fire and he felt a shiver of dread as he remembered the inferno. There wasn't much hope that many animals would have survived. Yet, some had been spotted, so he tried his best to remain positive and prayed they managed to find them.

It didn't feel like Christmas this year. Sam tried to find her festive spirit, but there just didn't seem to be the same vibe about this year.

Before the fires, the family had planned on a big Christmas gathering down at Burrumba. Mackenzie and Brooklyn were supposed to come, as well as her brothers' kids, so all the cousins would finally be together for the first time in years. But plans had changed.

Thanks to the fires, Jo and Thomas now had to go to their daughter Lucy's place to lend a hand with the clean-up down south, and both of Sam's girls had decided not to go away for Christmas this year, either. They would spend the day with their father.

'I'm sorry, Mum, but there are too many things on up here that I can't miss. I promise I'll go down and visit Nan and Pop in the new year,' Brook had said when Sam had tried to pin her down for a time to leave.

Even Kenzie, whom Sam had always counted on to be reliable, decided to stay home.

Sam was upset, but she missed Jack too much to let it weigh on her.

She should have had the house on the market by now. But she didn't. She found herself delaying—she wanted to get a gardener in to tidy up the landscaping and then realised the rooms really should have a new coat of paint. She wanted to make sure she got as much as she could for it; after all, this was her nest egg, the key to starting her new life. It was important. But deep down, she knew that it was the uncertainty kicking in.

Brook's reaction to her news had thrown her. She told herself to ignore the outburst—that it was just Brook being a drama queen—but that familiar twinge of guilt had begun to poke its head up again lately and at night she found herself defending her reasons for such a huge life change. *Was* she abandoning her kids?

It was also not helping that Jack hadn't been able to come up before now and meet the girls in person. He was busy rebuilding his own life, she understood that, and it was hard for him to leave right now. But it only added to the uncertainty.

She wanted the girls to get to know him, and so far that hadn't happened.

Sam had hoped that Christmas would finally be the time it all fell into place, but that seemed unlikely now. She was feeling fed up and annoyed by everything, which wasn't like her, especially at Christmas, her favourite time of the year.

Earlier, her mum had called to say her sister had had a nasty fall and she and Sam's father were going to have to go down to the Central Coast to lend a hand for a week or so until they sorted out some home care for her—which meant Christmas was officially cancelled. Then Jack had called and pretty much sealed the deal that this was the worst Christmas ever.

'It's all right,' she said after Jack told her that Cilia didn't want their girls going up to him this year while everything was still so traumatic after losing the house. 'I can see how she would be worried it would be too sad for them,' Sam ventured, although she also knew that Jack needed his kids around him at this time more than ever. He'd been through so much, and having his daughters with him would have helped take his mind off some of the endless worries he was dealing with trying to rebuild his property.

'She wants me to go down there.'

'How do you feel about that?'

'Frustrated. I spoke with the girls, and they're upset about seeing the place after the fires—and I understand. I still haven't got used to it and I see it every day. It probably is too soon for them to come back here, but I can't imagine not seeing them for Christmas.'

'I think you should go,' Sam said, even though the thought of not seeing him made her miserable. 'You *need* to see them. You need a break from all the work you've been doing.'

'I was thinking maybe you could come with me, but I still haven't told them. It's not that I've been avoiding it,' he said quickly, 'I just wanted to do it in person while they were here, but now they're not coming.'

'It's okay. I think they probably need your undivided attention.' Sam tried not to feel hurt. But he was right—if she went down there with Jack, and the girls didn't take it well, it might sour the relationship forever.

'I really hate not spending Christmas with you like we planned, though.'

'I'll be down there soon and we'll have every day together,' she said, forcing a cheeriness to her tone she was far from feeling. 'Just go and see your kids. Besides, it'll give me more time to get things sorted out here so I can get down there faster.'

She hung up feeling deflated and miserable. It wouldn't feel like Christmas back home in Burrumba anyway, she tried to console herself. The blackened remains of bushland and the continued heat would only sap any semblance of festiveness. It would also be hard to celebrate when so many people had lost so much. Nope—better to just wipe Christmas this year and plan for a better, brighter one next year.

'I've got an early Christmas present for you,' Jack announced two days later.

'Really? What?'

'How would you like some guests for Christmas?'

'Who?' she asked, her mind starting to buzz.

'The girls and me,' he replied, his initial excitement now a little dulled.

'You're bringing them *here*?'

'Surprise,' he said a little hesitantly.

It was certainly that. Just when Sam had finally accepted that she would be alone for Christmas. 'But you said you couldn't get the girls for Christmas this year?'

'I spoke to Cilia, and she was happy for them to be away from Burrumba. I told the girls about us. We've had a long talk and they're very excited to head up the coast and visit. If it's okay?' he added, sounding unsure.

'Of course it's okay.' Sam finally recovered from her initial shock. 'It's more than okay! You just surprised me. Wow. This is so exciting.' She felt a slightly hysterical smile fix itself on her face.

'This is fucking terrifying!'

'They're a couple of baby teenagers,' Chelsea said calmly on the other end of Sam's frantic call as soon as Jack hung up. 'You've handled teenage daughters before. You've got this.'

'Those were *my* teenage daughters . . . these are someone else's. I probably can't threaten them like I could my own.'

'No, probably not, but you know kids—they're always little angels for other people. They'll be fine,' Chelsea soothed, and Sam could picture her friend waving a blasé hand in the air.

'It's not them I'm worried about. What if they hate me? I don't want to be a wicked stepmother.'

'Would you calm down? They're not going to hate you—you're unhateable. Everyone loves you. Just be yourself.'

Chelsea's words were still ringing in Sam's ears two days later as she waited at the airport arrivals gate, searching for Jack in the surge of travellers filing out through the open doors.

She spotted him, a head taller than the crowd around him, dressed in a light blue button-up shirt and jeans, carrying a large duffle bag over one shoulder. God, she'd missed him. She saw him eventually find her and for a moment as he smiled across at her, she forgot how nervous she was about meeting his daughters. Jack was here and everything was right again in the world.

He dropped the bag and leaned down. There was an awkward moment when Sam went in to kiss him but he pulled her into a kind of sideways hug, patting her on the back like some long-lost war buddy. As they pulled away, he gave a quick, nervous glance beside him and cleared his throat. 'Sam, this is Bianca and Tasmin.'

Sam mentally smoothed her hair into place and adjusted her pride before smiling at the two girls who were openly scrutinising her. 'Hi, girls, it's really lovely to finally meet you. How was your trip?'

'Dad bought the cheap tickets, so there was no food or drinks,' Bianca announced bluntly, clearly unimpressed by the whole ordeal.

'We sat behind a man with smelly feet,' Tasmin added.

'Oh dear.' Sam winced sympathetically. 'That doesn't sound like much fun at all. How about we go out for lunch, then? You must all be starving.'

'Yes,' Tasmin agreed vivaciously. 'We *are* starving.' Her blue eyes lit up, and Sam laughed at her infectious smile. She turned her eyes onto the older sibling and felt her smile freeze. Unlike her sister, Bianca stood regarding Sam with a bored, petulant expression, one hip kicked out, arms folded across a ripped midriff T-shirt that had 'whatever' scrawled across it in a very angry-looking font.

Sam's gaze skittered back to Jack's and she saw a hint of apprehension hidden just under the surface of his eyes; clearly he felt out of his depth here too. She summoned her best we-got-this-gosh-darn-it smile and saw a faint glimmer of relief flutter across his face in response. 'Well, let's go eat!'

Jack fell in step with her behind the girls and bent down close to her ear as they headed out. 'Is this a bad idea?'

Sam shook her head and her smile softened. 'Not at all. It's going to be fine. We just all need to settle in a bit. You'll see.'

'Christ, I hope so—so far everything I've done is wrong,' he muttered.

'We'll have a great Christmas. I promise.'

If there was one thing Sam knew how to do, it was Christmas. She had this covered.

'Wow, this place is awesome,' Tasmin gaped as she walked in the front door of Sam's house. 'It's like Christmas threw up everywhere!'

Sam's proud smile teetered slightly, but seeing Tasmin's wide-eyed look of awe made her think it might have been a compliment.

'What do you reckon, sweetheart?' Jack asked Bianca, who'd just walked inside, dragging her suitcase behind her.

'That's a lot of Christmas,' she murmured, slowly sliding her sunglasses on top of her head. Sam didn't get the same feeling about Bianca's reaction.

'Sam, this is seriously impressive. I hope you didn't go to all this trouble just for us?' Jack said, taking in the decorated stairs and entrance hall complete with Santa on a throne surrounded by his elves and reindeer in a nook under the staircase.

'Oh, no. I do this every year.' She'd always gone all out for Christmas, but this year was a bit more last-minute than usual. After Jack's call, Sam had gone into a panic and put up . . . well, *everything*. She'd been like a madwoman, only finishing the last of the decorating two hours before she'd had to head into the airport to collect them.

'How about I show you to your rooms, girls?' she offered, leading the way out to the rear of the house. 'I've given you the two rooms down here. There's a connecting bathroom between them and you should have everything you need in there.'

'Where's Dad sleeping?' Bianca asked, arching an eyebrow in a manner that belied her fifteen years.

'Ah, I've got him in the guest room upstairs.'

'Go put your suitcases in your rooms,' Jack said, nodding towards the open doors.

'If you want, the pool's out the back. You're welcome to go for a swim.'

'Yes!' Tasmin said, fist pumping the air. 'Come on, Bee!'

Bianca rolled her eyes as she reluctantly followed her younger sister, but she didn't argue. Maybe the pool would be Sam's saving grace.

'Please show me my room,' Jack said, lowering his voice.

Sam stifled a giggle as he took her hand and pulled her towards the stairs. 'Certainly, sir. It's right this way.'

She led him upstairs and opened the door to the office, where she'd made up the sofa bed for him. 'Sorry it's the office, but I'm told the sofa bed is really comfortable.'

Jack kicked the door shut with the heel of his boot and pulled her close to kiss her. When they pulled away, Sam struggled to catch her breath. This was ridiculous! She was a grown woman of two adult children, but right in this very moment, she could have been a teenage girl again—tingling and prickling all over with a burning need to lose herself in the man before her.

'I wanted to do that at the airport,' Jack said, resting his forehead against hers. She'd missed this—the closeness, the comfortable completeness of finding her other half.

'I'm glad you didn't. I think Bianca would have turned around and caught the first plane home.'

'I know she's acting a bit . . .' He paused, seeming to search for a word. 'She just takes a little bit to warm up to new people. She'll come around.'

'Oh. Yeah. Of course,' Sam said in an offhand way. She tried not to dwell on the fact that his daughter seemed less than impressed by her. 'We've got the next few days to get to know each other.'

'By the time we leave, they'll love you as much as I do,' he promised, kissing her once more.

The door swung open and Bianca stood there, leaning against the doorframe. 'Tasmin didn't bring a towel.'

Sam sprang away like she'd accidentally touched the electric fence around her dad's bull paddock. 'Oh. No problem. I'll get her one. I was just showing your dad his room.'

The silent stare Bianca gave them spoke louder than any disapproval she could have voiced as Sam walked past her, relieved to get out of the room. *Are you seriously going to allow this kid to treat you like a child?* she silently berated herself. A quick glance over her shoulder as she reached the bottom of the staircase confirmed the teen was watching her with a suspicious frown. It was only the first day. Things were bound to get better. Surely?

'Brook, remember all those times I could have sold you on the black market but didn't, and you were looking for a way to repay me?' Sam asked her daughter, after sneaking into the bathroom to make an emergency FaceTime call.

'Ah, no,' Brook answered, tossing her long hair over her shoulder. 'I don't recall ever giving you any trouble, Mother.'

'Right,' Sam answered in a deadpan tone. 'Well, anyway, here's your chance to make it up to me.'

'Why are you whispering in the bathroom?'

'I don't have time to explain. I need your help.'

'Doing what?'

'Jack and the girls are here. They hate me. Help!'

'Wow. When did that happen?'

'It was all very last-minute.'

'I'm sure they don't hate you . . . Wait, you didn't try to be all sugary and sickly sweet, did you? Cause that's how Taylor acted when we first met her at Dad's and it was *super* annoying.'

'I wouldn't say I was *sickly* sweet . . .' Sam started.

'Did you do that weird, high-pitched-voice thing, like when you talk to a cute puppy?'

Sam gave a dismissive snort. '*No.*'

Brook stopped walking and stared down at the phone. 'Mum, kids pick up on fear. It's like with a substitute teacher in class—they know how to pick off the weak ones. Look,' she said, softening her tone at her mother's slightly horrified expression, 'just be yourself. You're a great mum, and if those brats can't see that, then they don't deserve you in their lives.'

'They're not brats,' Sam said quickly. She didn't need to put any more obstacles in the way of future blended-family happiness. 'But thank you.'

'Let them pick out their Christmas gift,' Brook said suddenly. 'Like you always did with us. That was the best, getting to choose our own outfits to dress up in on Christmas Day. At least they'll like what they pick and you won't ruin everything by choosing something uncool.'

'I never chose uncool outfits for you two.' Sam frowned a little.

'Trust me—let the brats pick out their own stuff. It's a sure-fire way to score points.'

'They're not br—' Sam started before Brook cut in.

'Sorry, Mum, I have to go. I'm meeting the gang. I'll talk to you tomorrow.'

The screen froze on the image of her youngest daughter waving before it went blank and Sam gave a frustrated sigh.

'Dinner smells good,' Jack said, coming up behind her in the kitchen.

They'd swum most of the afternoon and laid about on the deck chairs. Tasmin was funny and charming. She was curious about everything and asked a million questions, and Sam couldn't help but love her wide-eyed innocence about the world.

Bianca, however, remained aloof. Sam knew it would take more than one visit to crack this particular egg, but they only had a few days. Sam saw a bit of her father in her—the thoughtful way she seemed to sit back and take everything in—but she suspected there was a lot of her mother in there, too. Sam hadn't known Cilia well, but she'd seemed a nice enough person—and she must have been if Jack had decided to make a life with her. Sam and Jack had spoken about their respective spouses, and Sam knew that Jack had been gutted when Cilia left him, but she suspected they'd been drifting apart for a while before that. She knew that Jack took commitment seriously, and as she watched him with his children now, she could see just how much he missed not having them with him every day.

'I thought maybe the girls and I could go shopping tomorrow,' Sam announced as they ate dinner that evening. 'Then we could head to the beach in the afternoon?'

'I don't get an invitation to come shopping?' Jack asked, lifting an eyebrow.

'You hate shopping, Dad,' Tasmin reminded him as she buttered her roll.

'You can come along if you want,' Sam offered, knowing exactly how much he would detest walking around a huge shopping centre.

'No,' Bianca jumped in. 'He'll only keep asking if we're done and *how much longer?*'

Sam's spirits lifted slightly. Bianca sounded almost . . . friendly. 'Well, we don't want that,' she said with only a hint of apology towards Jack.

'Fine, then,' he sighed. 'You three go off and have fun . . . I'll find something to keep me occupied.'

Later, when they finally had a quiet moment together once the girls went to bed, Sam brought up the shopping trip again. 'I hope you didn't mind me asking to take the girls tomorrow? I'm just trying to find something in common with them and I thought maybe some last-minute Christmas shopping might help break the ice.'

'I think it's a great idea, and you couldn't have picked a better activity—they love shopping and I never take them.'

'I have had daughter experience,' she reminded him. 'Shopping can pretty much fix anything; it's a cure for teenage heartbreak *and* the blackmail reward for cleaning a bedroom.'

'I don't for a moment doubt you'll have them wrapped around your little finger by the time you get back,' he murmured. 'Just like you have their father.'

For the first time all day, they were free to enjoy each other without the hovering pressure of kids walking in on them, but they'd agreed, for this trip at least, separate bedrooms would be the best option. It was a big enough adjustment for the girls just being under a stranger's roof. But it definitely was not the most favourable option when Sam missed Jack so damn much. It was torture finally having him so close, and yet so far.

Sam took the girls to the large plaza, which, had they come from Burrumba, would have been *completely* impressive; but they lived in Newcastle, so it was probably not quite so exciting. Still, a shopping centre was a shopping centre and the smell of a sale still beckoned. They roamed from store to store and Sam asked them to each pick out an outfit for their Christmas present—which she told herself was not bribing them for their affection, it was simply being practical.

The shopping spree was a hit, and both girls were happy that Sam had let them choose their gift, although it did slightly backfire when Bianca held up a very short pair of ripped denim shorts and a faded, dirty-looking T-shirt that resembled the rags Sam kept under her laundry sink. 'Ah, I'm not sure your dad would be happy with those shorts . . . what about a skirt?' Sam suggested, turning to a rack behind her before realising they too all looked more like belts than skirts. In fact, the whole shop had a grungy, angry feel about its fashion. *Who the hell even decided this is fashion?* she wondered, hating that she sounded like her own mother had when Sam was a teenager. 'Or maybe we could look in another store?'

The crestfallen face Bianca gave her plucked at her heartstrings and she found herself reconsidering. 'But okay, if that's the outfit you want.'

Beside her, Tasmin gave a churlish snort. 'Dad's gonna freak when he sees that,' she warned in a sing-song voice.

'Maybe we can talk him around,' Sam said, trying for a confident tone but already bracing for a major fallout.

'Good luck,' Tasmin sympathised, idly flicking through the racks. She'd already chosen her outfit, a pair of denim overalls—ripped, of course, because clearly no one wanted anything that actually looked as though it might be new—and a plain white T-shirt. 'Are you sure you just want a T-shirt?' Sam had asked.

'She's got no style—she's always been the same,' Bianca said, shaking her head slowly at her younger sister.

'I do so have style. Just because I don't like showing off my boobs and backside to boys,' Tasmin taunted and Sam stepped in, quickly dismantling the potential argument as swiftly as a bomb technician disabled an explosive. She just hoped Jack was in a good mood when he saw what she'd bought his eldest child to wear.

On the drive home, Sam took them along the prestigious Hastings Street with its glamorous boutiques beside Noosa's main beach. Leafy pandanus trees lined the street, lending a tropical, laidback resort feel to the shopping strip. They parked and she showed the girls her old shop, which had been renamed but not entirely rebranded.

'You used to own this?' Tasmin asked as she licked her ice-cream, trying to catch it before it ran down her hand.

'Yep.'

'Do you miss it?' Bianca surprised her by asking.

'Sometimes,' Sam answered and realised that this was the first time she'd returned since selling it and she actually did miss it, but not the stress that had come with it. It was a nice realisation.

'It's pretty cool.'

Sam stifled a smile, not daring to show just how chuffed the small comment made her feel. She decided to quit while she was ahead. 'We better get home and see what mischief your dad's got up to while we've been away.'

'I can't wait to show him my new clothes,' Tasmin said with a skip in her step as they returned to the car.

'I can't wait to see his face when he sees mine,' Bianca said, sending her an innocent grin in the rear-view mirror as Sam slid into the driver's seat.

'Ah, let's not ruin the surprise. Besides, I have to wrap them and put them under the tree. They're your Christmas presents.' *Small victories*, she told herself calmly. *Small, small victories.*

In the end, Christmas Day went off splendidly. They spent it eating and swimming and lazing beside the pool, and in the afternoon they went for a long walk along the beach, which dazzled them with a perfect sunset to end the day. Jack had handled the fashion choices a lot better than Sam had expected. It seemed he was resigned to accept the fact he was outnumbered, and unequipped where fashion was concerned.

The time had gone too fast. Much too fast. The next day they would drive back to the airport, ready to head home again. And Sam would once again have to say goodbye to Jack.

Jack couldn't believe he'd done something as impulsive as booking three tickets to the Sunshine Coast. It had cost him a not-so-small fortune, with all the connecting flights and Christmas-holiday price explosions, but he didn't care. Cilia had given him a window of three days with the girls, and he knew exactly what he wanted to do with them.

He'd be lying if he said it hadn't also been for him—he missed Sam in a way he hadn't thought possible to miss another person before—but it was also important to him that she met his girls.

They had taken the news better than he'd expected, which was a nice change. He knew Bianca wasn't thrilled by the idea of this new arrangement. It wasn't anything she said so much as the change in her manner. She'd become quieter, which was always a sign she was withdrawing into herself to try to deal with something.

He'd tried to reassure them and explain how important Sam was to him, while at the same time making sure they understood he would never stop loving them. They'd been through a divorce and had already adjusted to their life being turned upside down once, then again when Cilia and Paul got together. He'd hoped by now another change wouldn't be so strange for them, but it was going to take time to adjust, for all of them.

Sam had been great with them—he'd been grateful when she'd taken them shopping, helping them buy gifts that made Christmas Day extra special. Whatever happened while they were out seemed to make things better. Bianca was less uptight, and Sam looked a little more relaxed.

And now they were at the airport waiting to fly home and he felt like they'd hardly had any time alone together.

He watched as both girls hugged Sam goodbye. Bianca's hug may have still been a little stiff, but it was a vast improvement to when they arrived.

'Girls, what do you say?' he prompted.

'Thank you for having us,' Tasmin said.

'And for taking us shopping—Mum wouldn't let me buy those shorts last week, and now I have them,' Bianca added.

'What?' both Sam and Jack chorused. Sam looked a little pale all of a sudden.

'Just kidding.' Bianca grinned, and Jack shook his head. 'Seriously, though, thanks for making Christmas kinda cool. I didn't think we'd have much fun this year.' She glanced across at her father. 'We really wanted to come and see Dad, but with everything burnt . . .' She wiped her eyes quickly, and Jack felt his throat close up as Tasmin stepped closer and slipped her hand into her big sister's. 'I'm glad we came up here instead.'

'I'm really glad you all came up here, too,' Sam said, reaching out to squeeze both girls' hands, before they moved across to wait at the gate.

Teenage daughters were certainly no walk in the park, Jack was discovering, but there were times like these that his heart swelled with pride. *I'm the luckiest bloke around*, he thought, feeling a wave of unexpected emotion and clearing his throat. He wished Sam was coming with them, but he fought the urge to beg her like he wanted to, instead pulling her close and burying his face in her hair as he held her tightly.

'I love you,' he said softly. 'Hurry up and come home.'

He felt her squeeze her arms tighter around his waist and heard a small sniff before she nodded against his chest. 'I love you, too.'

As the plane lifted off the tarmac, Jack leaned back against the head rest and closed his eyes. He didn't want to see her fade into a tiny speck below as they pulled away and left her far behind. Until she was back home with him, he would always feel like he had a gaping hole inside him.

He wasn't sure how many more times he could bring himself to say goodbye to her.

'I miss you,' Sam said as she sat on her back deck three days after Jack and the girls had left. She'd finally finished all the odd jobs she'd been putting off and had an appointment with the real-estate agent to come around and take photos of the house. It was exciting and a little scary, but she couldn't wait to tell Jack.

'I miss you, too,' he said with a sigh.

'You sound like you've had a hard day?'

'Sorry, yeah, I'm stuffed. Fencing didn't used to feel so hard when I was younger,' he joked, although she suspected he was only half kidding.

'You've never had to fence a whole property from scratch, though.'

'Yeah. True. That's great news about listing the house. Hopefully it'll sell fast.'

'Do you think you can manage another trip anytime soon? I'm really hoping to get the girls here together one weekend.'

She was becoming increasingly frustrated with both her daughters. Ever since breaking the news about selling the house and moving, there seemed to be a decided lack of communication. She knew having other stuff to do for Christmas had been a snub; neither of them had tried especially hard to get here while Jack and his girls had visited. She was going to have to address it very soon—the last thing she wanted was to leave when everyone was upset. It had to stop.

'I don't know when I'll be able to get up there again, Sam. Things are pretty busy down here.'

'I know,' she said, trying not to sound as miserable as she was feeling. He had a lot to do, she understood that, but lately he seemed a bit distant. She worried that he was taking on too much with the rebuild and not asking for enough help, but every time she tried to bring it up, he shut her down. 'Mum said there's been a few meetings happening at the hall about financial help and grants for farmers.' She hesitated briefly before adding, 'And counselling. Have you been along to any? Is there anything that might help you there?'

'I heard about them. I was too busy to go along.'

'I think there's another one coming up. Mum said she was helping cater for it.'

'Yeah, I'll see. Listen, I gotta go. I'll call you tonight when I get back to the house, okay?'

'Oh. Sure. Okay. I miss you.'

'Miss you too,' he said before hanging up, leaving Sam to stare at the phone thoughtfully before she went back to her packing.

Something had changed since Sam went back to the Sunshine Coast, but Jack wasn't sure what. She was still talking about *when* she was moving down, not *if*, but there was something he couldn't quite put his finger on that troubled him.

He knew she was anxious for him to meet her girls. He wanted that too, and he was planning on going back up, but there was just so much to do. Sometimes the sheer enormity of what he faced overwhelmed him. He occasionally found himself wondering if it was even worth it. He knew he should probably talk to her about it—really talk about it—but instead he found himself brushing over the details. She had enough to worry about at the moment and it wasn't like she could actually *do* anything.

He knew part of the reason he shut her out was because he'd been raised to believe he should be able to deal with all this stuff on his own. He was the fixer, just like his father before him. His dad was the kind of man who just got on with whatever needed doing. They'd gone through tough times growing up, times when money had been tight and beef prices low, when hail had destroyed their winter food and left them with huge feed bills, when expensive machinery up and died and needed to be replaced—all causes of extreme stress for their family, but never once had he seen his old man reach out and dump all his problems on anyone else. He would just get up earlier, work harder, do whatever it took to fix what needed fixing. *He never lost everything, though*, a small voice reminded Jack now. And that was true. Jack had wondered many times since this all happened what his dad would have done. He wouldn't be sitting down in some doctor's office talking about how he felt—Jack knew that much.

Besides, he had people he could talk to—the RFS were all about talking everything out nowadays, and there was a never-ending supply of handouts and flyers shoved in his letterbox from different organisations offering the community help—but talking wouldn't solve his current situation. Only hard, draining, physical labour could fix what needed mending right now, and it was all he knew how to do. He would just have to deal with all the other stuff later.

Thirty

'Sorry, Jack. We won't have any more in until next week. We just can't keep up with demand at the moment and sourcing stuff has been a nightmare,' Ted from the feed store said wearily. It seemed everyone was in a permanent state of exhaustion lately.

Jack had run out of wire for the fencing, and another delay was the last thing he needed. The longer he waited, the harder it would be to track down his missing cattle. On the upside, it now meant he had some forced downtime on his hands.

He could head up the coast. The thought of seeing Sam again went a long way to soothing some of the sting the halt in progress had caused, and by the time he arrived home he was actually looking forward to it. He took out his phone and dialled the number, grabbing his overnight bag and stuffing clothes in as he waited for the video call to connect.

'Hey.' Sam's bright smile lit up the room. 'I was just thinking about you,' she said, then narrowed her eyes. 'What are you doing?'

'Packing,' he said with a grin. He watched her eyes open wide as understanding dawned.

'You're coming up?'

'I am. I can't do anything more here for a few days, so I figured I'd use the time to come and annoy you up there.'

'Feel free to come and annoy me as much as you like.' She beamed, and his heart did a flipflop when he thought that in a few hours' time he would have her in his arms.

'I'm leaving right now. I'll see you soon.'

As the towns passed by outside his window, he felt some of the tension he'd been carrying begin to ease. The knots in his stomach lessened and for the first time in weeks he was filled with a renewed optimism about the future. After this visit, Sam would know how much he missed her and they would get their plan back on track. Everything would fall into place. It had to. He couldn't imagine a future any other way.

Jack felt his heart kick out of rhythm for a second as he relived that moment the door opened and he saw her again.

She was stunning.

For the briefest of moments, he'd been uncertain of his welcome. There'd been a flicker of something—uncertainty, maybe, in her eyes—and the fact she was wearing make-up and a summer dress had momentarily thrown him, but then she'd reached out for him and everything was okay again. It was more than okay. It was perfect. He held her in his arms and he felt complete once more.

He'd been moping about for the past four weeks like some love-sick bastard. Miserable that she wasn't there and restless because he worried that maybe she was beginning to regret her decision and realise how much she'd missed her life up here.

'I had every intention of *not* jumping your bones the minute I laid eyes on you, you know,' he said now as they lay in her bed, still fascinated by how soft her skin felt under his fingertips.

'Oh, really?' she replied lazily.

'I usually pride myself on my self-discipline and restraint.' He grinned at her un-ladylike snort and loosened his hold as she turned to look at him.

'I, for one, am glad you didn't employ your usual restraint,' she said, smiling.

'I missed you, Sam.' He'd meant it lightly but was unprepared for the intensity that swiftly followed. 'The place doesn't feel the same without you.' It wasn't just the fires that had changed everything . . . it went deeper than that. Without her, he'd lost the new spark she'd lit inside him, a spark that hadn't been there in a very long time. For years he had just existed, and it wasn't until Sam came back into his life that he realised how much happiness he had missed out on. It made the loss of her so much harder to bear.

'I missed you, too,' she said softly, touching the stubble on his face. 'More than I thought it was possible to miss another person.'

Her words went a long way to easing any remaining fear he'd had about her changing her mind, and for the first time since arriving he allowed himself to relax a little.

It was an afternoon like he'd never experienced before. Suddenly, he had no stock to tend to, no fencing to do, nothing that needed his attention except Sam, who managed to distract him over and over again. He couldn't think of a time when he'd lazed about in bed in the middle of the day. Was this what normal, non-farming people did?

He wasn't sure he could handle all this free time. Then again, he thought as Sam stretched out beside him, maybe he could get used to it if he really had to.

It was late afternoon and Jack was asleep beside her when Sam's phone rang. Her eyes rounded as she saw it was a video call from her girls. Grabbing the phone, she slipped on her dressing gown as she hastily made for the sliding glass door to her bedroom balcony to take the call.

'Hello,' she said, plastering a smile on her face as she quickly finger-combed her hair into some kind of order.

'Are you sick?' Brook asked abruptly.

'No, why?' Sam asked, adjusting the neck of her silky dressing gown as unobtrusively as possible.

'It's barely six o'clock and you're in your pyjamas. Were you asleep?'

'Oh ... um, no. I just decided to have an early shower. I might have a movie-in-bed night tonight, I think.'

'Hi, Mum,' Kenzie said, appearing on the screen briefly, carrying a mug. 'Are you sick?' she asked.

'She says she isn't, but she's acting weird,' Brook said.

'I'm not sick, I'm just having an early night,' Sam corrected warily, mindful of keeping her voice low.

'And why are you whispering?' Brook asked.

Sam heard the sound of the door sliding open at pretty much the same instant she heard Jack's voice. 'There you are,' he said.

And there *he* was, in all his glory, silhouetted in the doorway like some big, naked, hunky sex dream . . . on camera.

'Mum!' Brook's outraged voice seemed to echo off the concrete walls of the balcony.

'Oh shit,' Jack whispered, slamming the door shut. Sam almost tripped over the hem of her long dressing gown as she jumped to her feet guiltily, like she'd just been caught in a surprise police raid, unsure which way to run.

'I can't believe this is happening again,' she heard Brook say in a disappointed tone normally used by a parent to their child.

'Look, I appreciate this is a bit awkward. Yes, Jack is here. He came to visit and to meet you two in person. I was planning to call you about coming to dinner tomorrow. I'd really like you both to come. Think it over and let me know. I love you.' She said it all before disconnecting the call, too freaked out to continue the conversation.

When she'd got herself back under control, she stood up and went inside to find Jack sitting, now partly dressed, on the end of the bed, his head hanging and his loosely linked hands between his knees as he stared at the floor.

'You okay?' she asked as she approached him, placing her phone on the dressing table.

'I can't believe I did that again. They probably think I'm some kind of pervert.'

Sam bit back her smile at his mournful description. 'It was an accident. You didn't know I was on the phone.'

'Once is an accident. Twice, and standing there bare-arsed naked in front of your kids, is just . . . humiliating.'

'They couldn't see anything. It was dark,' she said, trying to comfort him.

'I could see them pretty well. Well enough to see the look of horror on their faces.'

'They were just shocked at seeing a man in my bedroom.'

'A naked man,' he pointed out darkly.

'Well, if you're going to have a man in your bedroom, having one naked is probably the best kind you can have,' Sam said, trying to lighten the mood. Judging from his frown, though, it wasn't working. 'Look, I've told them about dinner, and it's up to them. If they decide not to come, we'll do it another time.'

'My visit was supposed to reassure them that I was a nice bloke and put their minds to rest about who their mother was getting involved with.'

'And it will. We'll all look back on this in a few . . .' She saw his frown deepen. 'One day. And we'll laugh about it.'

He gave a noncommittal grunt in reply.

Sam let out a frustrated breath. 'I give up,' she said, turning away.

'What?'

'I'm so sick of being the negotiator stuck in the middle of all this. If I'm not reassuring *you* that everything's going to be okay, then I'm reassuring *them*. Just once, it would be nice to not have to worry about who the hell is currently having a meltdown.'

'Sam . . .'

'I know you must feel really awkward, and I get that two grown daughters are a lot to deal with. But this is *our* relationship. Not theirs. I need you onboard if this dinner is going to be a success. Not sulking up here.'

'I'm not sulking,' he said, sounding offended.

'Good. Then you can help me make something to eat because I'm starving and I really don't want to discuss any of this again tonight.'

'Okay,' he said carefully. 'You're right, we can't do much about what's already happened. We'll just have to move forward.'

Sam ignored the fact that Jack sounded about as enthusiastic about that prospect as a dog being dragged to the vet to get neutered, and was just glad that they could put the whole incident out of their minds for five minutes. Tomorrow was going to be another day and she was sure she would be a mess of nerves, but even if it killed her—or them—she was going to hash out some kind of truce. One way or another, everyone was going to get along. Or else.

Thirty-one

When the front door opened late the next afternoon, Sam had already had a glass of wine to calm her nerves.

'We're out here,' she called from the back deck, fixing a smile firmly in place as Brook and Kenzie came to the back door and she stood to greet them. Brook was looking every inch the bronzed beach worshipper that she was, dressed in her best coastal-chic attire of lacy white top and loose linen pants, pulling the look off effortlessly with her coffee-coloured hair falling in loose waves around her shoulders. Kenzie looked equally beachy in a pair of short overalls with a bright, oversized yellow T-shirt underneath, momentarily reminding Sam of Tasmin's choice of outfit at Christmas. Kenzie's lighter honey-caramel hair was scooped up in a messy bun, yet still somehow managed to look nice—something Sam had never been able to manage with her own hair. While Kenzie wore a smile, Sam noticed how drawn her eldest daughter looked;

she'd lost weight since the last time she'd visited. She had never handled stress well, and last year had been particularly gruelling with the added pressure of doing her internship on top of everything else. Still, after receiving her final results just before Christmas, and doing so well, Sam had thought Kenzie would be back to her old self by now.

'Mackenzie, Brooklyn—this is Jack.'

'Nice to meet you, Jack,' Kenzie said, stepping forward with a small, shy smile.

'Good to meet you too, Mackenzie,' Jack said, clearing his throat quickly as he stood and shook her hand.

'Call me Kenzie. I usually only get Mackenzie when I'm in trouble.'

'Jack,' Brook said, with only the slightest hint of aloofness in her tone when he turned to look at her. 'Nice to see you . . . with clothes on,' she added, then flashed a brilliant smile. 'I'm kidding,' she said before her mother could cut in. 'I'm glad we've finally got the chance to meet.'

Sam sent Jack a quick glance and managed a somewhat reassuring smile before taking a seat beside him.

'So,' Jack started, clasping his hands together, 'can I get anyone a drink?'

'Sure. I'll have a wine,' Brook said.

'What about you, Kenzie?'

'Oh, I'm fine thanks. I'll just have water. I'm driving,' she said with a small wave of her hand.

Sam waited until the door closed behind Jack before sending her youngest daughter a raised eyebrow in warning.

'What? I was nice,' Brook said defensively.

'I mean it, I'm not going to put up with anyone making *anyone*,' she stressed, 'feel uncomfortable today.'

'Okay, geez.'

'How are you?' Sam asked Kenzie as she took a seat across from her. 'How's work?'

'Yeah, fine.'

Jack returned and put a stop to any further questions as he placed the drinks in front of the girls. 'Did you want me to put the barbie on yet?' he asked Sam, still looking a little nervous.

'Ah, sure.' It was a little earlier than she'd been expecting, but she figured he needed something useful to do. She got up to bring everything out, but he waved her back.

'I can handle it,' he said confidently.

As Jack cooked on the barbecue, he seemed to relax, and pretty soon he was almost back to the capable Jack she knew and loved.

'So, Kenzie,' Jack said, 'your mum's been telling me you did really well in your exams.'

Kenzie shrugged. 'I probably could have done a little better, but I'm pretty happy with it,' she said.

'Sorry, I forgot to ask—what was the degree you were doing again?' Jack said, pausing as he placed the meat onto the sizzling hotplate.

'It was in Event Management and Marketing.'

'That's right,' he said with a nod. 'And you've been doing an internship, I hear? That's got to be pretty exciting.'

'Yeah. I was really lucky to get it,' Kenzie said, and Sam could have hugged them both for having such a normal adult conversation.

'That's great. Congratulations.'

'Thanks.' Kenzie smiled briefly before looking down into her glass.

'Your internship should be almost up by now. Have you heard anything yet?' Sam asked.

'Yeah, they offered me a position,' Kenzie said, glancing up at her mother.

Sam blinked at her uncertainly. 'When? Why didn't you tell me?'

'Oh, the other day. I'm still thinking about it.'

'Still thinking . . .' Sam's words faded out. What was there to think about? Kenzie had been raving about her work-placement company for months. She'd been excited about how far she could go with them if she was offered a position. 'What's changed your mind?'

'Nothing's changed, I'm just weighing up my options . . . you know.'

'Not really. I thought this company was at the top of your wish list?'

'They are. Can we not talk about it right now?'

Sam lifted an eyebrow slightly at her daughter's out-of-character tone. 'Okay. We'll discuss it later,' Sam agreed calmly but sent her daughter a look that warned her they *would* be talking about it.

To her surprise, Brook picked up the slack in the conversation and got things back on track, asking Jack about his daughters.

'Bianca and Tasmin,' he said, taking his phone out to bring up some photos.

'Wow, they're both really pretty,' Brook said, after taking the phone from Jack. 'Tasmin looks a lot like you.'

'My mum says the same thing. Poor kid,' Jack added. 'This meat and the . . . tofu things are just about done,' he said, eyeing the meat-substitute sausages Sam had added for Brook warily.

'Those would be *my* tofu things,' Brook said, with a slightly narrow-eyed glance. 'I should have known a beef farmer would turn his nose up at them. Have you ever tried it?' she dared.

'Can't say I've ever had the urge,' Jack said doubtfully. 'But each to their own. I just don't understand—if vegetarians are so dead against meat, why do they make tofu *sausages*?'

'Okay, plates?' Sam cut in, handing the girls a plate each.

Later, as she sat down, her glance fell on Kenzie's near-empty plate. 'There's plenty of food,' she said, her nurturing instincts zoning in on her eldest.

'I had a big breakfast and I'm still full. Don't fuss, Mum.'

Fuss, worry . . . it was all the same and Sam heard the faintest flutter of a little red flag inside her head. She *was* concerned. Her daughter's weight loss and the stress she'd been under was reminiscent of the lead-up to her year twelve exams. That period had led to Kenzie being put in hospital after she'd fainted at school, and the full extent of how she'd been internalising her stress, which had led to a lack of appetite and severe weight loss, had been revealed.

She should have been checking in on her. Sam had been so distracted by her own problems, she hadn't followed up on all the excuses her daughter had been giving her about why she couldn't make it to get-togethers lately. Well, that ended tonight, she vowed silently. Tonight, she'd find out what was going on.

Jack allowed himself to breathe out a slow breath. Now that they'd got the introductions done, he felt a bit better. Earlier, he'd been sweating like a colour-blind bomb technician and thinking about faking a reason to leave, before giving himself the pep talk about them only being two kids. There shouldn't be anything scary about meeting two young women . . . except there was. Especially when his future happiness would be heavily influenced by these particular young women. He needed them to like him.

He'd tried to be careful about the whole vegetarian thing. He'd already had a brief introduction when Bianca decided to give it a go after watching an animal-rights documentary. It stung a little that a kid of his could suddenly lose sight of a lifetime of being a farmer's daughter and believe everything the documentary had broadcast—especially when she knew how much care and work went into animal welfare on their property—but he knew that all kids needed a cause, something to rebel against, and thankfully it had only lasted six months.

He wasn't about to get on his bandwagon and ridicule Brook's reasons for becoming a vegetarian—that was her choice. And he needed to keep the peace.

He knew he wasn't the only anxious one today. Sam hadn't been her usual chirpy self either, which only added to the pressure. Her kids were her world—just as his were to him.

He got it. But they weren't talking about young, impressionable kids here. These were adults. He wanted to feel secure enough in their relationship to know that it would survive even if Sam's daughters flat-out refused to accept him in their lives, but he couldn't shake the feeling that maybe it *wasn't* strong enough.

The fact that she still hadn't listed her house for sale added to his growing concern. He felt awkward bringing it up, though; the last thing he wanted was to come across as a whinger, constantly hassling her about when was she coming back. It wasn't like he didn't have enough to keep him occupied. The fencing alone was going to take another couple of months, then there was the whole insurance headache to sort out. He had plenty to deal with, but he would rather deal with it with Sam around. He missed her. It seemed stupid to think he'd lived most of his adult life without her, and then after less than four months he couldn't seem to remember how to function without her there by his side.

Thirty-two

Sam stood after they'd finished the meal and began to collect the plates. 'Kenzie, could you give me a hand bringing these in and serving dessert?' she asked, before sending her younger daughter a firm glance. 'Brooky, why don't you tell Jack about your tourism course?'

'I can give you a hand,' Jack said, making to stand.

But she shook her head and waved him back in his seat. 'You cooked. It won't take long.'

She didn't give any of them time to argue before she turned away with a stack of plates and lifted an eyebrow at Kenzie to follow.

For a moment neither of them spoke as they fell into the routine they'd had for years, packing the dishwasher and putting away leftover food. It almost felt like old times—before Kenzie grew up and left home.

'So, what's going on?' Sam finally asked. 'And before you say nothing, let me warn you, we're not leaving this kitchen until you tell me.'

Silence fell between them before Kenzie eventually looked up, her eyes bright with unshed tears.

'I really stuffed up, Mum.'

Sam felt her heart plummet. She dropped the tea towel on the bench and immediately gathered her daughter into her arms. She couldn't recall the last time Kenzie had cried—not like this, with heartbroken sobs. 'Whatever it is, we can fix it,' she soothed, praying to God that was the truth. Sam's thoughts raced at a million miles an hour, imagining unthinkable horrors as she waited for Kenzie's tears to slow. She handed over the box of tissues from the bench beside them.

'Start from the beginning,' Sam prodded gently, despite the fact that internally she was panicking at the unknown.

Kenzie wiped her eyes and tipped her head back, taking a deep breath. 'I'm such an idiot, Mum,' she said, and again tears began to flow.

'Hey,' Sam said, taking her daughter's shoulders and ducking her head to make Kenzie look at her. 'Take a breath and tell me what's going on.'

'I met someone,' she finally said, and for a moment Sam was tempted to breathe a sigh of relief. Maybe Kenzie was just worried she'd get a lecture about not focusing on her career. But something warned her it was too early to breathe that sigh just yet.

'I've been really stressed over the last few months—like, *really* stressed. I didn't want to say anything, because I knew you'd worry,' she said, quickly waving away Sam's protest. 'Anyway, I got talked into going out one night. It was so out of character for me, but I did it. I was in the middle of exams ... it was so stupid ... but I just—' She paused, searching for the words. 'I sort of snapped or something.' She stared up at her mother almost in disbelief. 'It was as though I was someone else. I let my friends talk me into going to a club, and we danced and drank ... *a lot*,' she added, and dropped her gaze. 'I felt out of control. I hardly ever drink, but that night I just didn't care.'

Sam tried to keep the prickling sensation that was slowly moving up her spine at bay. Maybe this was Kenzie just being Kenzie. She had always been an over-achiever.

'Okay,' Sam said calmly, hoping this was where Kenzie said, *that's it*.

'I met up with a guy,' Kenzie said, and that prickle down Sam's back grew stronger. 'It was nothing. I mean, I never just hook up with random guys, but I was having so much fun, and drinking. He was a backpacker over here on holiday.'

Sam watched as Kenzie once more dropped her gaze. 'I thought it was just one night of harmless fun.'

'Kenzie, what happened?' Sam asked when Kenzie's words faded and she continued to stare down at the floor.

'I'm pregnant.'

Sam felt the air leave her body in a silent rush and sank back against the bench, clutching the edge for support.

'I'm sorry,' Kenzie said, finally lifting her eyes to reveal a look so devastated that it stole any hope of Sam finding the right words.

Sam pulled her daughter back into her arms and held her tightly as Kenzie cried. She felt numb.

'Are you sure?'

'Yeah. I did a test. Actually, I did five, in case the first four were wrong.'

'How long ago was this? That you went out?'

'A few months.'

'You've known for a while, then?'

'Yeah.'

'And you've been to a doctor?'

Kenzie nodded, wiping her eyes quickly.

'So, they would have told you that you have options?'

'I went through the options,' Kenzie said quietly, before taking a breath and straightening her shoulders. 'I can't get rid of it, Mum. I thought about it, but in the end I . . . I don't know.' She shrugged. 'I think I'd always look back and feel guilty. I don't think I could live the rest of my life wondering what might have been.'

'But you've worked so hard,' Sam said weakly, desperately trying to process the news and what it meant for Kenzie, for them all.

'I know,' Kenzie said, wiping away more tears. 'It couldn't have happened at a worse time.'

'Well, what about this guy. Have you told him? Who is he?'

'I don't know,' she said, her voice barely more than a whisper as she looked away. 'I don't remember his name—I barely remember what he looked like. He said he'd been backpacking around Australia for the last few months. It was his last night on the Gold Coast before he flew out from Brisbane. I don't even know what his accent was. I can't believe I was so stupid,' she groaned, clenching her hands together as she shook her head.

'Maybe we can find him, get a private investigator or something. Did you friend each other on Facebook, or get a phone number?' Sam asked but gave a resigned sigh when Kenzie just shook her head despairingly.

'I fell asleep, and he didn't stay. Mum, I've been over this again and again. I know how disappointed you must be in me. I'm disappointed in myself. I can't believe I did something so stupid, but now I just have to deal with it.'

'Is this why you haven't accepted the job offer?'

Kenzie gave a small wince. 'There's no longer an offer. They withdrew it when I told them I was pregnant.'

'They *what*? They can't do that.'

'They did. Well, technically they said the job had been given to someone else . . . but I guess I can understand their logic. There's no point hiring someone who would only be there a few months before having to take maternity leave.'

'We could fight this,' Sam said, frowning. 'You worked so hard and they were so impressed with you. They can't discriminate against you because you're having a baby.'

Kenzie shot her a look that clearly said she thought her mother was being naive. It might even have seemed comical at any other time. Not so much now.

'I'll be okay. I can do this on my own.'

'You won't have to,' Sam said firmly. 'You're not on your own. You have family.'

'I know,' Kenzie said with a weak smile. 'It'll be okay. It's just not how I thought things were going to play out.'

'Does your father know? Does Brook?'

'I haven't told Dad yet. I was planning on telling you both at the same time. I just hadn't worked up the courage to do it. Brook knows. She's been really great, actually. I'm sorry, Mum,' Kenzie said miserably, biting her lip. 'I've really let you down.'

'You haven't let me down,' Sam said, hugging her once more. 'It's just hard to remember you're an adult now and not my little girl who needs me to jump in and fix everything.'

'Not even you can fix this one, Mum,' Kenzie said despondently. 'If it's all right with you, I think I might go to bed. I seem to get morning sickness at night; go figure.'

'I did too,' Sam said with a faint smile. It felt surreal that she now had a pregnancy story in common with her daughter. As she watched Kenzie leave the kitchen, Sam felt herself rooted to the spot. Her legs didn't feel up to supporting her, and after a few minutes of staring blankly ahead of her, she used all her remaining strength to force herself back outside.

'Where's Brook?' she asked, finding Jack alone at the table, pouring a glass of wine.

He handed it to her with a sympathetic look. 'Sounded like you could use this,' he said. 'Brook decided she was going out because she wasn't, quote, "hanging around for the fallout".'

'You heard, then?' Sam asked.

'Some of it. Sorry, I probably should have closed the door or something but I wasn't sure if you might need . . . back-up.' He shrugged awkwardly.

Sam gave a weary smile. 'You didn't have to close the door. You're not a guest.'

'I'm also not exactly family. I understand if you'd prefer me to go home early so you can concentrate on the girls.'

'No,' Sam said, feeling an unexplainable panic race through her at the thought of him leaving. He'd just got here. They'd barely spent any time together. 'I'd really like you to stay. If you want to, that is. I mean, I think I'm still in shock and need to process everything, but I'd really like you to stay.'

'Okay,' he agreed calmly, but she saw a shadow of something pass across his face, and another tingle of warning began to tap her on the shoulder. But she pushed it aside. There was far too much happening right now to deal with any more borrowed trouble. Instead, she took a sip of her wine.

'So, Kenzie's expecting a baby,' she said after a moment.

'I take it this wasn't planned.'

'No,' Sam replied dryly.

'And the father of the baby? Will he step up?'

'It sounds like he won't have the chance to. Apparently, he lives overseas and they barely knew each other.' Sam let out a long breath and closed her eyes. 'It's just so not like her. Kenzie's always been this super-disciplined, mature kid. Even when she was little. She always kept her room spotless and everything had its place. For her tenth birthday, she asked for a label maker—that's how organised the kid was. I have no idea where she gets it from. I mean, I like a clean house, but Kenzie has always been on a whole other level. It was nothing to find her pulling out kitchen cupboards and reorganising them on her school holidays—seriously? Who even does that?'

Jack chuckled but let Sam continue.

'This job has been her entire focus since about year nine when she decided what she wanted to do. I just can't believe that literally only weeks after finishing her degree, she'd do something so . . .' She paused. It had been irresponsible, but it was also just a mistake. Kenzie was a kid. Unfortunately, though, it was a mistake that would change her entire life. 'It's just so unfair.'

'Has she decided to keep the baby?' he asked hesitantly.

'Apparently.'

'How will that play out? With no support from the father?'

Jack's question was a fair one, but it sent a fresh wave of anger through Sam. 'She'll get by. She has her father and me here to help out financially if she needs it.'

'What about other support? Babies are pretty hard work. I remember the sleepless nights and constant worry. I can't imagine doing that alone.'

Sam thought back to when her girls were babies, and she gave a small snort. She may have been married, but in those early days she'd practically been a sole parent. Andrew had slept through the long hours of crying and constant night feeds and nappy changes. He'd taken to sleeping in the spare room for the first few months each time she'd returned from the hospital with a baby. He claimed it was because he had to be able to function at work every day and he had never done well when he was tired and irritable. The thought outraged her now, but her twenty-something-year-old self had been too busy adjusting to motherhood to argue, and keeping the peace had been a lot easier than demanding her husband's attention.

Now, whenever she thought about those days she mostly felt embarrassed. Somehow, without even realising it, she'd fallen into a trap. Money and luxury had been as seductive and addictive as any drug. Her life had been easy. She got to stay at home with her kids, dress them in cute matching outfits, buy whatever she wanted and enjoy mothers' group long lunches at expensive restaurants. Kenzie would have nothing like that ahead of her as a single mum. But she *would* have as much support and hands-on help as she needed.

'Kenzie will be fine,' she added firmly. She would make sure of it.

Thirty-three

Jack had sat at the table after Sam had not-too-subtly taken Kenzie to the kitchen to get to the bottom of whatever had been going on, and he had tried not to listen in on the conversation taking place inside.

He'd instead focused on Sam's youngest daughter as she chatted about her tourism course, trying to keep up with her, but when the voices in the kitchen began to rise, it was impossible not to overhear.

At the first mention of pregnancy, Brook had stopped talking, and Jack had almost knocked over the wine glass he'd been reaching for at the time.

'Yeah, nah, that's my cue to leave,' Brook had said, before disappearing around the side of the house, leaving Jack alone on the deck and unsure what to do.

In the time he'd sat there, the implications of the situation had time to sink in. What would he do if one day Tasmin or

Bianca announced they were pregnant? He felt a cold sweat break out on his top lip at the very thought.

He knew that Cilia would always be there for her kids, as would he in whatever capacity they needed him to be, but he suspected his girls would most likely turn to their mother for practical support. Most women did. After all, that's what mums were for. It would be only natural in this circumstance for Kenzie to need her mother. His earlier unease made a quick reappearance. There was no way that now, with a pregnant daughter nearby, Sam would want to move away.

How could he expect her to? It was a crushing blow to any remaining hope he had for the future they'd been planning.

When eventually Sam returned to the deck, he'd been struggling to remain calm. He'd wanted to ask what this now meant for them, their plans, but he managed to restrain himself. There was a lot more at stake here than just his and Sam's future—a hell of a lot more—but he knew that this was going to change everything.

'What do you need?' Jack asked now, quietly.

He saw her soft smile as she closed her eyes, and it tugged at his heartstrings. They'd only just found each other after decades apart and he could already feel their newly forged bond slowly beginning to unravel. Then she opened her eyes and looked at him.

'You,' she said simply. 'I just need you, Jack.'

'I'm right here,' he said, reaching for her hand.

'It's been a lot to deal with,' Sam said, tiredness etched on her face. 'Let's just go to bed.'

They switched off lights as they moved through the house and up the stairs, Sam's hand firmly in his own. When they reached the bedroom, she went to the window and stopped, looking outside. He slipped his arms around her and pulled her back against him snugly as they both gazed out over the backyard garden brightly lit by silver moonlight. If he didn't know better he'd swear he was looking out at some swanky resort in Bali. Beyond the garden was the canal, and the narrow strip of water glistened, the small ripples on the surface catching the moonlight, making it look like a giant, writhing reptile winding its way between the banks of the expensive, perfect homes that backed onto it. He wondered if she was thinking about how she would miss this view if she sold her house. He couldn't blame her. This place was like another planet compared to the simple country life back in Burrumba.

'It's certainly beautiful here,' he said, hoping his voice sounded less jaded than he was feeling.

'Yes, it is,' she sighed, and his heart plummeted a little more. 'You know, ever since I've come back, I stand here at night and look out there, wishing you were here with me, just like this,' she said, turning her head to look up at him. 'And now you are.'

'And now I am,' he agreed simply. 'Listen, Sam, about tonight . . . I know you're going to have a lot to think about.'

Sam turned in his arms and slid her hands up to cup his face. 'I don't want to think about any of that right now,' she said, cutting off his words. 'I just want to be here with you, like this, okay?'

Her eyes held a plea that went straight to his core. He knew they would have to talk about it, eventually. They would have to make plans and discuss how all this was going to affect them. But right now—call it cowardice or maybe just plain selfishness—he was taking her diversion and running with it. Lowering his head, he kissed her and felt her body meld to his in a way no one else's ever had. They were the pieces of a jigsaw puzzle—the only bits that truly fitted together the way they were supposed to. They had each other, and right now that was the only thing he needed.

For the most part, they managed to enjoy their brief time together. Sam played tour guide and took Jack to as many places as they could squeeze in, making plenty of memories to take away. She scrolled through the photos on her camera on the drive home and found herself smiling. Her happiness was tinged by the knowledge this would be all she had of Jack once he went back home, until they figured out when they could see each other again. While he'd been here, though, everything had felt so right.

Their farewell had been hard. Beneath the surface lay the unexploded bomb that was Mackenzie. They hadn't discussed it since the night she revealed she was pregnant—there was nothing to discuss, yet. Everything was up in the air until she and Kenzie could sit down and make some big decisions.

'Everything will be okay,' Jack had said, holding her tightly before he left. 'We'll figure this out.'

She'd smiled and nodded confidently, as confidently as she could muster, given she had no idea how the hell any of this was ever going to be okay. As hard as she fought against it, the truth was that nothing was going to be the same. Everything had changed and she was terrified she was losing sight of the future they had dreamed of together.

Over the next few weeks, Sam found herself avoiding the phone. Chelsea had called and left messages; her parents were starting to get persistent about when she was putting the house on the market and what was happening, and she found herself turning her phone off rather than having to deal with the endless questions when she had no answers to give. She'd told no one about Mackenzie's situation. It wasn't her news to share, and there was still no firm decision on what Kenzie was going to do.

After Jack left, Kenzie came back to stay with Sam for a few weeks. Her nausea had worsened, and she spent most of the day locked away in her bedroom. After a week of indulging her, Sam finally decided it couldn't go on any longer.

Taking in a couple of dry crackers and a cup of black tea, she sat on Kenzie's bed and instructed her to nibble and sip.

'I can't, Mum.'

'You can. This was the only thing that helped me through my morning sickness with you and your sister. Once you finish that, go and have a shower and wash your hair,' she said gently.

'What's the point? It's not like I'm going to see anyone. I can't get a job, and everything I've been working for all this time is now useless.'

'It's not useless. You've got your degree. You'll get a job, it's just going to take a little longer. You should be proud of yourself. I know I am.'

'Oh yeah, there's so much to be proud of. A daughter who's gone and got herself knocked up, lost her dream job and ruined her life.'

'Now you sound like Brook,' Sam said with a small smile.

'I've ruined everything, Mum,' Kenzie said as fresh tears fell from her eyes.

'Everything is *not* ruined. It's just changed the timing and direction a little bit.'

'What am I going to do, Mum?' Kenzie asked, and her sorrowful look chipped at Sam's heart.

'We'll figure it out. You're not alone.'

'I heard you and Jack on the phone last night,' Kenzie said after she took the first few nibbles of a cracker. 'You were so happy around him. You were the happiest I ever remember seeing you when you were down at Nan and Pop's, too. You've lost that, and it's because of me.'

'It's not because of you,' Sam protested. 'We just have a lot to work out.'

'You need to put the house on the market, Mum.'

'I will, when the time's right,' Sam said, straightening the bed cover beside her. 'There's no hurry.' She'd been holding the real-estate agent off about the final listing until she knew for sure what direction Mackenzie's plans would take.

'The time *is* right. I don't want you staying here because you feel like you have to. I'll be fine.'

'I'm not going to leave you here,' Sam chided gently.

'Mum, I'm an adult. I'm about to become a mother,' Kenzie said, pausing and placing a hand over her stomach. 'I have to stand on my own two feet.'

'And you will. But you don't have to start right now. There's no hurry to sell. Jack's not going anywhere, and I don't have another property in mind to buy yet, so everything's fine.'

'Except, you're sad.'

Sam blinked a little uncertainly. She'd been trying hard not to show how much she missed Jack or how scared she was about what the future might now hold for them, but clearly she hadn't been hiding it as well as she thought she had.

'I'm not sad,' she said, reaching out to gently tuck a loose strand of hair behind her daughter's ear. 'Yes, I miss him, but we'll work everything out, so stop worrying about it. Now,' she said in a firmer tone, 'when you finish your tea, get up and take a shower.'

'Okay,' Kenzie said, more resigned than enthused by the idea, but at least she'd agreed.

Later, when she came out dressed in a simple summer cotton dress with spaghetti straps, her blonde-streaked hair pulled back into a ponytail, she had a little more colour in her cheeks.

'I thought we could go down to the beach and get a bit of sun—maybe go for a walk?' Sam suggested as she finished cleaning the kitchen.

'Okay,' Kenzie agreed with a small shrug. 'But do you mind if we do it a bit later? I think I need to visit Dad and tell him what's going on.'

'Do you want me to come with you?'

'No. I'll be okay. I just thought he should probably know. He's been hassling me about the job offer, so I should probably tell him why I'm not taking it.'

'You know, Kenz,' Sam said thoughtfully, 'I've been thinking about that whole thing. Why don't you start up your own business?'

Kenzie looked at her blankly. 'Me?'

'Why not? You could be your own boss. Work around your pregnancy. I'm pretty sure you could do most of it online, right?'

'Well, technically, I suppose I could. But I don't know anything about running my own business.'

Sam gave her a wide smile. 'Then it's a good thing I do, isn't it?'

'Wow,' Kenzie said, staring at her mother, and Sam could see the thoughts racing through her daughter's mind as she contemplated the idea. It was hard not to smile at that familiar look of concentration. God, Sam missed her kids being little. It seemed like yesterday, but here they were, young adults forging their own paths in life. Sam blinked away the tears she felt coming. 'Well, just think about it. There's no rush.'

'Yeah. I will. Thanks, Mum,' Kenzie said distractedly as she leaned in to kiss Sam's cheek. 'I'll be back a bit later. Love you,' she called on her way to the front door.

For the first time in days she seemed like the old Kenzie again.

Now, if only Sam's little pep talk could inspire some positive change in her own life.

Picking up a stack of washing to fold, she carried it upstairs to Kenzie's room and put it on the end of her bed. A wave of melancholic emotions unravelled inside her as she found herself repeating the same chore she'd done a thousand times for her daughters over the years. She sat down slowly on the side of the bed. *Her baby was about to have her own baby.* It seemed surreal. She thought back to her own mother shaking her head and saying how it only felt like yesterday that Sam and her brothers had been in nappies, and now here she was feeling the same way. It *did* feel like only yesterday! She was about to have a *grandchild*.

So far she'd shied away from thinking too deeply about how this whole thing would affect her—she'd been too focused on Kenzie—but now that things had settled down a little, she allowed herself to really consider it all. There was the initial resistance that there was *no way* she felt old enough to be a *grandmother*, but that was quickly swept aside as she realised . . . she was excited. She'd been mourning the loss of her own babies—the ruthless way age crept up on you, taking your children and turning them into adults practically overnight without waiting to see if you were ready to let them go—but now . . . there'd be a baby back in her life who she could dote on and love, and even more importantly, hand back to its mother! A smile tugged at her lips as she imagined that new baby scent and watching her daughter experience all the exciting firsts in her baby's life. She wiped at her eyes and stood up, straightening the bedcover before walking out of the room.

Two days later, things had settled into a new routine. Sam took Kenzie her morning dry crackers and tea, then they organised something fun to do for the morning before coming home to rest. Today, however, as they walked into the house after a trip to the beach, Sam's phone rang.

'Hi, Mum,' Sam said, 'how are you?'

'Hi, darling. Your dad's here too, we're on speaker.'

'Hi, Dad. How are my cows? Did you need my farm manager's advice about something?' Sam joked.

'Yeah—there's this one cow I just can't get any milk out of and I have no idea why,' he drawled.

'Have you checked it's not a bull?'

'Oh. Maybe that would explain why he gets so cranky . . .'

It was an old joke but it still made her smile. 'What are you two up to?'

'Well, the thing is,' her mother started, and Sam instinctively knew this was going to be a long conversation. Her mother's big ideas always started with 'the thing is'.

'We had a call from Mackenzie the other day,' she continued, and Sam felt a long breath escape her. 'She's very upset about everything, poor little mite,' her mother went on. 'But she was calling because she's worried about you. She wanted us to convince you to put the house on the market and move down here like you were planning to.'

'Mum, I can't sell up and move away now—at least not at the moment. Everything's so up in the air. Kenzie has to sort out what she's doing—I can't just leave her here to do it all alone.'

'We understand that,' her mum went on. 'Your father and I have been talking about it and we think we've come up with an idea. As much as your father complains, he really enjoyed our trip and we want to do more travelling, only, as you know, the livestock are a big commitment and tie us down quite a bit. And you know your father—he wouldn't leave unless someone he trusted was here to keep an eye on his precious cattle.'

Sam listened quietly as she processed what her mother was saying. 'You want me to move in with you and Dad?'

'Actually, we were thinking, perhaps you might like your own place? Somewhere Kenzie could move with you. Years ago we had a building envelope put in, thinking one day it might come in handy—to have another house on the place, a bit like a retirement plan. Neither of us want to go into a retirement village, so we figured maybe someday one of you kids might want to build and move out here.'

'We were actually thinking it might be Alex after he got out of the navy, but he went and got married,' her dad put in, soundly slightly disgruntled. 'But with everything going on, we just thought it might be something that was of interest to you.'

'We spoke to both of your brothers,' her mother added.

'Down the track, you could buy out our part,' her dad explained, 'which would go to your brothers, and you'd end up with a decent-sized property and an extra house you could either rent out or maybe use for one of the girls if ever they wanted to move down.'

'There's plenty of room here to live while you build, and we'd probably do a bit of travelling around Australia to get out of each other's hair,' her mum said. 'It would be lovely to have your company, too,' she added.

The aftermath of the fires was still a raw wound within the community, with so many left uncertain about their future. Sam knew from previous conversations with her parents and Jack that many of the families who'd suffered damage to their properties had decided to sell. For a lot of the older neighbours, including many of her parents' close friends, it had been far too close for comfort and they didn't want to face that kind of destruction again. It would take some time before life went back to any kind of normality again for much of the town.

Sam didn't know what to say. The idea had caught her off guard but it wasn't totally ridiculous. 'Wow. I'd have to think about it, but that's definitely something to consider,' she finally said.

'Lovely,' her mum said, sounding relieved. 'We'll understand if you don't want to do it. It was just a thought.'

'I'll definitely think about it,' Sam promised. 'Thank you.' She was constantly humbled by how amazing her parents were and how lucky she was to have them. They'd always been her rock, throughout her entire life and especially during and after her divorce. If she could be half the parents they were, she'd be happy.

They hung up, leaving Sam to ponder all this new information. Maybe there was some kind of road out of this mess after all.

Thirty-four

Jack sank the last post in its hole and rolled his shoulders in an attempt to ease some of their strain, hearing the various clicks and cracks that went along with moving parts of his body nowadays. He used to laugh at his father complaining about getting old—now look at him.

It had been two months since Sam left, and while he was starting to see progress around his property, it had been a slow and painful process. All around him, signs of new life were beginning to show. The trees had suddenly sprouted bright green masses of leaves—an explosion of lime green foliage against the stark blackened sticks of their trunks. The bush, like the people who lived in it, certainly was resilient. While the fires had smouldered across the ridges and valleys, it had been hard to imagine anything coming back, yet the bush was slowly regenerating.

He had managed to finish his fencing, and after an extensive week spent mustering alongside his neighbours, he had found the majority of his stock. It never ceased to surprise him—the survival instinct livestock seemed to have. While some farmers in the valley hadn't been so lucky, mostly due to not managing their fire plans early enough and instead locking animals away, Jack and the neighbouring farmers had managed to locate most of their wandering stock from the surrounding bushland and national park. Finally, there was a light beginning to shine at the end of a long and dark tunnel.

His love life, though, was not looking so optimistic, he thought as he threw his tools into the back of his ute and grabbed his drink bottle, taking a long drink of the tepid water inside. He hadn't been up to the Sunshine Coast since Kenzie announced her pregnancy. He wanted to give Sam and her kids time to figure out what they wanted to do without him hovering over them like a dark, annoying cloud.

He and Sam still talked every day and he knew she missed him, but she'd gone very quiet on the topic of moving, and he never quite knew how to bring the subject up without making her feeling pressured. He understood her distraction and that there was a lot going on up there, but it still stung whenever she mentioned the time they had spent together as a family—with her ex-husband and their kids—and told him that the announcement of Kenzie's pregnancy had actually brought them all a little closer. That had been a few weeks ago but it had stayed with Jack and fed the pessimistic voice in his head with all kinds of less than desirable outcomes.

He'd had a visit from his girls the weekend before, and it had felt almost like old times. He shared their pain at the loss of their home and he finally felt as though they were both really here of their own free will, not simply because they'd felt like they had to visit their old man. They'd asked about Sam: when she was coming back, and whether they would see her again. He hadn't had any answers for them other than: soon, I hope.

The sound of machinery operating once more drew his attention and he made a note to drop by to visit the Murphys later. For the past few weeks, he'd been hearing activity over the ridge and though this wasn't unusual considering everyone was in the process of rebuilding and repairing, he thought he should be a bit more neighbourly and at least offer some help.

He was pretty sure both Henry and Margaret knew he was avoiding them—he hadn't meant to, but it was hard to ignore their sympathetic glances each time he went over there. They always sounded positive that things would work out, but they also seemed on edge, and he wondered if maybe they knew something he didn't and just couldn't bring themselves to tell him.

As he pulled up back at the shed, his eyes narrowed slightly at the shiny car parked beside it, and for a moment he wondered who the hell was visiting. But then he saw her and his heart leapt into his throat.

Sam.

It took him a few long seconds to remember how to move, before opening the door and getting out. She was standing at the front of his makeshift house, and suddenly everything looked brighter. Her dark hair was pulled back by the sunglasses on the top of her head, and the pink dress she wore almost matched the bougainvillea she'd potted for him on the small deck he'd built.

'Hey, stranger,' she said simply, her face lighting up with a wide smile that melted him from the inside out.

'What are you doing here?' he asked, before swearing silently under his breath. 'I mean—why didn't you tell me you were coming?'

He heard the tinkle of her laughter as she put her hands on her hips and continued smiling at him. 'I wanted to surprise you.'

'Well, it worked.' *Jesus, did it what.*

As he reached her, he stopped a step below where she stood on his deck, bringing them to eye level. He still couldn't believe she was standing right there in front of him, smelling so damn good and wearing a sexy, amused smile.

'So, are you just going to stand there or are you going to kiss me?' she asked, tilting her head slightly as she held his gaze.

That managed to knock him out of his stupor and she gave a small squeal of surprise as he leaned forward and scooped her into his arms, then headed up the small step and inside.

There was no more conversation as they deftly removed their clothes before making it to the bed and rediscovering each other all over again. If this was a dream, he planned to make it a good one, but when they lay side by side afterwards, breathing heavily and laughing, he knew this was real and he rolled his head sideways to soak her in.

'Now, *that* was a welcome,' she said, grinning back at him.

'When did you decide to come down?'

'I've been planning it for a little while. I wanted to be sure everything was going to work out before I said anything, and then it all just happened so fast, so I decided I may as well just surprise you.'

'What do you mean by everything?'

'Well, Mum and Dad made me an offer I really couldn't refuse, but I had to sort out a few things first and make sure it could all go ahead,' she said. 'I didn't want to get your hopes up if it fell through.'

'What offer?'

'I'm building a house across the creek,' she said, biting her lip as her eyes lit up in excitement.

'You're doing *what*?' He rose, leaning on one elbow as he stared down at her.

She shrugged slightly, but she couldn't contain her grin of anticipation as she filled him in.

'That's . . . great,' he said as the shock wore off.

'And . . .' she continued, but her eyes lost a little of the excitement, taking on more of an anxious look, and he braced himself. 'Kenzie and I have gone into business together.'

'Business?' he asked, confused.

'Kenzie's going to move down here, with the baby. We're opening her event-management business. I needed something to keep me busy and she can work mostly online and have someone on hand to help out with the baby once it arrives.'

'Wow,' he said, trying to take it all in.

'It all happened pretty fast.'

'Sounds like it,' he said, trying to mask the fact he was struggling to keep up. 'So, you're going to build a house on your parents' property?'

'Yeah. Dad's already started clearing and levelled the plot ready for a slab. They're pretty excited,' she added needlessly.

'I know you were planning on buying a place and everything once you sold your house, but, well . . . what if you just moved in here instead?'

He'd been thinking about it a lot since coming back from the Sunshine Coast. He knew what he wanted. He wanted Sam—forever. It seemed like a waste of time to go through all the hassle of building her own place when he'd be building his and planning on living there with her.

As he watched her face now, though, his hopes began to fade.

'Jack, I think it's too soon to move in together. I mean, Kenzie's planning on coming back to have the baby. I don't think she'd do it if you and I were living together. I know it feels like we've been together forever, but it really hasn't been all that long.'

'I don't need more time to know what I want.'

'I don't either, but it's not about time to know what we want. It's time to get to know everything about each other. The small stuff. The important stuff. I'm moving back so we can be together, and take our time.'

'We've wasted nearly thirty years, Sam,' Jack said, hearing the urgency in his voice and not caring that he sounded like an impatient jerk.

'And we won't be wasting any more, but there's no hurry. I'm here.'

'But I want to make it official. I want to marry you, Sam. I thought you knew that?'

He saw her eyes soften and fill with tears, and a gentle smile touched her lips.

'That's what I want too . . . but not right now.'

He understood that it didn't seem like very long to be with someone before thinking about marriage—especially for him, after swearing off marriage forever—but this wasn't a normal situation. They weren't two strangers. They were two people who'd grown up together, who'd been madly in love. They didn't need the socially acceptable amount of time to get to know each other. 'I just don't see the point of wasting more time when we both know what we want.'

'I guess I'm not ready to give up my independence just yet.'

'How can you think I'd stop you doing anything you wanted to do?'

'You won't mean to,' she pointed out logically, 'but you will because going into marriage, that's what you do—you have another person to think about before making decisions, another person to consult. Besides all that, we have kids to think about. They don't share our history. I want your girls to get to know me without forcing myself on them, which is how it would seem if I was living with you.'

'I don't see it that way,' he said after a while, breaking the silence that had fallen between them. 'I'm sorry, Sam. I just don't. I'm ready to start a life with you now. I thought you felt the same.'

He saw a flash of hurt cross her face and he felt bad, but his pride was hurting too. He'd been patiently waiting for months, trying not to pressure her, trying his best to be understanding and give her some space, based on the understanding that she was coming back here to start their life together. But apparently, that wasn't the case. He pulled on his jeans and gathered his shirt and boots. 'I've got to finish up outside before dark. I'll be back in a little while.'

He felt bad as he closed the front door and left, but there wasn't anything he could do—he was hurt. For the first time since Sam had come back into his life, he wasn't sure where he stood with her, and it scared the hell out of him.

Still half asleep, Sam stretched out in the now empty bed and felt lazily at the pillow beside her where Jack's head should have been; it was cold. Then she remembered their argument. She hadn't meant to fall asleep, but obviously the drive down and all the excitement had taken a bigger toll than she'd anticipated.

She'd worried about keeping her news a secret from Jack, but she'd wanted to make sure it would happen. She desperately hadn't wanted to get his hopes up only to have something prevent it from going ahead.

She couldn't have done it if everything hadn't worked out the way it had with Mackenzie. There was no way she could leave her daughter to try to manage a pregnancy and baby alone. She knew Kenzie could have handled it if she'd had to, but Sam couldn't. She would have stayed. It wouldn't have been the end of the world, but it would have been at least another year before she would have felt okay enough to move away. Maybe she was just being an overprotective mother—she knew that women had babies on their own all the time—but if there was a way she could help her daughter have an easier time of it, then she would do whatever it took.

At first, Kenzie hadn't been sure that starting her own business would work, but what began as dipping her toe into the ocean to test the waters had resulted in her landing her first big job through a contact of her father. She'd coordinated a large corporate function with less than two weeks to prepare, and Sam had watched with a mixture of admiration and awe as her daughter calmly handled crisis after crisis and pulled together a product launch that was both innovative and stylish and ended up landing her another two jobs. 'Events by Kenzie' was up and running.

For now, Kenzie was running the business from her father's house, but she would move down to Burrumba once the new house was built. Everything seemed to be falling into place and finally Sam could think about a future that included Jack.

However, there remained one last issue between them, and Sam hadn't realised how upset Jack would be about it.

He hadn't made a secret of the fact he wanted her to live with him, and as much as she wanted that too, she also knew she wasn't ready to take that step yet.

She wanted the freedom of waking up in her own place to the crow of roosters and the purr of a cat—without needing anyone else's approval, or in the case of a cat, disapproval. Yes, she wanted to be here with Jack, but she also wanted her own space.

She had no doubts about their relationship, but they had a few hurdles to think about—namely, their kids. Sam didn't want to jump headfirst into such an important decision like living together without giving everyone time to adjust. After all, she planned on this being for the rest of her life; they still had plenty of time and she wanted to make sure it was done right.

The sound of boots being stomped outside made her hands twist together nervously. Jack had been disappointed earlier, and she got it, but she also knew she had a valid argument for taking things slowly.

Her nerves dissolved and a small smile crept onto her face as Jack walked into the bedroom carrying a bouquet of purple hydrangeas.

'They're beautiful,' she said, feeling her voice catch as emotion tugged at her heart. He really was the most perfect man.

'I'm sorry,' he said before sitting down on the side of the bed. 'I acted like a spoilt brat earlier. It just caught me off guard. I've missed you so much and now you're here, I just want to be with you. I guess deep down I'd convinced myself you'd changed your mind and weren't coming back.'

'I know it took longer than we were expecting.'

'I've been thinking about what you said, and you're right,' he said simply. 'I wasn't thinking about the kids. I was only thinking about myself.'

'Make no mistake, Mr Cameron, I intend to make an honest man of you,' Sam said, grinning, 'but I want to do it with the blessing of *all* our family. It's too important to rush.'

'We can wait as long as it takes,' he said, resting his head against hers. 'As long as we're together.'

Who would have thought, all those months ago when she'd agreed to come down and housesit for her parents, that she would end up staying for good? Or that she'd have gone through the devastation of the fires that had destroyed so much. And yet, through it all, she'd come full circle, back to the man she'd loved as a girl and now as a woman.

'I know when we originally planned that I'd come back, it wasn't with a daughter in tow, but I can't just leave her alone up there to fend for herself. This way, I don't have to worry about her, and I still get to be down here with you, and involved in a new venture, which I'm actually really excited about.'

'I don't care if you move in both your kids, your ex-husband and his child-bride as well, if it means you'll be here,' Jack said.

'Well, we won't get *too* carried away. Just one kid . . . and a grandchild,' she said, then stopped, shaking her head with a rueful smile. 'I can't believe I'm going to be a grandmother. I suddenly feel so old.'

'For a grandmother, you're kinda sexy, though,' he said, leaning down to kiss her.

'You think?' she murmured, eyeing him playfully.

'Definitely.'

It was a long time before they discussed anything else in depth, and he still couldn't believe that a day that had started out so normally could end with his greatest wish being fulfilled.

Epilogue

Sam stood in the doorway and soaked in the scene before her. Brook sat beside her sister on the lounge in their grandparents' house—in her arms, she cradled the tiny form of her baby niece.

It had been a huge few days since the trip into the hospital in the early hours of the morning and the very rapid arrival of the precious bundle now being adored by everyone around her.

Sam's parents beamed, proudly boasting that they were now great-grandparents, and the room had a festive feel that had been missing since the fires. Today, though, there was reason to celebrate. Baby Poppy was home from hospital, and everyone had come to meet her.

'Happy?' Jack asked as he came up behind Sam and wrapped his arms around her waist.

'Ecstatic,' she replied, leaning her head back against his chest. She had everything she could possibly want, right here in this room.

'I love you, Granny,' he said softly.

'I love you, Granddad,' she replied, elbowing him lightly. It was going to take a bit of time to get used to being a grandmother, but she'd already fallen in love with Poppy and she couldn't be prouder of Kenzie and how well she'd handled everything that had been thrown at her. Outside, the paddocks and garden were lush and green—a stark difference to how they had looked nine months earlier. The drought-breaking rain had finally come and with it, a surge of fresh hope. This was a new beginning for them all and Sam couldn't wait to see where the next chapter took them.

Acknowledgements

With thanks for their help with my research: Trudie Ryan, Elyse Evans, Trevor Stride, David Sinclair, Mark Farnsworth, Chris Knight, Kylie Smith, Claire and Ruth Beaver, Erica Foley and Sheralee Parkins. Lyn, as always, for her coffee debriefs and brainstorming, and to my kids and husband for listening to me talk out loud or ask for random word suggestions.

Writing this book sometimes proved incredibly difficult. My family were among the lucky ones whose property was thankfully spared, but so many in my community of the Nambucca Valley were not as fortunate. The stress the entire community felt at the time was something I've never experienced before. I was constantly worried about my livestock and my property, my children and our house. The lurking fires that surrounded us were an ever-present threat, and knowing that everything depended on which direction the wind decided to blow felt as though we were living in a lottery. It was the difference between losing your property or having it saved by, seemingly, divine intervention, at times.

However, in the midst of all this uncertainty and stress, we found heroes. The Rural Fire Service, of course, but also everyday heroes. Men and women who stepped up and just got on with it.

Our farmers used whatever they had on hand to hold back fires from not only their own properties but also their neighbours' and ultimately our small rural townships. Groups of neighbours who worked shoulder to shoulder around the clock to do what they could to help.

The local land services, council and showground committee provided feed and accommodation for every type of animal known to humankind at the showground and gave worried horse owners like me a safe haven for our four-footed loved ones.

I'm so grateful for the endless hours of volunteering from people who gave up their time to feed and clothe and comfort so many of our community who were suffering and to the businesses who helped out and supplied meals for exhausted firefighters. The amazing BlazeAid organisation who were absolutely vital in helping rebuild many lost fences in the district and who help thousands of farming and rural families across Australia after natural disasters. I know that our farmers can't thank you enough for the selfless work and support you offer each and every community you set up camp in. Thank you so much.

I was never so proud of our amazing community.

At the time of writing this book, eight months after the worst of the fires ripped through our valley, many of the people who lost homes were still living in tents and caravans with no running water. The devastation and heartbreak didn't end once the fires were finally contained. The lost lives, livestock, property and wildlife will never be able to be replaced.

Before the fires came, our farmers and rural communities were going through one of the worst droughts on record. Now more than ever before, we need to support them.

Wherever you can, please buy local. If possible, take a weekend away and stay in a small rural community. Buy from online platforms like #BuyFromTheBush and #OneDayClosertoRain to support businesses selling from rural Australia.

Below is a list of people who were just a fraction of the real-life faces behind the story. People who inspired not only me but our whole community with their bravery and selflessness. You can find some of their photos and stories on Instagram and Facebook.

The Lower Buckra/Argent's Hill crew, otherwise known as The Red Hot Crispy Crew, contained the following legends who worked tirelessly around the clock to keep their homes and community safe.

Wade and Donna Olman, Jenny and Dan Argent, Bobbie and Ian Taylor, Kelly and Danny Taylor, David Foley—Captain of the Crispy Crew. Kris Cameron—The Water Boy—delivering food and beverages to the front lines at all hours of the day and night. Laura Graham—The Feeder, and the Voutier Boys.

The list of people to acknowledge individually would almost fill another book, and everyone has their own list of heroes, but you all know who you are and we are so very proud of you all.